What readers have said about
Spider Silk *and* **Stone Fly:**

"This quick read novel [*Spider Silk*] has such incredible details and character development...it just swallows you up.   **Pat from Massachusetts**

"Just had to let you know those [*Spider Silk* and *Stone Fly*] were the two best books I've read in awhile....When does the third one come out? Can't wait."   **Beverly from Oregon**

Stone Fly is "a really, really good novel! And a fun read!"   **Peter from Vermont**

"Just finished *Stone Fly*....What a great action-packed read. Looking forward to the next.
Can I expect BB back as Bud's deputy next time?"
Doug from Virginia

"...[*Spider Silk* and *Stone Fly*] just knocked our socks off! We really like your style and story line. Can't wait for your next offering. Hope it comes soon."   **Jerry and Pat from Oregon**

"I just finished *Spider Silk*....Gripping story meant I had to read it this afternoon. I will spend the evening reading *Stone Fly*. I need more!"
Marty from Oregon

Two protectors
on a lonely stretch of road...

"How would you set up an ambush, John?" Bud asked as the big pickup wound up the lazy curves beyond Summer Lake, heading for Picture Rock Pass.

John said, "Car wreck. You're a cop. You have to stop. So a car wreck gets you stopped, and a couple of flankers come at you from both sides. A third person is made up to look like a bloody victim. Not hard to do in the dark. Headlights would be all the special effects needed. Boom. You're had."

Bud nodded and asked, "How else?"

"Okay. Three cars...or big pickups. They box you, force you off the road and you're surrounded. Boom. Same story."

"Okay," Bud said. "A wreck, then. If there is a real wreck, we stop short and light the scene with our headlights and use the spotlight. Agreed?"

"I'd add one other detail. If it's still dark, you let me out about a hundred yards short of the scene and I'll flank them." He patted the duffel. "I can see in the dark."

"Okay. It's a plan."

BRIGHTWORKSPRESS

BLOODSTONE

Bright Works Press
Redmond, OR 97756
www.brightworkspress.com

© 2010 Rodney D. Collins
All rights reserved

This is a work of fiction. Names, characters, places, and incidents are the
product of the author's imagination
and are used fictitiously. Any resemblance to actual
persons, living or dead, or events is entirely coincidental.

Cover design by Val Stillwell and Anne Starke
Growth Collaborative • Eugene, Oregon
growthcollab.com

Editing, book design & production by Long On Books
www.longonbooks.com

ISBN: 979-8-9895768-1-4
Library of Congress Control Number: 2010911807

Printed in the United States of America

to Vi

ACKNOWLEDGMENTS

Bloodstone came harder than *Spider Silk* or *Stone Fly*, but finally, thanks to the patience and the timely help of family and friends, *Bloodstone* is ready for public debut. I give special thanks to Vi, my lifetime companion and friend.

Thanks to Peter Flowers, my friend of thirty-five years. As with *Stone Fly*, Peter labored to read, criticize, and give me useful, intelligent mark-ups without killing my enthusiasm for the book.

As always, thanks to Eva Long, friend and editor. If my stories improve, she is an important reason for the improvement.

Thanks also to Val Stilwell and Anne Starke for their intriguing cover art.

And finally, thanks to Bud Blair fans for demanding a sequel to *Stone Fly*. Here you go. Enjoy.

Bloodstone

*LEGEND HAS IT
that when Christ was crucified, the blood from his wounds dripped onto the green jasper ground, spotting it red and forming the bloodstone. And it was believed that if a bloodstone was covered with the herb heliotrope, the owner became invisible.*

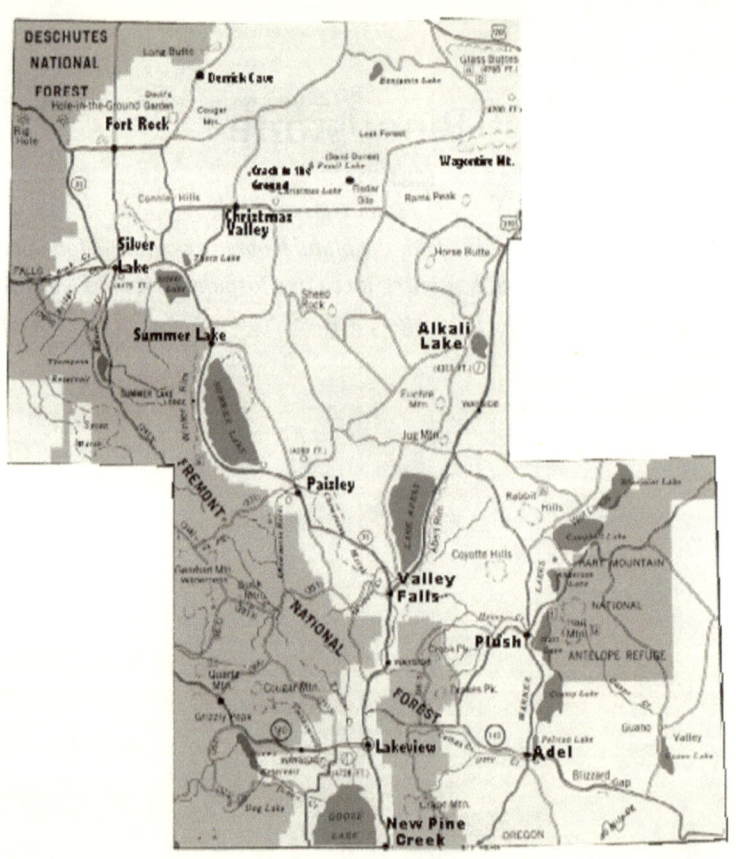

Lake County, Oregon

Prologue

THE SHAGGY, GRAY-HAIRED, UNKEMPT FIGURE OF Bobcat Larson stopped behind a lean six-foot juniper that somehow grew out of a crack in a low basalt bluff. He pulled his greasy, flat-brimmed leather hat lower, and squinted against the rays of a setting sun. Without looking back, he motioned Bud and Roger up beside him.

Bobcat pointed at a boot print and some scuff marks where the man they hunted had skirted the low bluff and slid down the dusty, pine needle-covered bank. He studied the tracks and then eyeballed the far edge of a scab-rock flat decorated with cheat grass and struggling sagebrush. "There's your varmint," he whispered.

"Where?" Bud whispered back.

"At the base of that little cliff over there… across the clearing… in the shadow just to the right of that leaning pine tree."

"I see him," Roger said quietly.

Bud took the small ten-power binoculars from his shirt pocket and glassed the hiding place of Bobcat's "varmint." The man they hunted was sitting behind a fallen pine about thirty inches in diameter, his back up against a small ledge, a rifle across the dead tree. He appeared to be staring at the ground—like he was trying to figure out what to do next. "Yeah, there he is," Bud said, "And he's not looking too good."

"I wonder," Bobcat speculated in a whisper, "if he knows a cougar is about to have him for supper. Look right above him…about ten feet…on that little ledge."

"Damn," Bud whispered back, "I want that guy alive."

Roger peeled off his jacket, wadded it up in a ball, and dropped to the ground in a prone shooter's position. He pushed the bundled jacket out in front him a little, then nestled the barrel of his rifle on the makeshift rest.

"You gonna shoot the varmint or the cat?" Bobcat whispered.

Roger didn't say anything. He just adjusted the scope for eight-power magnification, found his target, and then concentrated his attention on the head of the big yellow cougar. "How far is it, Bobcat?" he asked.

The old hunter squinted and stared, estimating the distance.

"I'd say about two hundred and forty yards…maybe two fifty. Hard to tell in this light."

Roger's big frame seemed to settle into the ground. He took his time, setting his sight picture to allow for bullet drop, took a deep breath and exhaled slowly.

The binoculars gave Bud a clear view. He watched the cougar twitch its tail and then bunch its legs up under its body, like a house cat getting set to pounce on a mouse.

The muzzle of the .308 belched fire, the heavy report rolling through the pine timber, and then the cat twisted and fell sideways off the bluff. The cougar's one hundred and twenty pounds of dead weight smashed into the wounded legs of an average-sized man who began screaming like a rock concert fanatic. Judging by the screams, Bud thought the guy's terror trumped his pain.

Bobcat grinned. "Where'd you hit him?"

Roger stood up, brushed the dust off his knees, picked up his brown khaki jacket, and then grinned at Bobcat. "I was aiming for his right eye."

"Did you hit it?"

"No. I think I shot him between the eyes."

Bobcat slapped Roger's meaty shoulder and said, "Well, son, if you practice enough you might just make a shooter yet." And then he let out a whoop and a laugh and danced an old man's jig, thin arms and legs pumping in time to some tune that only Bobcat could hear.

Bud watched the exchange between the lean, seventy-something, retired government trapper and Deputy Roger Hildebrand, shook his head and said, "Roger, what the hell did you do for the military? Between the eyes? At two hundred and fifty yards?"

Roger just shrugged and said, "Anyone in my unit could make that shot. It's no big deal."

Bud stared at Roger for a long five seconds, and then just shook his head and pointed across the clearing at their quarry. "Let's go get the guy and see if we can get out of here before dark."

Bobcat nodded, and without looking at Roger, he asked, "You want the tail or the scalp?"

Chapter 1

HE AWOKE TO THE SMELL OF fresh coffee and a soft voice saying, "Morning, Sunshine." He rolled over on his back and looked up into a pair of beautiful, smiling green eyes.

He grinned and said, "The future Mrs. Blair, I presume."

"Not if you don't get up and get going."

"Don't want to." He patted the comforter and said, "Let's just stay here and have breakfast in bed."

"Not today, but tomorrow you can bet on it…tomorrow."

He spread his arms out on the bed and intoned, "Alas, my fair maid, I fear that man is born to sorrow."

"If you don't get moving, I'll give you some sorrow." She grinned, set a cup of coffee on the bedside stand, pulled his old blue bathrobe up to her chin and crossed her arms. "I gotta get. When are you picking me up?"

"You sure you gotta go?"

"I'm sure."

"Dang. Well, first I have to question those two idiots Stone Fly left me. Then I have my report to write. Then I have to call Bruno and see if he can fly us to Yakima. I'll do that when I get to the office."

"And if Bruno can't fly us up?"

"I'll rent a really, really fast car."

"Call me when you know. I'm worried about Mom. I called her yesterday and she kept repeating herself. I'm going home to pack some things. Call me."

She leaned forward, kissed him on the forehead, and then left the room. A few minutes later he heard the engine of her Toyota pickup start up, and then the crunch of tires on gravel as she backed out of his driveway.

ASA CONNOR, OWNER-EDITOR AND, AS HE frequently put it, chief cook and bottle washer of the Lake County News, was waiting on the sidewalk when Bud backed into his reserved "Sheriff" parking spot.

As Bud stepped out of his pickup, looking fresh and ready for the day—boots polished, starch in his khaki shirt—Asa said, "Good morning, Bud. Brought the latest edition for your approval."

"Hell, Asa, you don't need my approval."

"I'd like it if you'd read it anyway. Scooped the big boys on this one. Had it out on the AP wire before they ever knew what hit 'em."

"Come on, Asa. They were all over it before I called you."

"Yeah, but they couldn't quote the sheriff of Lake County."

"How have they treated me since?"

Asa grinned. "Why you are the fair-haired boy, the type of law enforcement officer this country needs. You broke up a big terrorist operation and saved hundreds, maybe thousands, of lives. Nothing but praise for you and your injured officers. Trouble is, it'll probably go to your head, because it actually happens to be true."

Bud sighed and shook his head. "Come on in. I need a cup of coffee. Want one?"

Coffee in one hand and a cinnamon roll in the other, Bud studied the big picture of the bomb crater, and read the lead story in the Lake County News. He snorted at the headline, and read it aloud. "Sheriff's Department Wins Gun Battle with Terrorists."

He shook his head again and said, "Good Lord, Asa."

Asa looked peeved. "What would you have me say, Bud? 'Sheriff's Department Makes Nice?'"

The article was an almost exact quote of Bud's angry statement to the some hundred or so reporters from the national and local press that thronged to the blast site, keen on finding enough sensational news to feed what Bud termed "a blood-thirsty public." Competition to be "first" had led The Oregonian to speculate about terrorists in advance of any solid evidence, and it had pissed off Bud to the point that he broke his own first rule: Never talk to the press.

FRIDAY MORNING, ACTING ON AN ANONYMOUS tip, Lake County Undersheriff Sonny Sixkiller, Deputy Roger Hildebrand, Deputy Larae Holcomb and State Trooper Charles Prince stopped a hay truck approximately two miles north of Fort Rock.

As the officers approached the truck, three unidentified individuals with automatic rifles fired at the officers. State Trooper Prince was hit by a bullet. His vest protected him, but the impact ruptured his spleen. During the firefight, the assailants detonated explosives hidden in the truck. The assailants were killed and all four officers were injured by the blast.

The officers were taken by both Oregon Air Life and ambulance to Saint Charles Medical Center in Bend. State Trooper Prince was reported to be in stable condition following surgery. He is expected to make a full recovery and return to duty following a period of convalescence.

Deputy Larae Holcomb was treated for a broken ankle, cuts, bruises, and contusions. Her condition is listed as fair. Undersheriff Sonny Sixkiller was treated for a minor head wound from rock shrapnel. Deputy Roger Hildebrand was held overnight for observation and then released.

An FBI forensics team examined the blast site, a crater estimated to be ten feet deep and 100 feet wide. They collected soil samples, the body of one assailant, other evidence, and left by helicopter. There is no word yet from the FBI as to the identities of the assailants, but witnesses said the body recovered at the scene appeared to be a foreign national of Middle Eastern origin. According to Lake County Sheriff Bud Blair, the weapons used by the assailants were AK-47s.

In a statement to this paper, Deschutes County Sheriff Cal Redmond gave high praise to Sheriff Blair and his officers. "Sheriff Blair marshaled his resources skillfully and organized a textbook operation. There was no way these guys were going to escape. Thanks to Sheriff Blair, we had a cork in the bottle almost from the beginning. I think that's why they killed themselves. They knew there was no way out."

In addition to injuring the officers, the blast also started a sagebrush fire that spread into the pine timber north of the blast site. According to Bureau of Land Management (BLM) and Forest Service estimates, the fire was held to about 500 acres due to quick action by Forest Service and BLM retardant planes."

BUD LOOKED UP FROM THE PAPER, sipped his coffee, then spun around and stared at the big Lake County map on the wall. He was seeing a bloodied Deputy Larae Holcomb, her ankle obviously broken, gashes in her lower calves, blood coming from each ear, dazed, confused, nearly unconscious.

And he was seeing the bulky frame of Deputy Roger Hildebrand rising from the sand like a phoenix, dusty, and slightly befuddled. He had been protected by a low berm of dirt, but the concussion had knocked him out.

He also had a flash recall of Bremerton Detective Gino Maretti swatting him on the back of the head and telling him, "We ain't got time for no weepies."

He shook it off and turned back to Asa. "I didn't tell you everything."

Asa sniffed, and said, "Like who Deputy Larae Holcomb is or where she came from?"

Bud nodded. "New to us, did lots of undercover work in the Sacramento area. Good cop. I had her working undercover in Fort Rock as a bartender. She was trying to sniff out a meth lab. Anyway," he continued, "we had a lot of help from an NCIS agent…a real agent, not some desk jockey. He tipped us off. He was hunting his sister's killer and unearthed this people-smuggling operation by accident. And he took down four of the assailants by himself."

Bud shook his head and chuckled. "I found two of them, arms wrapped around a big ponderosa pine, tied wrist to wrist. They were still quarreling with each other like a couple of old hens when...uh...I brought them in. Still have them in our fine jail."

Asa gave a small smile. "Mid-Eastern?"

"No. Just a couple of dumbshit baddies from the Seattle area."

"I heard the other bad guys were Mid-Eastern."

Bud's tone was challenging. "Where did you hear that?"

"Well, from a friend who watched the whole thing from the top of Fort Rock."

"Won't wash, Asa. The distance is too great to make out that kind of detail through the best of binoculars."

Asa grinned, ran a hand over his close-cropped gray hair, and then said, "It seems your watcher plan worked. My friend got suspicious of Cowboy and stayed up late one night. Sort of sneaked in and took a peek. Said he saw two or three people who looked like Arabs."

"And he just happened to give you a phone call."

"That's the size of it. Wouldn't give me a name."

"I'll give you one: Stone Fly."

"Is that the NCIS agent who took down the four bad guys?" When Bud didn't answer, Asa nodded to himself and said, "Now the question is, why do that?"

Bud thought about the computer disc in the small fireproof safe hidden in his cabin out at Dog Lake. Yeah. Why would Stone Fly trust me with information he wouldn't share with NCIS?

Bud shrugged. "Maybe he doesn't trust his own organization. And, maybe he wants our citizens to realize those boys are waging war on us. Maybe. Or maybe he believes a small town editor hasn't been corrupted by political influence and will tell us the truth."

Asa rose and said, "Elliptical thinking is what we have here. We'll be doubling back on ourselves before you know it." He pointed to the paper. "Enjoy the article about Lake County's heroes. Sit still, I'll let myself out."

Bud looked up at him. "When you going to Bend?"

"Tomorrow. Prostate comes out the next day, two days in St. Charles and then I'll stay in a nice suite at the Shilo for a week to ten days. Catheter time. They don't want me traveling until I'm healed up."

"And Agness is taking you up?"

Asa grinned. "Yep. And when I come home, she's taking me to Reno."

Bud got up and shook Asa's hand. "Good luck, my friend. And congratulations to you and Agness."

Asa closed the door and Bud grinned at the thought of five-foot-three-inch Agness and the tall, lanky editor getting married. Bud liked them both. As the postmaster for Lakeview, Agness was also a fountain of information and a quiet political power in the county. A sensible, intelligent power, Bud thought.

Chapter 2

A GREEN, HOODED SWEATSHIRT KEPT THE morning chill at bay as John Bernard—aka "Stone Fly," aka "Gar"—elbows propped on a weathered wooden picnic table, drank his morning coffee. A trickle of cold smoke drifted from the fire ring between his green scabrous sixteen-foot camp trailer and the picnic table.

The scratch of tiny claws alerted him to an expected morning visitor. A golden-mantled ground squirrel worked his way across the table in quick starts and stops, wrinkled his nose, and then reached out and snatched the peanut from John's palm. The squirrel skittered across the table, jumped to the ground, and raced to the top of a two-foot chunk of gray basalt. The squirrel sat upright, stared at John while it cracked the shell, and stuffed its jaws with peanuts.

John chuckled. "You remind me of some people I met in Afghanistan. You're greedy, suspicious, and untrustworthy. I think I'll call you Idi Al Greedy."

His pine-sheltered campsite overlooked the mirror surface of Timothy Lake a dozen miles south of Mount Hood, and he watched the morning sun slowly color the treetops on the ridges sheltering the lake. A feeding fish arched from the still surface, and the sound of the splosh came quietly across the lake a full second later. The expanding rings disturbed the reflected picture of the shoreline trees, and then sank back into the lake.

A white car-topper boat putted along the face of the dam at the west end of the lake. John recognized the boat as the same one he had seen each of the past three mornings. He put down his coffee mug and lifted the binoculars from the table. Nothing suspicious there. Just an older man trolling for trout…alone.

Sorrow, and a sense of great loneliness suddenly hit him, followed almost immediately by anger. Sorrow for his dead sister, raped and killed by Crazy Charlie, anger at a once-upon-a-time friend and teammate. John dismissed the fact that two sailors had killed Dena. Crazy could have, should have stopped them. The fact that Crazy killed both sailors later on made no difference. He was the big boar in the pig sty.

John shook off the feelings. In his business you had to develop a certain sense of fatalism or go crazy…or quit. He turned back to the squirrel.

"You know, Greedy, I'll bet you that old man has outlived his friends. Either that or his friends are too bunged up to go fishing." He smiled and added, "Or he could just be an old curmudgeon."

It was John's private game, the challenge of profiling people, inventing histories—all without knowing a single thing beyond physical characteristics and behavior in the setting of the moment. It had served him well from time to time. And it amused him when he discovered his intuitive guess turned out to be right—which it was—a large percentage of the time.

The cell phone had been off for the past three days, but his R&R was over tomorrow, so he had grimly, reluctantly, turned it on last night, wondering as he did if he shouldn't just quit and go do something else.

And that thought brought back a clear picture of Larae Holcomb tending bar at the Christmas Valley Lodge. Honey-blond hair and bright blue eyes. A little taller than average, with a compact athletic figure. She was almost beautiful. And when she smiled, her whole face lit up, and she was beautiful.

He sat at a back table in the Christmas Valley Lodge and watched her every Saturday night for over a month as she tended bar. And he was there to stop Cowboy from raping her in an after-hours attack in a moon-lit parking lot.

The squirrel was back for more, so John swung his legs over the built-in bench and headed for the camper to get another handful of peanuts. He didn't quite make it past the fire pit before the cell phone vibrated in his pocket.

He pulled the phone out, flipped it open and scanned the incoming number. He growled into the phone, "Amanda, I'm still on R&R."

Special Agent Amanda Spear, NCIS, headquartered in Silverdale, Washington, smirked at the sound of his voice. "Not any more. And I've been calling you for three days. So...for three days you've been AWOL."

"So fire me."

"I remember some mornings when you were glad to hear my voice. But now...I have to wonder if you're just a natural born asshole or if you have to work at it?"

"You make it easy, Amanda. So why are you calling me?"

"I want you to scoot back to Lakeview and keep an eye on Sheriff Blair...cover his back..."

He paused, letting that information percolate through his brain. "Okay, but the sheriff strikes me as perfectly capable of taking care of himself. Why the sudden interest?"

"Where have you been? Haven't you been reading the papers?"

"No."

"Well, what the hell have you been doing then?"

"Just feeding the squirrels." And taking care of some private grief.

"Look," she said, "for the moment, Lake County's sheriff is one of the best known people in the world His picture has been on the front page of all the major nation-al and international newspapers...even on Al Jazeera's website. Especially Al Jazeera. And we received a tip that he's now a target."

"From Middle Eastern terrorists, the Mexican Mafia, or druggies?"

Special Agent Spears hadn't answered, and in truth, John knew that she didn't need to. His mind flashed back to Cowboy's barnyard, two EMTs loading Crazy Charlie on a gurney and sliding him into the back of an ambulance, and with lights flashing, heading for the little city of Bend some sixty or so miles away.

"Is that what Crazy's telling you?"

"He's dead, John. It looks like the EMTs killed him with an overdose of Cardizen, a cardiac drug, drove the ambulance to the hospital in Bend, then simply walked away."

"Damn! I knew there was something wrong about that whole thing…about the EMTs…but I was too tired to think straight." He stopped talking for a few long seconds, then said, "So someone arranged a phony ambulance pickup and killer EMTs in less than an hour? And what about Cowboy?"

"The docs patched him up, and he'll live. But he's not saying anything. I think he'll talk eventually if we can guarantee his safety. The problem is, even though he and his minions were smuggling people, guns, explosives, and drugs through the county, I don't think he knows a lot beyond his piece of the action."

John digested this new information, wondered briefly about who could organize a snatch operation in less than an hour. He nodded to himself, and asked, "Amanda, do we have a mole?"

He heard a slight tremor in her voice. "John, I think it's more than that."

"Okay. So tell me."

He heard her take a deep breath, and then ask, "Do you trust me, John?"

"That's a strange question, Amanda. Any reason why I shouldn't?"

"I suspect the SAC thinks I'm the mole."

"Want to enlighten me?"

"What's your location?"

"Are you kidding?"

"You got your other phone?"

He stopped breathing for a long three seconds. "Got your other phone" was her code for "they are probably listening." He just said, "Shit."

She broke the connection.

Twenty minutes later, Idi Al Greedy was busy at work on a big pile of peanuts his benefactor had left for him in the center of the picnic table.

Chapter 3

Bud drank the last of the cold coffee in his mug and munched on a stale day-old cinnamon roll while he reread the action report it had taken him two hours to write.

"Too many players," he grumbled, "but I think I've covered the basic action." He took the report to Karen Highsmith and asked her to make the requisite number of copies.

Suddenly he was bored with the whole thing. He pulled the phone directory from his top drawer and looked up the number for Kowalski's Air Service.

Bruno's wife, Julia, answered on the second ring.

"Mrs. Kowalski, this is Bud Blair. I was wondering if Bruno could fly me and Nancy Sixkiller to Yakima this afternoon."

"Let me get him on the radio. He had a charter to Reno this morning. I'll get an ETA for Lakeview."

Bud's Call Waiting beeped, but he ignored it while he listened to Mrs. Kowalski talking to Bruno. He could hear enough to know Bruno would be back at about 11:00 a.m.

"He can give you a ride to Yakima at noon. Will you want him on standby in Yakima?"

"Wonderful! Yes, we'll be on the ground for a couple hours, and then we need to get back here."

"Okay, Bud. You're booked. Do you want an estimate of charges?"

"No...today it doesn't matter."

She hesitated and then asked, "Ah...how're the boys doing?"

"Boys and girls, Mrs. Kowalski," he said gently. "Boys and girls, and they are doing just fine. We'll all be back to normal in just a few days."

Deputy Michele Trivoli, Bud's acting undersheriff was leaning against the door jamb when he hung up. "I just had a call from Special Agent Spears. Wants us to ship Harley Spencer and Donald Brice, aka Chase, to Springdale. NCIS is assuming custody."

He shook his head. "No. NCIS can't have them. Call 'em back and tell them they'll have to get in line. Howard is talking about charging them with criminal conspiracy, assault with a deadly weapon, sale of drugs, attempted murder, and riding an ATV in a restricted area. When we're done, then NCIS can have them." And then he grinned.

Michelle frowned and said, "What's to smile about?"

He shook his head at the memory of finding Harley and Chase, tied wrist to wrist, hugging a big pine tree right where Gar had left them. They had both pissed their pants and smelled ripe. "I hope they've had a shower."

Michelle smiled. "First thing Karen made them do. Howard wants to sit in on the questioning."

"Has he reviewed the transcript of the recording Gar made of those two babbling idiots?"

She nodded. "Yes."

"Okay. Get Howard over here and let's do it. And close the door on your way out. I've got some private calls to make."

HOWARD FINCH, LAKE COUNTY DISTRICT ATTORNEY, his mop of hair in need of a comb and a haircut, pushed the call button on the inner door leading from the main offices of the Lake County courthouse into the sheriff's office. Karen Highsmith turned to see who was at the door and then pushed the latch release.

"Good morning, Karen. I'm about the county's business."

She eyeballed his blue blazer, pale yellow shirt, and red tie—Howard's version of official attire—and wondered once again where he had learned to knot a tie. His was always askew. Or maybe, she thought, he doesn't care.

She nodded at Bud's door. "He's on a call. Have a chair. Want some coffee?"

"No. He's expecting me," Howard said, pushing past her into the short hallway leading to Bud's office.

Howard knocked and without waiting for an invitation, opened the door in time to hear Bud say, "I owe you one Cal...again. Thanks. I'll let Deputy Trivoli know what's going on. I'll call when I get back from Yakima." He waved Howard in, put the phone back in its cradle, and pointed to a visitor's chair that carried the scars of boot heels on its wooden rungs.

"You ready, Howard?"

"Let's talk about this first. I read the transcript of Mr. Spencer and Mr. Brice's...ah...encounter with...Gar? Stone Fly? What are we calling him these days? Our esteemed NCIS agent."

Bud grimaced and said, "I'm in a pickle here, Howard. He was undercover. He wasn't really, officially ever here. I don't think legally we can use the recording in court. So...I think we have to get each of them to sign the transcription as a personal statement. If we can do that, it'll hold up in court, and we won't have to reveal our source. We also need to offer them a chance to have an attorney present."

"I thought of that," Howard said. "I asked the judge to have a public defender available if that's what they want."

"Who?"

"Meryl Saunders."

"Don't know him."

"Her. Young. Just passed the bar. She's going to work for Randolph Elkins. Randolph tells me she is pretty sharp...graduated third in her class."

Bud's face broke into wry smile. He looked sideways at Howard and said, "I always wondered just how tough the bar exam actually was. Can't be too tough. All the attorneys I know passed it."

Howard started to respond, stopped, and then nodded. "Good one, Bud. I can use that...when we try you for being a frivolous asshole. Remember, judges were attorneys before they stopped working for a living."

"I keep forgetting, Howard. You're the only district attorney I know who charges people with spitting on the floor."

"Gotta give the opposition something they can win, Bud. Left hook, right cross, that's my motto."

Bud looked at the short, pudgy figure with his mop of curly blond hair, and just grunted.

Michelle, who had returned to stand in the doorway shook her head, and interrupted with, "Chase is waiting in the interview room."

Bud nodded. "Good. How long has he been there?"

"Just a couple of minutes," she said.

"What do think, Howard? Make him wait a few more minutes?"

Howard looked at his watch and said, "I'll be back in fifteen. Got some calls to make."

Michelle headed for her desk when Bud stopped her. "Any word on when we'll have Roger and Sonny back?"

"As a matter of fact, Captain Delaware from the state police called this morning to assure us they will conduct a quick 'use of deadly force' review. Said it wouldn't take more than a couple of days. He has already pulled together a lot of information. And then Sonny and Roger can return to duty."

Bud nodded approval, and caught himself staring at this tall, slender, dark-haired young woman, aka "Trigger Trueshot." He just couldn't help it. Whenever he looked directly at her, he almost always came up with a clear picture of her in a shooter's stance, banging away at Bill Casey because she thought Casey had killed her sheriff.

"Where is Lonnie, by the way?" he asked her.

Lonnie Beltram, one of Bud's reserve officers had paid his own way to the police academy in Monmouth, and had graduated in the top ten percent of his class. He was looking for work in Eastern Oregon—only in Eastern Oregon. No westside jobs for him. In the meantime, Bud kept him busy part-time as a reserve officer.

"Bud...what were you thinking? I could see something in your eyes."

"Well, to be honest, I was thinking about being pinned to the ground by a dead horse and watching my junior officer banging away at Bill Casey with a pistol. And I was remembering how you blushed when I asked you about dating Trooper Prince. Put that together, and we have what I would call a touch of irony. Wouldn't you agree?"

"I sent Deputy Beltram up 395 to Paisley…just to fly the flag. We don't want the bad boys to think we're understaffed."

"Changing the subject, are we?"

"Yes."

"Well, then let me share some good news-bad news. I'm leaving at noon, and I won't be back until this evening."

Michelle looked a bit worried. "Where are you going?"

He suddenly grinned like a school boy. "Yakima, back here, and then on to Reno tomorrow."

"That's just plain stupid."

He frowned.

Michelle got red in the face and amended, "Not getting married. You can marry whoever in the hell you want. I don't give a damn. If you think leaving now is such a great idea, why don't you just resign and let me handle things. We have a homicide to solve, we have three officers out of action, and you want to go chasing your… damned ego!"

Bud was too stunned by her outburst to respond, and he watched in amazement when she shouted, "I quit!" She slammed the door on her way out.

He leaned back in his old captain's chair and rubbed his forehead, wondering what that was all about.

He rocked forward as Michelle Trivoli, Italian ancestors undoubtedly applauding her hot-blooded outburst, came storming back into the room.

She slammed a paper on his desk, a computer copy of Al Jazeera's lead story. "I downloaded it this morning. Read this and then tell me you have time for romance." She crossed her arms and waited until he rocked forward and spun the page around.

He was red-faced when he finished reading a front page article headlined by the picture of a rough-looking sheriff from Lake County, Oregon.

Michelle waited calmly for the angry explosion she was certain would be aimed in her direction. Bud glared at her, took a deep breath, frowned, and then reached out and wadded the page into a ball, his knuckles white from the pressure of squeezing the crumpled page.

He kicked the wastebasket across the room, threw the paper wad in the same general direction, sat back, turned his chair around, and looked at the cork bulletin board behind him, the surface covered by a big map of Lake County, full of red and black pins— black ones for cases solved, red for ongoing or unsolved cases. There were dozen of black pins and a handful of red ones.

Finally he nodded, turned around and growled, "You can't quit until I fire you…and I'm not going to do that…just yet. But I am going to Yakima to meet my future mother-in-law. An hour-and-a-half up, two hours on the ground, an hour-and-a-half back. Five hours. I'll be back this evening."

"And then?"

He took a deep breath, and then patiently explained his plan. "I'm not leaving you without resources. I just got off the phone with Sheriff Redmond. He'll have two…not one…two Deschutes deputies patrol Silver Lake, Christmas Valley, and Fort Rock for the next two days. Starting tomorrow, they will check in with you, the undersheriff of Lake County, to plan a patrol pattern. Basically they will work for you."

Her relief softened her features, and he pointed to the visitor's chair. She sat down, and he tossed her a note pad. She fished a pen from her shirt pocket and started taking notes.

"Their names," and he pushed a note card across the desk. "Also," he continued, "the Oregon State Police is sending a trooper to temporarily staff the Lakeview office. I don't know who they are sending, but that officer will be here by this evening. And, Trooper Hansen from Burns will patrol as far south as Alkali Flat each day. You are also authorized to keep Beltram on the rolls for the next thirty days. You will also have the backing and support of the Lakeview city police. Now if you can't manage with that, you are free to go ahead and quit."

She shook her head, looked him in the eyes and started to say, "Bud, I'm so..."

He held up his hand and stopped her. "No. I'm the one to say I'm sorry. You haven't had a break, have you?"

She shook her head and tried hard not to let tears erode her composure.

"Michelle, you've got fifteen minutes to talk about it."

Somehow the tears got the best of her. "Bud," she choked, "I just feel...like they violated everything I hold dear. You know, I thought our people were all dead. My heart just stopped. Damn, we're the good guys and here they are trying to kill us!"

He resisted the impulse to hold her, to offer comfort, and offered a tissue instead. He felt like kicking himself for not realizing much sooner that she hadn't had anyone to talk to—to decompress. He had Nancy, and just telling her about the explosion and the injuries to his officers had helped him start feeling normal again. This young deputy didn't have that luxury. And he should have known it. Even though she wasn't really alone or abandoned, he knew she felt that way.

A soft knock on the door was answered by Bud's "Busy!" But Karen Highsmith pushed in anyway. Her eyes were red from crying. "Sorry," she said, "but you two can't part company. We need you, Michelle. I need you." And she broke into to tears again.

"Oh shit," Bud said. He wasn't comfortable with tears, so he did the only thing he knew to do. "Stop it. No one is going anywhere. We're just having a hard time in here, but we'll get through it and get back to work. We're a team, and we stick together."

Chase got to stew for an extra thirty minutes before Michelle and Howard questioned him. Bud chose to watch through the one-way glass.

He was an easy interview. He didn't want an attorney present. What he wanted was protection. "They gonna kill me," he sniveled repeatedly.

"So, help us," Michelle would counter.

After forty minutes it was clear that he had little new information to offer except that he had seen a visitor at Cowboy's ranch. "This big Mexican guy," he kept saying. "Big shot. Telling Cowboy whose cow ate the cabbage."

"What did they talk about?" Howard asked at one point.

"Didn't hear the words," Chase said, "but the Mexican was yelling at Cowboy. And Cowboy, he took it. I did hear Cowboy say he wasn't cool with doing that kind of thing, but the Mexican said something else, and I heard Cowboy shout something like 'All right, I'll do it.'"

On a sudden impulse, Bud hurried back to his office and started leafing through the FBI's wanted posters. Several carried pictures of Hispanic felons, some Colombians, some Mexican nationals, some homegrown Latinos. All were wanted for major crimes: kidnapping, assault, criminal conspiracy, drugs, extortion, prostitution, theft, murder. He knocked on the door to the interview room and let himself in. Without preamble he put a dozen posters on the table in front of Chase.

Chase pulled them around and held each on at arms length. "Can't see to read without my glasses." Bud pulled a ten-dollar drugstore pair from a pocket and handed them to Chase. Michelle glanced at Bud and raised her eyebrows. She could tell by his frown that teasing him about his eyesight wouldn't be a good idea.

Chase sorted through the stack and then handed one of the posters to Bud. "Yep, that's him. That's the guy telling Cowboy what to do. Scary looking dude, ain't he? I told Harley we shouldna gotten mixed up with Cowboy. Now look at us. Dead. Just dead. That's what we are. These ol' boys don't mess around. They just kill you."

He started to sniffle, and Bud just looked at him with disgust. He'd had all the tears he could take for one day. "Shut up, Chase. You cry and I'll kill you myself."

Howard and Michelle looked startled, but Bud winked and nodded for them to follow him outside. When the door closed behind them, Bud held up the flyer and asked, "You think he's telling the truth?"

Howard nodded, and Michelle said, "I think he truly believes they'll try to kill him, and we are the only safety he's got. He's desperate and will probably say anything to get us on his side."

"Okay," Bud said. "Did he sign the statement."

Howard waved a copy. "Got it right here."

"Then let's try Harley. Get him to sign a statement, get him to describe this guy. Don't show him the flyer, but if what he says matches the flyer, we can maybe start to believe them. Okay?"

Howard and Michelle nodded.

An hour later, both Chase and Harley were locked in a back cell, and Howard had the judge's order to hold them in protective custody. Michelle's job was to work out the finer details as to what they were witnesses to.

Bud called Michelle into his office. "You gonna be okay?" She nodded. "Me too, I think. Now…I'm still going to Yakima…but Sheriff Cal Redmond will be sending two Deputies down to haul Chase and Harley to the Justice Center in Bend." She started to say something, and Bud held up his hand and stopped her. "I don't think we can keep them safe here. Too open…too close to the street. And I want you to lock the station down. No one gets in until you okay it. If I thought it would do any good, I'd post a sign saying Harley and Chase aren't here.

"What we can do is tip off Carol Connor that the suspects in the Fort Rock drug running operation have been transferred to another facility we aren't at liberty to disclose. She can run a short article in the Lake County News. That might—emphasis on 'might'— keep the opposition from storming the jail or blowing up the courthouse.

And see if the radio station will cover the story about the transfer on an hourly basis for the next couple of days."

Michelle nodded and then swore. "You're scaring me, Bud."

"I think I'm starting to get scared myself. But we have to keep our eyes open and keep on doing our jobs just the same. Let's keep our watchers alert, and when Roger is returned to duty, let's get him down here for backup for you and Lonnie. Okay?"

"Good idea, Bud. And I think I'll break out the AR-15s, just in case."

"You okay if I'm gone for the next six or seven hours?"

She gave him a thumbs-up. "I'll be okay, but I think I'll get Lonnie back in here."

"Good. And I want you to put a report together about what Harley and Chase told us, who they identified…" And then he just ran down. Just stopped talking and grimaced. "Well…bullshit," he said softly and pushed his chair away from his desk.

"Bud?"

"Hell. I can't do it." He looked at her and said, "I thought if I got you some backup it would be okay to be gone for a few hours." He shook his head. "I can't do it. I've got to see this through. If something happened to any of you and I wasn't here, I don't think I could live with it."

He walked over to the wadded piece of copy paper, picked it up and smoothed it out on his desk top. Seeing his own picture staring back at him, he picked up the paper and tacked it to the cork bulletin board. Then he angrily punched the speed dial for Nancy's cell phone.

"Sheriff?"

He looked up at Michelle, and saw her mouth the words, "In person," before he heard Nancy say, "Hello."

"Uh, hi! Nancy, I've got some bad news."

"You can't go, can you?"

"No. I want to, but I can't be gone right now. We need to talk."

"So come to the house, Bud, and we'll talk. I think I understand."

Chapter 4

Ruby crossed her long legs and leaned forward in her chair. "Normally I'm not a nosey person. I really believe in live-and-let-live. But the loud parties, the coming-and-going at all hours of the night often kept me awake. And so I started keeping a log." She shrugged. "It was something to do. Anyway, when a U-Haul truck backed up to the door and four big, strong men began loading the truck with filing cabinets, computers, boxes, etcetera. I first thought he was simply moving into a new office. But then they started bringing out those little closet things...you know...the kind that people use to move clothing they want to keep hanging up..."

"You mean a wardrobe?" Ed Hoosier asked.

"Right," she said, "wardrobe. Or in this case several wardrobes, and some big coolers." She leaned back and dug into a front pants pocket and handed Maretti a folded piece of notebook paper. "So...I wrote down the license number of the truck, and I took pictures of the men. I knew that might be dangerous, but it just didn't feel right. I'm glad to be rid of such a noisy neighbor, but if he's been up to criminal mischief, then I want him punished. Actually, I'd dearly like to keep him awake for a year or two."

That brought the expected chuckles.

Maretti finally stopped staring at her long, lovely legs and asked, "Did you ever file a nuisance complaint with the city?"

"Just once. My cat was run over not too long after that. I could see where someone had come all the way up on the sidewalk to hit her. That scared me."

"Why are you talking to us now?" Grandfield asked.

She sat back in her chair and looked over their heads, seeing something no one else could see. Finally she said, "Well, I bought a new alarm system, I installed remote cameras, and I own an H&K .40-caliber handgun. I practice with it at least twice a week. I'm getting so I can hit what I aim at. He just pushed me too far."

They all chuckled, and Amanda gave her a high-five. "Way to go, girl!"

Mrs. Goldstein blushed a bit, and then simply said, "Thank you. My husband thinks I'm nuts, but his work frequently takes him out of town. He's missed a lot."

Maretti looked at the smooth skin of her attractive face and thought, Yes, he has.

THEY TOOK AWAY COPIES OF HER log book and the pictures Ruby printed for them, each picture neatly dated on the back and signed by her. Grandfield used her computer and typed out a statement which she signed. Amanda called in the license plate number from the truck and asked for a trace.

A glum Maretti said he wouldn't be satisfied until he had examined the house. "We got a search warrant, don't we?"

So he and the two FBI agents satisfied some primal urge and kicked the front door in, and then "processed" the scene. The furniture was still in place, the refrigerator was still stocked with food, a load of laundry was in the washer waiting for transfer to the dryer, and the heat pump was still running. But the office, the bathrooms, and the closets were empty.

They met back in the entry. "You know what I think," Payne said to his FBI partner, "We all should get a forensics team here and run every little old fingerprint we can find. Get DNA if we can. We might not be able to track this Pettibone dude, but maybe we can track some of his associates."

Hoosier nodded and pulled a cell phone from an inside jacket pocket.

While Hoosier talked on the phone, Maretti asked Agent Two, "Do your boys work fast, or do they keep you waiting forever?"

"They're pretty fast. And when you go to court, the FBI's evidence is solid gold. We take some pretty hard hits from the movie crowd and from the press, but people still have a lot of confidence in the integrity of the FBI."

Maretti nodded, and then added, "If only you weren't such arrogant assholes…"

"I know what you mean, but there's some pretty good old boys… and gals…working for the Bureau. And we ain't got a lock on arrogance. Take yourself for example."

Maretti started to take offense, but something in the tilt of Payne's face, the start of a grin made Maretti snort. And then he laughed. "Yeah, but I ain't prissy like some of you guys."

'Now don't get us confused with that NCIS dude…what's his name? Warren. Yeah, that's it. Now that is some prissy dude. I knew a guy like that one time. This old boy could tear an automobile engine apart, rebuild it, and stick it back in a car without getting his hands dirty. I swear. He could do it in a white shirt and come out spotless. Now me, if I so much as walk by a car, the grease just comes flying at me like flies to honey."

Maretti laughed and said, "Yeah. In my off time, when I have any, I'm restoring an old 1950 Ford two-door sedan. Can't find my bench for all the grease rags."

Hoosier walked over. "You two done shootin' the bull?"

Maretti took offense. "And the point of your question, Agent Number One?"

"Special Agent Ed Hoosier," Hoosier corrected.

"Yeah. But you're Agent Number One to me, and this is Special Agent Payne. He hasn't caught the FBI bug yet. You know…the one that turns people into officious assholes…so I actually remember his name. And that surprises me, it does."

Detective Grandfield had quietly entered the door. "You at it again, Gino?"

"At what?" Maretti huffed.

"Making friends.

They congregated at the Bremerton city police station in downtown, back in the same squad room where they had started. Seated around a Formica-topped folding table, Amanda at the flip chart, they recapped.

"We know what?" Amanda asked.

Maretti snorted, and Ron thought, Here he goes again.

Amanda pointed the marker at him. "You were about to say, Detective Maretti?"

"I was about say, Special Agent Spears, that what we know is somebody tipped off Pettibone. He cuts and runs, makes sure there isn't anything incriminating for us to find. Since Grandfield and I didn't call him up and say, 'Oh, by the way, that leads me to think someone from NCIS or...and this I don't think is too likely...the FBI...is ratting us out.'"

His voice rose several decibels, and he smacked the table with a beefy hand. "And it's not the first time, Agent Spears!"

Her face turned red, and she stammered, "I...uh...I don't know what you are implying, but I don't think I like it."

Maretti glanced at the two FBI agents as if to say, "You getting this?," and then stared a hole in Agent Warren, while he asked Grandfield—rhetorically, of course—"Ron, who knew we had an ambulance coming to pick up Crazy Charlie? Who was afraid Crazy would talk? Who killed him? Who knew we were going to search Pettibone's place? Who has the organization and the resources to carry out a snatch job in less than an hour?"

He waved a hand at the chipped, tape-scarred walls of the squad room. "It sure as hell ain't the Bremerton city police. And the FBI wasn't in the picture until after Crazy was dead. So, somebody, maybe even one of you," and he pointed first at Toby Warren and then at Amanda Spears, "is working for the opposition."

Amanda shook her head. "We only invited you in as a courtesy. It's not your case."

Maretti rocked back in his chair, stared at the scratched Formica, picked up his heavy, white U.S. Navy surplus mug, and looked back up at Amanda, his dark brown eyes sparkling with amusement.

Grandfield mentally shook his head, and thought, You love this, Gino, you grandstanding jerk, but I'll be darned if it doesn't work for you.

"Nah, I don't suppose it was you, or," he pointed to Agent Warren, "Candyass over there. Too close to the action in Christmas Valley, not enough time to orchestrate the hit. But I'll bet dollars to donuts someone you told, or someone listening to your phone calls, is working for the opposition."

Toby Warren, who in truth was somewhat intimidated by Maretti, finally spoke up. "I don't like you, Maretti. And I resent your accusation that NCIS has been corrupted by...by...I don't know who."

"And that's what we need to find out, because you got a mole, boy, deep inside NCIS. No doubt about it."

The room went dead silent for a few seconds. Finally, Agent Payne, who was a bit like Maretti and couldn't stand very much silence, said, "Well, partners, let's assume Maretti is correct. And let's assume for the moment that Agents Warren and Spears are as clean as fresh laundry. Agreed?"

They all nodded except Amanda who was glaring at Maretti, half-turned like she was thinking about pulling her weapon and shooting the bastard.

"Good," Payne said, ignoring Amanda's non-response. "So, how about doing some old-fashioned police work. Why don't y'all proceed with what you were doing, Agent Spears, before our wop-a-cop got going? Let's see what we can do with what we know for now."

Maretti turned to Payne who was sitting on his right and said in a fairly loud aside, "Wop-a-cop? The Mob ain't gonna like that."

Grandfield muttered, "There he goes again. There isn't any Mob, Gino."

I<small>T WAS AFTER NINE WHEN THEY</small> finished listing what they knew. It was a pretty short list, but at least they had a direction to follow.

On the chart Amanda listed:

–Photo of Pettibone-Pacific NW Washington law enforcement agencies as person of interest - FBI
–Fingerprint and DNA search - FBI
–U-Haul trace — Bremerton City Police
–Photo of truck driver and helpers to Bremerton City Police as persons of interest - BCPD
–Interview U-Haul rental agencies in the Bremerton area — BCPD
–Check with private aircraft charter services — NCIS
–Visual identity check — NCIS
–Background check on Pettibone — FBI

Maretti made a mental note to put Grandfield on that one as well.

It was Special Agent Ed Hoosier who looked at each of them, and then asked "Anything else?"

Nobody volunteered anything new. Finally, Toby Warren cleared his throat and said, "I wonder who is going to inform Homeland Security."

Payne said, "We'll take care of that. You just keep an eye out for your mole."

"Let's do a progress check tomorrow," Amanda directed. "1600 hours all right?"

"Where?" Payne asked.

"How about right here? I don't think we should use the phone to conference," Maretti stated.

FROM AN UPSCALE HIGH-RISE APARTMENT IN downtown Seattle with an unobstructed view of Puget Sound, Basil Pettibone called his former friend and current criminal employer, Kevin Ross.

"I told you not to call me," Kevin snarled.

Basil shrugged and said. "I'm on a use-and-toss phone. Untraceable."

"You idiot! That's fiction for novelists. Any call can be traced."

"Mister Congressman," he sneered, "I'll make this quick. I'm going to disappear for a while. Some nosey NCIS cops raided my house. My girlfriend got word to me, so I moved all of my records before they got there."

"Where did you move them?"

Pettibone hesitated and then lied. "I destroyed them. I'm out. My friend and I are going to retire to a nice warm climate."

Actually, he thought, we're going to find a quiet island in southeast Alaska and turn hermit for a while.

Former Congressman Kevin Ross, who two years earlier was forced to swap his high office for a high-priced drug rehabilitation center, grunted and said, "You quit when I tell you to. Not before."

"Who's talking? My college buddy Kevin Ross, famed campus drug dealer? Or Bloodstone, international arms dealer, slave trader, dope pusher, and cocaine addict?"

"I'll kill you, Basil. Promise."

Basil laughed, but it was a nervous laugh. "Do you want to know how I found your Bloodstone code name? One of your goons forgot his cell phone. There was a text message. I traced your number. Cost me $5,000 in bribes to a computer nerd who works for a cell phone company. But I found you."

"You just signed your death warrant."

"Well, before you kill me, tell me…what's the significance of Bloodstone?"

"Bloodstones make people disappear."

"I thought it made them invisible. I looked it up."

"Yeah, but this Bloodstone makes people disappear. Which is what is going to happen to you, Basil."

"Who's gonna do that, Congressman? You personally? Or that army of thugs you employ?"

"You'll never know."

"And you'll never find me. And you sure as hell won't find that last shipment of money I was holding for you. Well, gotta go, Kev. Catch you on the flip side, old buddy. I can't say it's been fun."

Ross just stared at the phone before shutting it off. He walked across the room to a set of double doors that opened out on a third floor balcony jutting out over the waters of Puget Sound. He threw the cell phone as far as he could in the general direction of Seattle. He watched the phone arc out over the water, splash and then sink.

"You idiot, Basil! We had a sweet deal going, but you can't keep your mouth shut or your pants zipped."

He walked back to his office and parked his boney ass on the edge of the big teak desk. "Maybe it's time to quit," he said out loud. "Yeah, and do what? Ortega won't stand for that. But then again, maybe it's time to rid the world of that grease ball."

He walked around the desk and reached for another cell phone. A woman with a Middle Eastern accent answered. Without preamble Bloodstone said, "I got a job for you. It's worth $50,000."

"Doing what?"

"What you do best."

"High profile?"

"Very."

"I don't do high profile for less than $100,000."

Bloodstone snorted and then laughed. "Deal."

"In advance," the woman said.

"After," he countered.

The line was quiet for a good twenty seconds, and then the woman asked, "When?"

"I'll send the details to your Fedex mailbox."

The woman hung up without another word.

Bloodstone paced the room and then skipped down a wide staircase to the foyer of his mansion that sat perched on the east side of Bainbridge Island.

He opened a side door to a servant's suite and said, "Frank, turn off the damned TV and get in here. I got some people I want followed."

Chapter 5

AND IT WASN'T JUST THAT HE was on administrative leave from the City of Portland Police Department—again. He was sincerely worried about his old partner, Sheriff Henry (Bud) Blair.

The big, handsome Black detective, Dell BeBe, known to his friends as "BB," sipped his coffee and stared again at the newspaper clippings scattered on his dining room table. There were news photos of the blast crater that BB had downloaded and printed from major national and international newspapers, papers like the *New York Times*, *London Times*, *The Christian Science Monitor*, and several non-English papers. And each edition had a front page picture of a haggard Bud Blair standing on a stepstool while he gave the press the "what-for."

BB couldn't read the text of the non-English papers, but the photo of his old friend was front and center on most of them also. The one that worried him the most was an English translation of an Al Jazeera article. Words like "false claims," and "infidel" hammered at BB. *They gonna try and kill Bud for damned sure*, he thought. *And I just can't let that happen.*

He picked up his cell phone and hit the speed dial for Bud's cell number. He could barely hear Bud say, "That you, BB?" over the engine noise of a diesel pickup.

"Honky? I can hardly hear you. Where you at? Can you hear me?"

Bud's voice was clearer as he answered, "Yes. That's better. You were breaking up. What's going on?"

"Call me when you get to wherever you're going."

"That's it?"

"Call me," BB directed and then hung up.

He hit another speed dial number. "Yo," he said on the pickup. "Six-thirty," and hung up.

He looked at the grandfather clock sitting in the living room corner of his small but somewhat elegant apartment overlooking Portland and the waterfront. He felt at home in this room—leather couch and recliner, Navajo rug, onyx mantle above a gas fireplace, with several expensive, nicely framed prints on each wall, prints from Western artists like Ray Eyerly, Remington, and Bev Doolittle, and an original J. C. Smith he'd found at an art show over in the old Coliseum. The Smith was a simple painting—winter colors, depicting a tilted windmill in a snowbound field of tangled barbed-wire, an open gate, and dark sagebrush. The only personal touch was a large framed picture above the mantle, a picture of his son, Brian Dell BeBe, Lance Corporal, U.S. Marines, smiling, holding a rifle in one hand and signaling "V" for victory along with a crowd of other dusty Marines dressed for war. Somehow the photo was in harmony with the theme of the room.

The clock chimed the half-hour. *Okay*, he thought. *Five hours to the meet.* He heaved himself upright, stacked the clippings in a file folder and walked down the hall to a small bedroom that served as his office. He slid the file into a small fireproof metal box, and then locked the box in the bottom drawer of a metal three-drawer filing cabinet.

"Habit," he muttered in mild disgust. "Nothing in there that didn't come off the Internet. Oh, well."

He grabbed a dark blue windbreaker off the hallway coat rack, and patted the inside pocket to make sure his peacemaker was there, a small .22 Beretta that he could almost hide in his hand. Out of habit, he left a tell-tale—a small piece of monofilament fishing line closed in the door. If anyone opened the door, the fishing line would fall to the floor. Not foolproof, but it made him feel better.

He walked down the hallway to the elevator which took him to the parking garage.

MAX, Portland's version of D.C.'s metro system, dropped him at the Lloyd Center, and then he hoofed it "home" a few blocks north into his old salt-and-pepper neighborhood of older well-kept homes. He had attended Grant High School a dozen blocks east of the neighborhood, and at six-two, weighing a lean two-fifteen, he had made a name for himself on the football field as a high school running back, receiving a football scholarship to Oregon State University to boot.

The walk and the familiar neighborhood eased his tension somewhat. At least he had a plan, was doing something. The forced suspension without pay from his job as a homicide detective was wearing on him. And the business about Bud's high profile was scary. No street cop wanted his mug in the paper. And BB knew that Bud was at heart still a street cop. "You shouldna talked to the press, Bud," he muttered to no one in particular.

The Rock of Ages church stood in muted gray-green splendor on a corner surrounded by homes whose owners were waging a gallant fight against decades of rainy weather, ice storms, and cold east winds that belted a winter song down the Columbia Gorge. The building had the feeling of a quiet, humble neighborhood church with a touch of subdued dignity: stained glass windows down each side of the two-story building; a bell tower for a crown; neatly kept grounds; a modest rectory attached to the rear. But no parking. As Reverend T. J. Wildish put it, "You come to church, you walk. Christ did."

Century old trees stretched over the narrow streets to intertwine in green cathedral arches. Insistent trees roots buckled sidewalks in front of three-story homes that had been "discovered" by a new generation of young middle-class professionals whose bidding wars for the once-and-soon-to-be-again elegant homes had driven the prices to astronomical heights.

BB remembered his parents paying $18,000 for one of these "relics" that now brought $750,000 even in this depressed market. Just the increase in property taxes had driven many blue-collar families out to the suburbs where housing was more affordable.

He shook his head, mentally shrugged and thought, *That's the way of the world. You can fight it, but all you get is the right to cuss it. We're all conservative when it comes to changes in the world of our childhood.*

Early afternoons were always quiet ones for the church, so he turned down a narrow sidewalk past the glass-covered reader board that declared, "He is the Resurrection and the Light." He smiled at the worship notation: "Sunday Service — 10:00 A.M. Until I'm Through— Reverend T. J. Wildish."

He knocked on the kitchen door of the rectory.

T. J. peeked through the curtain on a side window, and then hurried to open the door.

"Lordy, lordy, if it ain't the prodigal son, hisself!" He gave BB a big hug, the top of his head barely even with BB's shoulders, and then stepped back. "Come on in."

T. J. poured them both a cup of coffee and sat down across the kitchen table from BB, staring up at his old friend through his bifocals. "I haven't seen you in church lately, BB."

BB tried to stifle a grin and failed. "Well, Reverend, I've been sorta busy. And I think I've heard all your sermons, anyway."

"Not true, my son, not true. I gain new insight every time I read the Good Book, and every time my flock discovers a new sin. Why just the other day, I discovered a new way of looking at the sin of covetation. Yessir, a new way of looking at covetation."

BB looked skeptical. "T. J., I've read quite a few books, and I've listened to a lot of lectures, and even a few sermons, but I've never heard the word covetation."

T. J. just looked smug. "New one, huh? That's because you have not been coming to hear my sermons, which are the fruit of my experience, and the guide to salvation and everlasting life."

"I think I can figure it out for myself. Covet as in desire. Covetation as in wanting something really, really bad. Sinfully bad. Right?"

"You got it. Now this Sunday, I'm going to excoriate my flock for the Sin of Covetation." He rose from his chair. Right hand on his chest, left arm raised toward the sky, he intoned, "We live in an age of greed, and greed is godless covetation." The Right Reverend Thomas Jefferson Wildish plopped back down in his chair. "What do you think, BB? If I have to, I'll scare them into becoming righteous beings."

"Wow. I'm impressed, T. J. It scares me in ways you can't imagine. And to think you could barely read when you finished high school."

"Don't rub it in. I caught up wichya. But that's not why you came to see me, is it?"

"No. Are you still on the Portland Ministerial Council?"

"Yes, of course."

"Good. Are the mullahs still on the council?"

"You mean our Islamic brethren?"

BB shook his head. "No…they're not my brethren, T. J. I mean those asshole Muslims mullahs who preach hate against any non-Muslim, of any race, and who recruit young Black men into a pseudo, plagiarized religion and turn them against all humanity. Especially American humanity. That's who I mean!"

"Strong words for strong beliefs. I'd say you missed your calling," T. J. murmured with a look of admiration for BB's soliloquy.

BB looked grim. "I'm not filled with 'covetation' for their souls, T. J. I'm in the business of retribution."

"What is it you think they've gone and done, BB?"

"I can't prove it, but I know those bastards intended to use the explosives they touched off down in the desert…intended to set them off in my town. In Portland. Against the people I live with. And I'm pretty sure they now intend to kill my old friend Bud Blair."

Thomas Jefferson Wildish nodded. "Okay. You don't need to ask. I'll put the word out. I know some brothers who deserted the true church. A few still talk to me. I'll see if I can find out what's going on in the Muslim community. They ain't all blood thirsty, like some."

BB nodded. He picked up his coffee cup and noticed the genealogy charts spread out on the kitchen table. He pointed. "What's all this?"

T. J. looked a bit embarrassed. "Research."

"Into what, Wildman?" BB asked.

T. J. sniffed. "I don't go by Wildman anymore. Not since I was saved by our Lord Jesus Christ. So knock that off. What I'm doing is researching my family history. Mama was always convinced we were related to Thomas Jefferson, so I aim to find out."

BB snorted. "Yeah, and he was a slave owner."

"I know, but he was also President of the United States."

BB shook his head. "By the way, where's Tubby?"

'You been away too long, BB. Tubby is grown now, graduated last year. He's a marine gone off to fight the godless infidels in Afghanistan. Just like your Brian."

"I'm embarrassed, T. J.. I didn't know. Give him my best. I'll say a prayer."

"You...praying?"

"Only for others."

"Well, you best say a prayer to our Father for yourself. It's okay to ask for help. Sounds like we gonna need it. And I'd say you need it especially right now. I saw in the papers that you been suspended...again. Want to tell me about it?"

BB shook his head, and then sighed. "I hit an undercover cop in the mouth. Hard enough to bust some teeth. He was sassin' me, wouldn't tell me what he was doing hanging around with some hookers. Started calling me names. I can handle being call a pig... got used to hearing that from the hippies years back...but when he started to question my sexual orientation, I'd taken all the crap I was going to take from that asshole. Next thing I know, Internal is running an investigation, a stolen driver's license winds up being 'found' on my garage floor, and I'm on admin leave."

T. J. nodded. "You have a history of violence, BB. It just caught up with you."

"I'm in a violent business in a violent world, Wildman...I mean Reverend."

He rose, held out his hand and said, "Got to go. I'll check back with you. And thanks for the coffee."

"Give me a couple of days, BB. I should have something for you by then. And I'll say a prayer."

Chapter 6

THE SUN WAS BURNING A HOLE in the desert sky before Larae's system finally worked free of the drugs in the pain pills she'd taken the night before. When the throbbing ache in her ankle brought her awake, she was sweating, momentarily disoriented, and close to panic.

She gingerly swung her feet out of bed and onto the carpeted floor of the small back bedroom at the rear of the Christmas Valley Lodge. Staring at the room, trying to remember where she was, Larae finally got her bearings, and her pounding heart slowed to a more normal rate.

She took a deep breath and looked at the walking cast on her right ankle and the bandages wrapped about both legs. "What a mess," she groaned to herself, "and I can't even take a shower." But she was hungry—the first good sign in four days that she was mending—so she set about the business of using a toothbrush at the sink in the small bathroom, took a spit-bath, used lots of deodorant, and tugged uncooperative sweat pants over the cast. Satisfied she had done what she could with her hair, she slipped into a tank top that exposed a coiled cobra tattoo glaring on her left shoulder, and stumped down the short hall to the dining room avoiding the ugly aluminum cane the hospital had given her.

Dressed in cowboy civvies, Deputy Roger Hildebrand was sitting at the counter next to Wally Pidgeon, a small, spare man with thinning gray hair who retired to Christmas Valley ten years earlier. "For the view," he often explained to visitors.

In spite of themselves the tourists almost always asked, "What view?" Wally would sweep his arms in grand gesture and answer,

"Why, the view of miles and miles, of course." And then he always laughed at his own joke.

If the tourists didn't get the joke, he would explain they were standing on the bed of an ancient lake that had once lapped the edge of the mountains; that without the several thousand acres of irrigated farm and ranch land in Christmas Valley, all they would see were sand, rock and sagebrush, "for miles and miles."

Despite his habit of mooching free coffee almost every morning at the lodge, Wally had become Billie's best friend, the twenty-year gap in age not withstanding.

Billie Thompson, owner and operator of the Christmas Valley Lodge had joined them and was leaning over the counter listening to Roger give his version of the exploding hay truck. The enlarged photo lying on the counter showed a dramatic birds-eye view of the raw crater left by the enormous release of energy in an explosion that simply vaporized the hay truck and the terrorists.

Wally had his glasses pushed back on his forehead, squinting to make out the detail in the photo. Roger didn't comment, just pushed the photo to his right, a bit closer to Wally.

At the sound of Larae's entrance, Billie looked up. "Morning, Larae. How you doing, honey?"

"Just peachy." Larae sat down on Roger's left and gingerly inched her foot under the counter, only banging the walking cast against Roger's ankle once.

Roger winced, and said, "You mad at me?"

"Not yet," she groaned, "but I could get there in a hurry if you don't stop playing footsies with me."

Wally chuckled, and Billie reached for a heavy mug. "What you need, honey, is some coffee to get you going. You hungry?"

"I think I could eat the north end of a south bound skunk."

Billie headed for the kitchen. "Sounds like you're starting to heal up. Good appetites are a sign of improving health," she tossed back over her shoulder. "Eggs, bacon, and hotcakes coming up."

Larae took the cup in both hands and sipped at the coffee. She nodded at the photo. "I saw the picture the Bend Bulletin ran, but I was loopy from the drugs. Where'd you get that?"

"A friend of mine works for the Forest Service. One of their planes took the picture, so…I got a copy from him."

"Can I see it?"

"Here. Do you remember what happened?"

"It's coming back." She studied the photo and said, "I don't see our vehicles in this picture."

"No. Our rigs had been moved by the time the picture was taken. Sonny's rig had to be towed out, the state police came and drove Trooper Prince's cruiser away, and Bud used my pickup to get home after the fuss died down."

She nodded. "I seem to remember Bud coming to see me. He had a woman officer with him. Was that Michelle Trivoli?"

"One and the same."

Wally inched his chair a little closer and reached across to pull the photo in front of Roger. "Okay. Now. Go through it, step-by-step. I want to know how this all came down."

Roger glanced at Wally and then said, "Okay, Mr. Pidgeon. Here's what I think happened. I was told by Michelle that an NCIS special agent was flying into Lakeview, that a meet was set for 11:00 A.M., and that I was to get Larae in uniform and take her with me to Lakeview."

Wally looked glum. "One of the saddest days of my life. My beautiful Sweet Mama…my friend…turns out to be an undercover cop." He sighed, "Oh well, it was fun while it lasted."

Larae leaned forward and looked intently at Wally. "We're still friends, Wally. And you're still my bouncer until Billie says otherwise. I might quit this cop business and just tend bar."

Wally shook his head. "No. You won't quit. It's in your blood. Trust me."

Roger leaned back and glanced from Wally and then to Larae. He nodded. "Yep. Wally's right. You're too good a cop to just walk away."

"Good?" she snorted. "Look at me. Busted ankle. Both legs wrapped in gauze from crotch to ankle. Busted ear drum. A really good cop? Wow!"

Wally frowned at her outburst. "I never thought my Sweet Mama would go around feeling sorry for herself."

Larae clamped her mouth shut, her bright blue eyes squinting daggers. And then her shoulders slumped. "Damn you, Wally. Can't a girl have a little let down after being blown up?"

"Not my girl," he countered. "Besides, you were only almost blown up."

She stared and then started to smile, and then broke out in a broad grin. "You old reprobate. I could get to like you."

"You need that, I think," Roger added. "Maybe I need that, too. We did some PTS debriefing when my team left Kuwait. It wasn't a whole lot different than this. Just talking…punch and counter punch. Cry a little. Laugh a little. Get it out on the table. Look at it, move on."

Larae nodded. "Okay. So go through it again. Start where we found the hay truck."

"You don't want the prelim?"

"No. It doesn't matter to me."

"Well, it matters to me," Wally muttered.

"Okay. Maybe it matters to me, too," Roger agreed.

Billie called from the grill behind the service counter. "Louder. I want to hear this." She used a large hotcake turner to flip a row of sizzling bacon.

"I think that when Larae pulled Gar's fingerprints and we tried to run them through AFIS, things really got stirred up. Seems that Gar's fingerprints were classified. Our access was blocked, and Bud got a call from NCIS in Springdale, Washington, that a Special Agent was flying to Lakeview post haste to find out where we got the prints. I think they wanted to find Gar."

"Gar…as in our bottle-and-cans man?" Wally asked.

"I'd say that information is probably classified, but I won't deny it."

Billie hollered over the service counter, "I just thought he was a hippie. We get those here in Christmas Valley, you know. Deadbeat loungers."

Roger nodded. He skipped past the part where he had accused Larae of withholding information.

"Anyway. We were almost to the top of Picture Rock Pass... Deputy Sixkiller right behind us in his vehicle...when we got a call to check out a hay truck just north of Fort Rock. We had zero intel. But good soldiers that we are, we complied. State Trooper, Charlie Prince caught up with us at Fort Rock."

He looked at Larae. "Do you remember us finding the hay truck?"

She nodded. "Yes. I remember some people helping Cowboy change a flat tire on the hay truck. It was stopped where the crater is." She pointed to the photo. "I also remember a small plane crashing in Cowboy's hay field. Sonny sent me to check it out. There was a body in the plane and a blood trail leading towards Cowboy's house and barnyard."

She took a deep breath, "And when I came back up the road, you were in a firefight with some bad guys."

Billie slid a plate of bacon, eggs and hotcakes in front of Larae, wiped her hands on her apron, and lifted the coffee pot to pour herself a cup. "To think this happened in Christmas Valley," she murmured.

Roger ignored Billie and said, "And then you ran wide," and he pointed to the east side of raw crater, "and took up position here."

"Yes!" Larae said excitedly. "Now I remember. And then Sonny told us to take cover. That the bad guy was holding a detonator. So I dropped into a slight depression in the ground...the only real cover I could find. And that's the last thing I remember until I woke up in the hospital in Bend. Oh, wait a minute. I remember talking with you on the radio. You were off to the west of the truck. The bad guys were shouting to each other in a foreign language. Yes. That's right. And you thought it might be Farsi."

Roger nodded. "I'm pretty sure it was. I don't speak Farsi except a few words...like halt, surrender, water...basic stuff. I think they were deciding to try and kill us along with themselves."

Billie stepped back from the counter, arms crossed, just staring out into sunlit parking lot without really seeing it, trying to imagine the scene.

And Wally rocked back on the stool and just shook his head. "What did they intend with the explosives?"

"We don't know. Best guess? Some large urban target where they could do lots of damage and kill as many people as possible. Which city, which target, we'll probably never know."

"And kill themselves in the process," Wally added. "How do you fight that kind of thing in a big porous society like ours? How do you counter people who don't care if they die as long as they can kill you in the process?"

"One at a time, Wally. One at a time," Roger intoned.

Roger's cell phone rang, and the tension broke. "Morning, Ms. Undersheriff Trivoli," he said. "How may I help you?"

He listened for a few seconds, and said, "Hold on a second." He pulled a small leather bound notebook from his shirt pocket, clicked his pen, and said, "Okay. Go ahead."

Larae, relieved at finally being able to remember the events leading up to the blast and her subsequent injuries, turned her attention to her plate and fell to devouring the breakfast Billie had fixed for her. Billie and Wally looked on in approval at the evidence of a good appetite. And their collective worry changed to something nearly like parental love. Billie winked at Wally and they both smiled.

Roger flipped his notebook shut and said into the cell phone, "Will do. Bye."

He caught the look that passed between Wally and Billie and nodded. He silently thought, *Me, too,* and nearly blushed when he realized how deeply he felt for his injured partner.

"Well," he cleared his throat, fighting the lump there that threatened to betray him, "I have to be in Bend at 0800 tomorrow morning. The state police are fast tracking the admin hearing. If all goes well, I could be back on duty by this time tomorrow."

Larae looked up, smiled and mumbled, "Great," around a mouthful of hot cakes.

Chapter 7

A<small>N EXPENSIVE, POWERFUL LAPTOP RODE SAFELY</small> and dry in the man's backpack. In contemporary parlance, the thirty-year-old looked like a nerd. He was wearing wrinkled, baggy, green shorts, a University of Washington sweatshirt two sizes too big, and gold rimmed glasses. His black hair was two months past needing a trim. Scuffed black high-tops rode above his ankles, and his muscular legs sported knee-length gray socks. In a habit peculiar to residents of the Pacific Northwest, he wore no hat in spite of a persistent light drizzle that coated his hair and dripped off his glasses.

In the University of Washington district, he was just another poor starving student on his way to the library, a study session, a student tavern—some place students spent their Saturdays. Only his age, a worried frown, and the urgency of his pace marked him as suspicious.

He ducked under dripping branches and knocked on a Pilgrim's Gate set in a tall ivy-covered, weathered brick wall. A voice said, "Who?"

"Abdul."

"Last name," the voice said.

Abdul looked in both directions and then said in a whisper, "Mackenzie."

He heard what sounded like a key turning in a lock and the metallic slide of a bolt. The door swung inward and he stepped through to a stone flagged path that led to a three-story, ivy-covered mansion that overlooked Lake Washington. This was private property, but its proximity to the school and its brick construction suggested to passersby that it belonged to the University.

He turned and waited while the large man with close-cropped salt-and-pepper hair bolted and locked the gate.

He turned, smiled and shook his head. "Abdul McKenzie. What kind of a name is that?" He wrapped Abdul's hand in both of his big hands, grinning. "Did you get it?"

Abdul nodded and pointed at his backpack. "I did. You won't believe it when you see it. I didn't."

Bill Thompson, Special Agent in Charge, NCIS, Springdale, Washington pointed up the walk to the front entrance of the big house. "Come on in. I've got the coffee on. I won't guarantee it since I had to make it myself. My wife Dorothy is off to Florida to visit an elderly aunt who's ailing."

Thompson showed Abdul Abraham "Abe" McKenzie into the tiled entrance, a wide curved staircase leading upstairs on the right, a parlor on the left, and a long hallway straight ahead. An ancient brass chandelier, dusty with cobwebs hung from a ceiling two stories high.

"I'm impressed, Chief."

As he led Abe down the long hall, Thompson said back over his shoulder, "You should be. It cost me $4.5 million, and it's a wreck. But it has secrets that should work to our advantage."

"Uh…Chief. Where does a bureaucrat come up with that kind of money?"

Thompson pushed a swinging mahogany door open and walked into a large, very modern commercial kitchen. He pointed to a highly polished kitchen table next to a large cutting block that sat in the middle of the brightly lit room.

Abe pulled back a chair, set the backpack on the table, and sat down.

Thompson poured coffee for Abe, saw Abe shake his head no to the silent offer of cream, and added cream to his own mug of dark brew. He pulled back a chair and sat, cradling the warm mug in both hands, organizing his thoughts.

"Everything was built on a large scale when this baby was erected. It was copied after a larger mansion that one of the early lumber barons built in the late 1800s. This one has seven master suites, each complete with sitting room and bath. The big one has thirteen. This one only has two servant's quarters. The other has four. We do have a pool room, a small theater, and the basement came with a bomb shelter built during the 1950s. I use that as a wine cellar. I keep the wine for my guests...not that there are any. I prefer coffee. It's the darnedest thing in the world. I love beer, but it gives me a headache. Can't stand wine. And even the best whiskey taste like crap. You like wine?"

Abe nodded, and Thompson, said, "Good. I'll give you a bottle of that strange French wine my wife buys. Some of that stuff cost nearly two hundred dollars a bottle. Think about that. Two hundred dollars for a quart...make that a liter...of horse piss."

Abe looked slightly puzzled. "Chief? You haven't answered my question."

"Impatient." And then he laughed. "Take that damned wig off."

Abe grinned and pulled off the expensive but now dripping black wig. Underneath was short-cropped, brown hair. He took off the gold-rimmed glasses and stuffed them in the belly pocket of his UW sweatshirt.

"Better. Okay, about the money. It's my wife's money. We tried to keep it quiet for years. Didn't want to rub the noses of the power brokers in it. She inherited her money, about a hundred million of it, from a favorite aunt...who, by the way, inherited it from the lumber baron who built the big house. This one was built by a brother of the same lumber baron. Of course it didn't cost millions back then. Anyway, when it came on the market my wife came home, told me she was tired of trying to look poorer than we were, to stuff my damned ego up my 'you know where,' and that she didn't give a damn what I thought because she already owned this place. And I'd damned well have to commute to Silverdale."

Abe nodded. "You know I'll have to check all that out, don't you?"

Thompson snorted. "Of course I know it." He walked over to a desk sitting against the wall between tall rows of cupboards, pulled out two files from the top drawer and walked back to the table. "Here." He slid a thick file across the table. "This is the paperwork on the house. And this," he slid the second file across to Abe, "is the court recording of the will leaving my wife all of that lovely money."

"I still have to run my own check," Abe said almost defensively.

Thompson shook his head. "You can be a pain in the ass, Abe. Don't lecture me. I know the checks you have to make. Especially since…notice I don't say 'if'…we have a mole."

"Okay. Just wanted you to understand."

"By the way, how'd it go at the mosque?"

"As a third generation Lebanese American, I'm happy to tell you that the Imam is pissed. All those wonderful explosives and no Americans were killed." He paused and gave Thompson a questioning look. "When is the FBI going to take these guys down?"

"Soon. But we want the money source as well. And we want our mole. I believe it will all tie together and lead us back to Iran or Afghanistan. Big diplomatic coup if it does."

Thompson took another drink of coffee, set the mug down, and said, "Okay. Prelims done. What you got?"

Abe dug the laptop out of the pack, opened the lid, hit the power button and watched the computer boot up—for all of three seconds. He scrolled his files, hit Open, and turned the laptop to face the SAC, who held his breath a moment, then said, "Agent Tobias Warren."

Thompson read the file, muttered "shit" and turned the laptop back to Abe.

Abe's brown eyes were sympathetic. "Sorry, Chief. I just can't make it come out any other way."

Thompson slapped the table and said, "Damn, I hate this. We have to neutralize this agent."

Abe took a deep breath of his own and said, "I'm not an assassin."

"I don't expect you to be. I said 'neutralize.' I didn't say kill."

"Okay, then, Chief. This is what I suggest. You ask the FBI to put a tail on our agent. See if he leads us to Pettibone."

"Why not put Agent Spears on it?"

"Too close to Warren." Abe said, "He'd get suspicious."

Thompson nodded. "You're right. He would. But how about using those Bremerton detectives? Keep it totally out of federal hands. You act as the go-between. The only people who know will be you, me and those two? Right?"

"Wrong. He knows those two as well. I'm thinking we put Stone Fly or Bambi on this. Warren doesn't know any of the team. And any one of them is twice as good as Warren on his best day."

Thompson nodded. "Okay. I'll see to it."

Abe picked up his mug, sipped the coffee and stared at the ceiling, at the wall cupboards, the big grill—every place except at his boss.

Thompson looked at him, not talking, just speculating about what Abe might be thinking.

Finally Abe set the mug on the table, fixed Thompson with a level stare, and said. "I was excited when I found the money in Warren's bank account. And I was convinced he was our guy when I found the money had been moved to an offshore account. But it was too easy…like someone wanted me to find the money…to point the finger at Warren…somebody really good with computers." He dropped his eyes to the table and nodded to himself. "Yep…I think he's being set up."

"Think so?" Thompson asked.

"It sure feels like it."

"Okay, but we need to make sure."

"How we gonna do that, Chief?"

"I'll take care of it. In the meantime, I want you to do some digging into the backgrounds of our intelligence analysis group…see if any of them are having financial trouble, spousal trouble, drinking too much, gambling too much…using drugs or alcohol." His voice rose a decibel or two. "Hell, I don't know. Maybe they are pimps or racketeers on the side. But find me somebody who is vulnerable to blackmail or bribery."

Abe nodded and then took a deep breath. "Chief, there has to be somebody who is better at this computer shit than I am. I want a field assignment."

"No. I'm not asking."

Abe frowned and said, "Okay, I'll do what I can, but I need somebody who can really drive one of these things," and pointed at the laptop.

"Who do you know?"

Abe shook his head, "I'm not sure. Maybe someone from another law enforcement agency. Maybe a non-federal agency."

"Who do you trust?"

"I know this sounds far out. I read the reports from the various agencies on the Oregon bomb. They're all good, but one is exceptionally well written…vivid in description but still in an expository style. I'll have to go back and check on who wrote it, but I remember it was non-federal. There was something about the way the guy thought. And his report had pictures of the bomb crater, maps of the area, demographic information, that kind of thing. And he wasn't afraid to draw conclusions when the evidence supported it. I don't know what I'm saying. I guess I think the guy is a smart cop and a nerd all rolled into one."

Thompson got out of his chair and stood staring out the square panes of the kitchen windows overlooking a neatly kept flower garden. He turned to Abe and said, "Okay. You find this guy, you got 'em."

"Where we gonna work?"

"Upstairs. I have a nice office up there. You tell me what you need for computer power, I'll see that it's there."

Abe slipped a disc from the laptop and handed it to Thompson. "Here's your evidence. I've also downloaded this to a secure site. If anything happens to me, my source will contact you."

"Who is it?"

"Can't tell you, Chief. Wouldn't be secure otherwise."

"Abe, at the risk of sounding redundant, you can be a pain in the ass sometimes." He grinned. "Okay. Play it your way. Load up. I've got something to show you."

Thompson led him to a door in the corner of the kitchen and down a set of wooden steps. He flipped a switch and the basement was flooded with light. A heavy looking metal door was set in the Lake Washington end of the basement. There were no hinges visible. "That's the bomb shelter. I'll at least give 'em credit for more than paranoia. Damned thing has a back entrance. Here, I'll show you."

He opened a cupboard door and tapped six numbers into a keypad. There was an audible click and a pneumatic ram swung the heavy door quietly open.

Thompson led Abe into a fairly large room, an eight-foot ceiling, and maybe twenty-five feet wide and almost forty feet long. Shelves of vintage wine lined about twenty feet of one wall. The rest was simple smooth gray concrete.

Reinforced, I'll bet, Abe thought.

Thompson said, "I had all the bunks, tables, radios...all the junk torn out and thrown away. Did most of the work myself. Don't blame me for all the wine. I think my wife is planning a big bash... retirement bash for me maybe. Gonna invite the world, maybe. But this is what I wanted to show you." He fished a set of keys from his pocket and unlocked a smaller metal door set in a recess in the end of the room.

"Unknown to the world at large, a tunnel connects with a 3,000-square-foot carriage house at the bottom of the hill...which happens to belong to this house." He took two keys off the key ring. "This ordinary house key lets you in the back door of the carriage house. This other strange-looking monster," and he held up large bronze key shaped like a crucifix, "let's you into the tunnel and into this shelter. It works from both sides. Lock it behind you. And don't lose the brass key. It's the only one I've got. Maybe you can find a smith to make another one. At any rate, the vault can be opened from this side without a key. The code on the keypad is GOPHER. Cute, huh?"

Abe shrugged and decided, again, that his boss was just a little eccentric.

"You locate your guy. Bring him here through the carriage house. You'll find a garage door opener and a house key in a kitchen drawer. Even if you're followed, they'll never connect you to this house. And besides, you can leave by the Pilgrim's Gate and whoever follows you can wait down below until hell freezes over."

Thompson held out his hand and said, "Sooner the better. Leave by the carriage house. And don't forget to put your wig on. It's raining out there." And then he laughed at his own weak joke.

Chapter 8

PULLING HIS TRAILER BEHIND HIM, THE drive from Timothy Lake to Lake-view took John Bernard the better part of six hours. He grumbled at the delay for construction between Madras and Redmond, cussed the highway planners that squeezed traffic through the small city of Redmond, felt some relief when he found the expressway through Bend, and muttered at drivers who tailgated him down Highway 97 on his way to LaPine.

He was trained to plan, to plan again, to rehearse the plan, and then to execute the plan. Discipline was the bedrock of his craft. So it was totally out of character when he impulsively turned off Highway 31 just past the Horse Ranch R-V Park and onto the Christmas Valley highway. He knew it, but somehow seeing Larae again was more important than getting to Lakeview. The sheriff's a big boy, he rationalized. He can take care of himself for a few more hours.

ROGER HILDEBRAND AND WALLY PIDGEON HAD both left the Christmas Valley Lodge by the time John wheeled his pickup and trailer in an arc and parked on the edge of the big gravel parking lot. He shut the engine down, looked in the mirror at his growth of dark whiskers and thought, Oh well. I'll find my razor one of these days.

Billie was behind the counter taking clean plates, cups, saucers and silverware from the dishwasher when John opened the door. She recognized the blue sweatshirt and the blue eyes.

"Aha," she said. "The missing bottles-and-cans man. I know someone who will be glad to see you."

She poured coffee into a cup, set it on the counter, and said, "You sit right here. Don't go away."

She turned, pushed through a door near the end of the counter and walked down the hallway to Larae's room. She knocked and called out, "Honey? You awake? You got a visitor."

Billie could hear Larae groan through the hollow door just before the door knob turned and Larae peeked out. "What are you talking about, Billie?"

"Gar. It's Gar. He's here to see you."

"Oh my gosh. Wow! Look at me. I'm a mess." She ran her right hand through her hair.

"Never mind, honey. He isn't too fixed up himself."

"Okay. I'll brush my teeth and be right there."

John Bernard, who was known simply as "Gar" to the locals and as "Stone Fly" to his team, raised his eyebrows in speculation as Billie returned and walked behind the restaurant counter.

"She'll be right here."

"Uh…Mrs. Thompson, how…uh…how's she doing?"

"Oh, she's bunged up. And it'll be a while before she can take the cast off, but she ate like a starving hay hand this morning. That's a good sign. Where you been, by the way?"

"Feeding the squirrels. Feeling sorry for myself, I guess."

"Well, it's about time you got here. That girl has been worried sick about you."

John looked surprised. "Really?"

Billie shook her finger at him. "Yes. You just up and disappear, never leave word. Don't be doing that again or I'll sick Wally on you."

He grinned at the thought. "No ma'am, I don't want Wally after me."

"And don't you hurt that girl's feeling either."

LARAE PUSHED THE DOOR OPEN AND hobbled in.

John got off the stool and stood up. Larae didn't say a word, just gimped over to him and held out her arms, silent tears starting down both cheeks. He held her and she sniffed and whispered, "You smell like wood smoke. Where the hell have you been?"

Tears finally under control, Larae led John by the hand through the bar and out to the back patio. They sat in lawn chair recliners, sipped coffee, and watched thunder heads build in the north over the China Hat country.

"I've been thinking about a career change," John said. "Maybe buy me ranch in Christmas Valley. Find a woman who likes that kind of life. One who could stand living with me, of course."

"Or one you could stand to live with," she countered.

"Do you know anyone like that?"

"I might," she said, "but right now she's a little bunged up. If you talked to her in a month or so, she might have an answer for you. If you don't get yourself killed in the meantime. And if you actually do make a career change."

"Good point. What are you going to do, about the police business, I mean?"

"A ranch wife might need to work to bring in a steady income until the place started paying off."

"So you plan to stay with the sheriff's department?"

"Wally says it's in my blood. And I have to believe that what you do is in your blood, also."

"I hate to think this is all I can do," John muttered.

The ninety-minute drive from Christmas Valley to Lakeview, gave him ample time to sort through his feelings for Larae and her obvious attraction to him. But his own feelings were a bit harder to define, partly because he was trained to lock his feelings away. Sneaking into an enemy camp, playing possum for hours on end, watching and listening, as his unit commander put it, "like a fly on the wall," required something entirely foreign to the business of feeling. He felt a degree of modest pride to be dubbed "Stone Fly," but he didn't analyze why. Not something people in his business did.

"How do I feel about her?" he asked himself aloud somewhere along about the Summer Lake refuge. "Why do I have this urge to take care of her?" And then he snorted at the irony of that, because taking care of someone meant something entirely different in his line of work.

As he topped the rise north of town and started down the gentle grade to Lakeview, he saw green farm fields, cattle, a few horses and Goose Lake off in the south, looking more like a mirage than a body of water. Tree-shaded houses lined the east side of the highway, and in the distance rows of ancient trees marked the town.

John spotted an RV park just beyond the Hunter's Hot Springs and pulled in. The manager cast a skeptical look at the decrepit-looking trailer, but didn't object to a month's rent paid in cash. He told John to take spot sixteen, and waited until the pickup and trailer pulled away from the office before hurrying to find a phone.

THE RINGING PHONE DISTURBED THE CONCENTRATION of Michelle Trivoli, acting undersheriff for Lake County. She waited for Karen Highsmith, the sheriff's bailiff and unofficial administrative assistant to answer the phone, but after the fourth ring, Michelle decided Karen must be in back tending to her "guests" as Karen referred to the inmates.

She picked up the receiver and said, "Lake County Sheriff's Office. This is Deputy Trivoli. How may I help you?" She glanced at the caller ID and scribbled the number on a note pad while a male voice answered. "I'd like to speak to the sheriff."

"I'm sorry. He's not available. This is Undersheriff Trivoli."

"Well, this is Marvin Goodnough out at the RV park…north of town. It's probably nothing, but there's a guy out here I think you need to see. Scruffy sort, old pickup, beat-up travel trailer. When I asked for a credit card he just pulled out a bunch of bills and paid cash. Looks suspicious to me. Thought you might want to know."

"Thanks, Mr. Goodnough. We'll have an officer talk to him."

Michelle hung up and muttered, "Well. 'We'll have an officer…' That was optimistic. Sonny and Roger are on admin leave at least through tomorrow. Lonnie is headed for Quartz Mountain to check a burglary report. Bud's gone to talk to Nancy, and Larae is bunged up. That leaves me. I wonder if Gus Hildebrand is busy."

She hit the speed dial for the City Police, waited through two rings and heard a female voice answer, "Lakeview City Police."

"Helen? This is Deputy Trivoli. Is the chief there?"

"No, but I think he's across the street having coffee at Jerry's Café. Want me to fetch him?"

"Yeah. Ask him to call me. I need some backup."

AUGUSTUS (GUS) HILDEBRAND, LONGTIME LAKEVIEW CITY police chief, followed Michelle's SUV in his cruiser, a black Ford Crown Victoria, out to the RV park. Marvin came out of the office when he saw the two police vehicles. Michelle powered down her window, and Marvin said, "Sixteen. He's just setting up."

A bearded face greeted her knock on the trailer door. John Bernard said, "Shit," and then asked, "Is he okay? I tried his cell phone, but he's not answering."

"Please step out of the trailer and identify yourself," she ordered.

He smiled at the hefty figure of Chief Hildebrand, right hand on the butt of his pistol, standing beside his cruiser which, John noted, was blocking his pickup.

He stepped out arms wide and hands empty. He looked at her badge and said. "Okay, Officer Trivoli." He sighed and said in a tired voice, "How do I do this?" And then he said, "I was in Christmas Valley when the bad guys blew themselves up."

Michelle felt a small surge of adrenalin and a touch of panic that she pushed down. "Stone Fly?"

"One and the same."

Michelle's mind was racing furiously, partly out of fear for Bud, and partly from the excitement of actually talking to the mysterious Stone Fly. I need some way to verify this guy, she thought.

"Give me the one detail the press never reported."

"I have no idea what the press has reported. I've been camping. Totally out of touch with the world." He paused, and then asked, "Did anyone tell the press about Chase and Harley? The two guys I left tied to a pine tree?"

She let out a breath she hadn't realized she was holding. "No... they didn't."

"There you go then."

"Give me another name," she ordered.

He chuckled, and then said, "How about Gar?"

She wasn't totally sold yet. "Tell me about fingerprints," she ordered.

"You are hard to convince. That set off a hornet's nest, didn't it? All right. Sequence: Deputy Holcomb ships you a beer bottle carrying my fingerprints. You run the prints and find your access blocked. NCIS Special Agents Spears and Warren fly down.

"I peg the bad guys and call it in. Your unit responds. The bad guys shoot at the good guys. The good guys shoot back. The bad guys blow themselves up and hurt the good guys.

"I bring in Crazy Charlie. Sheriff Blair and I chopper out to pick up Chase and Harley. I borrow a quad and go on R&R."

"That'll do. I believe you. Why are you here?"

He let his arms fall back into a relaxed position. "Well, I'd rather talk privately," he answered, nodding toward Gus.

She said, "I must be crazy."

He shrugged and said, "After what your unit has been through, I'd be suspicious of anyone who comes to town looking like I do." He sniffed his right arm pit and wrinkled his nose. "Right now I need a shower and a shave."

He turned and put his hands behind his back, and almost whispered a command. "Now cuff me."

She thought quickly and said, "No. Lock your trailer and get in the front seat. We've already attracted too much attention. I don't think you want that. Let's play it like it is...a friend come to see Bud."

He said, "Maybe you're right. Small towns and busy bodies. Right?"

She sniffed. "Don't look down on these people. They are bright, loyal, and very protective of their town and their county. What you see as nosey is more than curiosity. It's our early warning system."

"Hence, the phone call from the park manager, right?"

She nodded. "I need to tell Gus. His son is Deputy Roger Hildebrand, one of the officers hurt in the Fort Rock explosion."

Gus's great, bushy eyebrows, just turning from black to silver, were raised in a question mark when she walked over. Quietly she told Gus that he was a friend of Bud's. That this friend had been camping, an explanation for his scruffy appearance, and that she was going to give him a tour of the town since Bud wasn't available.

She said, "Thanks for the backup. It made me feel better to have you here."

Gus looked skeptical, but shrugged. "Any time, but I have to tell you there's something about him that makes me uneasy. You be careful, girl."

With that he slid into the Crown Vic, hit the starter and drove the loop out of the RV park.

"No introduction?" John asked.

She shook her head. "Gus is notional and sometimes grumpy. I think he's pissed because I dragged him away from his coffee and pie. It could also mean that he doesn't like you."

John laughed, and shook his head. "You know, he may be a good judge of character."

Michelle stopped and powered down the window as Marvin came out of the office. "It's okay, Marvin. He's a friend of mine. Just scruffy looking because he's been camping," and she grinned at her smoky-smelling passenger. She looked up at Marvin and added, "But you did the right thing. Thank you."

The ride to the station was quiet until John said, "You didn't answer my question."

"Which question?"

"Is he all right?"

"Gus?"

"No, and don't play games with me. I mean the sheriff."

"As far as I know. Why?"

"I've been trying to reach him on his cell, but he's not answering."

She hesitated. "Well, he and Nancy were planning a trip to Yakima to introduce him to Nancy's mother. And then they were flying to Reno to get married. I mean, I'm sure that's what the plan was. Although he didn't say the word 'married' come to think of it. Hmmm."

"Don't get side tracked, Officer Trivoli. Let me lay it out: My boss told me to get down here to watch Bud's back. Only he isn't here. So," he hesitated as their vehicle drove slowly past the tree shaded cemetery, "I can't watch his back if he's gone."

"Then we'll have to find him, won't we?" she smiled sweetly.

Chapter 9

BB DIDN'T LIKE OPEN MEETING PLACES like parks or zoos or football stadiums. He always snorted in derision when he saw scenes in movies where the bad guys wanted to meet in open spaces. "Too easy to trap or kill," he said.

No, he liked middle-class, yuppy bars. Brightly lit, noisy, busy bars. Impersonal bars. Bars with few if any regulars. And he liked his snitches to clean up and blend in. That's what he liked about the lounge at the Portland Hilton. No local crowd. Strangers coming and going. Nobody making eye contact. There was always an element of risk, but the kind of people he was trying to avoid never came close to the place.

His snitch was late, not unusual for Cletus who had a dozen scams going at any one time, none of them involving violence, prostitution or drugs, but most of which were illegal in a fairly harmless sort of way. So BB sat in a back corner of the Hilton lounge, nursed a draft Heffy and watched the small crowd of customers, most alone or paired up with a business associate. None of them were familiar to BB, and none of them looked to be anything other than travelers killing an out-of-town evening.

BB knew Cletus scalped tickets for Blazer games and sold knock-off watches at twenty times what he paid. Cletus also had a half-dozen people working for him hawking umbrellas, flowers, walking canes, Blazer tees, caps and sweats that he imported from Thailand, and imitation leather belts, all sold from unlicensed tables at Max rail-line stops and parking lots near the Rose Garden, the Portland Trailblazers' home court. And he had friends among the Chinese gangs who steered Cletus to "good" deals.

Every year Cletus Enterprises paid the State of Oregon fifty dollars to be registered as a DBA, ostensibly an import/export business. And every year Cletus Enterprise showed a small profit and Cletus duly paid his taxes.

But the main product of Cletus Enterprises was information. In simple terms Cletus Falls was a paid informant for several government agencies like U.S. Immigration Services, the FBI, and almost every police agency in the greater Portland area. Since these agencies rarely shared information about their snitches, BB was one of only a couple of police officers who knew Cletus frequently sold them all the same information.

BB took a sip of beer and thought about the first time he had met Cletus. Five years ago, because he had once again been the subject of an article in *The Oregonian* about police brutality—undeserved in BB's opinion—his captain had assigned BB to investigate a complaint from one of the city's licensed vendors about an outlaw vendor at the Rose Garden. When he had walked up behind the sixty-five-inch Cletus, a young man whose ancestry appeared to be Asian and Black, and put a big hand on his shoulder, Cletus had started, turned and looked at him. "Who you?"

BB chuckled. "Why bro, if this was a bad movie, I'd say I was your worst nightmare. But this ain't a movie, so I'll let that pass." He flipped his badge open and then slipped it back in his pocket.

Cletus had just stared up at him and said, "Let me see that again."

"You're a cocky little bastard," BB said with a hint of a smile. But he dug the leather wallet out of his jacket pocket and showed his badge to Cletus again.

"What for is a big city detective rousting an honest businessman?" Cletus asked.

BB shrugged. "Good question, but I still want to see your license."

"Don't need one."

BB sighed. "Not true. The City says you do."

Cletus had shrugged and said, "If you let me go, I'll tell you something a lot hotter than an unlicensed vendor."

BB looked skeptical, but said, "What you got, Bro?"

"See that tall, Black dude with the white chick on his arm? He be the pimp and she be the trick. And that ain't all they do. He be a big time blackmailer. Gets the john into a room, sells him a little weed, lets the girl do the trick, and takes pitchers. Then shakes the john down for lots of cash money.

"Right now they be prospectin' the crowd, lookin' for an out-of-towner willin' to play around a little."

BB and stared hard at the little man and then decided he was telling the truth. He reached into his pocket, casually pulled out a roll of bills and slipped a fifty-dollar bill into Cletus's hand. "What's your name, boy? And don't give me no shuck and jive bullshit. And I want a cell number and an address. Otherwise, I'll take you downtown."

Cletus had hesitated before telling BB his name and address and then gave him a cell number. When BB thumbed the numbers into his cell and hit send, the phone in Cletus's pocket started playing a musical a jingle.

"Okay. Gather your stuff and split. I don't want to see you again."

"For another fifty, I got more information you might like."

BB used his cell phone to take a picture of the man and woman, and when Cletus laughed, he had kicked Cletus gently on the rump. A full sixty seconds ticked off the clock before Cletus had his folding table in one hand and a battered suitcase full of cheap, imitation Blazer gear in the other.

BB shook his head, and stared as Cletus swaggered through the parking lot until the small boy-man took his red and white Blazer jersey, blue sag-down-your-ass jeans, and high top black and white Nikes around the corner and out of sight. BB resisted the temptation to follow just to see if Cletus simply moved around the block and set his table up again.

"You need a daddy," BB growled to no one in particular.

When BB shared the tip with an old friend who worked vice, he discovered Cletus had already sold that information, twice. He just grinned and knew he had found a new snitch.

That had been five years ago, and Cletus knew that all BB had to do was pick up the phone to rat him out. So he worked pro bono for BB—except for an occasional dinner and a drink that BB paid for from bribe money furnished by the City. And BB had coached, wheedled, and threatened to the point that Cletus finally applied to the city for a vendor's license. But he wouldn't abandon his information dealing.

"Gots to pay for my eddication, somehow," he told BB every time BB chided him for his scams.

"And clean up that ghetto tripe you talk," BB would retort.

Now sitting in the lounge waiting, the vibration of his cell phone interrupted his reminiscing. Seeing the number, he asked, "That you, Honky?"

"Yeah. This is Bud. I'm sorry I didn't call sooner, but it got kinda busy there for a while."

"Where are you?"

"I'm in Lakeview."

"Okay," BB answered, "I'm going to suggest you not use that particular cell phone again. Buy a couple of those use-and-toss kind. And I'm going to suggest you find a safe place to hole up until I get down there to give you back up. I know these bastards, and they are big on revenge. They'll be coming after you, Honky, so don't let your guard down. And don't give me no crap about not needing my help. I know your department is down to practically zero officers."

"That won't last long." Bud said, "I should get two of my guys back in the next couple of days."

"Nonetheless, you listen to your old partner and watch your back. Keep an eye out for my old red Corvette. I'll be down. Got a couple of things to do here first, but I'll be down."

He could hear Bud let out a deep breath. "If I listened to you, BB, I could become paranoid. Sure hard to believe the bad guys would waste time on a high desert sheriff." The phone was quiet for a few seconds and then Bud added, "Okay. I'll do my best to stay alive, but I'm not going to hide. Let me know when you get here."

BB watched Cletus walk through the entrance to the lounge, and said, "I'll find you. Gotta go." And he broke the connection.

THE CALL FROM DELL BEBE TO Sheriff Bud Blair triggered a late generation satellite tracking system hidden in an old historic mansion atop the West Hills above the city of Portland. It automatically encrypted and transmitted a micro-burst message to a secure site at NCIS headquarters in Silverdale, Washington.

Chapter 10

NCIS SECTION SUPERVISOR DAN WITHERSPOON WATCHED as one of the printers in a room full of wall-mounted monitors spit out a deciphered record of Bud and BB's cell conversation. It was a flagged intercept. Witherspoon chewed a mangled toothpick, testament to a nicotine habit that kept him looking at a wall clock that seemed frozen in time.

Kathryn Lockwood, his number two, noted the tight look Witherspoon got when he needed a trip to the inner courtyard to feed his two-pack-a-day habit. And she pondered again why the few smokers in Silverdale were almost always in the information and analysis group. To her knowledge none of the special agents and none of the operators smoked.

"Log that and give me a copy," he said, and pointed to the printer.

Kathryn sorted the pile, placed a copy in a file folder and handed the folder to Witherspoon. He tucked the folder under an elbow, and headed for the communal snack counter. The last inch of coffee in the pot, maybe two hours old, looked and smelled like burnt rubber.

"Damnation," he grumbled, and, sans coffee, pushed through an unmarked exit out into the damp air of the inner courtyard.

Bill Thompson was sitting at a patio table, a cold cup of coffee on the damp metal surface. An unlit, well-chewed cigar rested in a battery-powered "smoke scrubber" ashtray. The batteries had long since corroded, but no one cared that it was useless.

"Got a light, Dan?"

Witherspoon put the folder down and fumbled a lighter from his shirt pocket.

He wondered if Thompson had been waiting specifically for him to take a smoke break. When the tip of Thompson's cigar was a red coal, he passed the lighter to Dan, and asked, "What you got there?"

"I'm not sure. It's low level stuff. The characters are interesting, but the conversation doesn't do anything for us that I can see." Witherspoon sat down and handed the folder to Thompson.

Witherspoon lit an unfiltered cigarette and took a deep drag, his synapses settling down, smoothing out, no longer demanding a nicotine fix.

Thompson read slowly, trying to hear the nuances of the conversation between Sheriff Blair and Detective Dell BeBe. Finally he put the pages back in the folder, stared at the tip of his cigar, and then asked, "Who ordered the surveillance?"

"Special Agent Spears."

"Why?" Thompson asked.

"Didn't give a reason. Special agents order and we respond. End of story."

Thompson nodded and rose. "Okay. Maybe she's in love again. Log that and send me a copy."

Witherspoon started to butt his cigarette, but Thompson said, "No hurry, Dan. Finish your cigarette."

Back in his office, Thompson dialed a number, listened for the call to be picked up, and said, "Abe, have you found our guy?"

Abe said, "Ronald Grandfield, a detective for the Bremerton City Police. He partners with another detective named Maretti."

Thompson snorted. "I know Maretti. At least I know of him. He keeps irritating our on-base NCIS agents in Bremerton. Seems to think there is some conspiracy to keep him away from our investigations."

"If I know our guys, there is," Abe said.

"Okay, Abe. You be at the house this afternoon. I'll have Detective Grandfield there. I'll also have our computer equipment delivered in an hour or two, so you might want to be at the big house a little early."

Without saying anything further, Thompson hung up.

Chapter 11

After a restless night and broken sleep, Maretti finally gave it up and rose at 6:30 A.M. A quick shave and a shower while his coffee brewer glugged and gurgled, a travel cup slopping with this vile bachelor brew—a double dose of Seattle's Best—and Maretti was headed for the station, his vintage Ford GT rumbling through the nearly empty streets of Bremerton.

He made a quick stop at a mini mart for gas, two maple bars, and a copy of the *Seattle Times*.

Even though he hated the Times and had in fact cancelled his subscription, he was a news junkie. And that meant buying the Times at newsstand prices. He recognized the absurdity of his behavior, but he kept thinking that the paper didn't know he still read the damned rag. So that counted for something.

The Bremerton City Police—that is Maretti and Grandfield—had drawn the unglamorous job of circulating pictures of the truck driver and the helpers who moved Pettibone out of the big house on the heights. They had also agreed to check with the truck rental businesses in Bremerton.

Grandfield walked in at 7:30, wrinkled his nose at Maretti's rancid-smelling coffee and set his cup of Starbucks on the table in the conference room. He nodded at Maretti and immediately walked to an overstuffed bookcase. A well-thumbed Bremerton phone book peeked out from under a stack of department memos, old newspapers, and the human detritus of a "paperless society."

He flipped the book open to the yellow pages.

Maretti looked at the list of assignments, drummed his fingers on the table and finally said, "Grandfield, I don't mind doing the grunt work, but I can't believe Basil Pettibone is stupid enough to hire locals…unless he was panicked. You agree?"

"I don't know, Gino. Criminals tend to get over-confident and make dumb mistakes."

"How many you got listed there?" Maretti asked.

"I count seven truck rental companies."

"Okay." Gino heaved up out of his chair. "Let's go see if we can get some Uniforms to chase this…show the photos, ask dumb questions like, 'You be an honest man?' I want you to dig into Pettibone's background, family, college, military service…anything you can find. You know how to do that?"

Grandfield started to say that he was a hell of a lot better than Gino at computer search, but he caught the amused gleam in Gino's eye and kept the comment to himself. "I can do it, Gino."

"Okay. I'm gonna go Bigfoot hunting, see what I can pick up."

"Bigfoot hunting?" Grandfield asked.

"Yeah. You know where you can find any Bigfoot around here?"

Grandfield thought the question was rhetorical, so he stayed quiet, hand on the door knob, poised to leave the conference room. When Gino didn't elaborate, Grandfield finally said, "No, I don't."

Maretti grinned. "I don't either."

Grandfield shook his head and pulled the door open. He looked back at Gino before closing the door, and thought, *Gino's just making noise like he always does.*

Maretti walked over to the easel and studied the list, trying to think of anything they might have overlooked.

The conference room phone rang twice before Gino picked it up. "Maretti," he said.

The voice on the phone was that of his chief's administrative assistant, a striking thirty-something, willowy redhead named Loretta Green. She always wore pantsuits that probably cost five hundred dollars a copy, had her short hair "coiffed" once a week, drove a silver BMW—an older one he had to admit in a fit honesty—and kept the captain's subordinates nicely in line. Maretti idly wondered how she managed to live so well on an AA's salary.

Green's peremptory attitude and her flagrant use of the chief's "shadow power" earned her a Gino Maretti sobriquet. "AA doesn't mean Administrative Assistant," he told Grandfield. "It means Arrogant Asshole."

Grandfield made the mistake of telling him that only men were assholes. He further asserted Ms. Green was good at her job, and then couldn't resist suggesting Gino was offended because she was three inches taller than Maretti. Grandfield never shared that particular observation with Maretti again. "Too risky," he told his wife. "He was so mad I thought he might shoot me."

"I HAVE A CALL FOR YOU," Loretta said. "Hang up. I'll put it through."

He waited until the phone rang before taking his finger back off the receiver button. "Maretti."

"This is Ruby Goldstein. I thought you should know that she just left here. She said she wanted to know if I had given her all the pictures I had taken."

"Who is she?" he asked.

"Oh, I'm sorry. That woman NCIS agent, Amanda Spears. I thought you knew."

"No, I didn't."

"Well, there was something almost frantic in her behavior...like she was afraid of something in the pictures I took." Ruby Goldstein paused. "So...I lied. I told her that she had all the copies of all the photos I had taken. And then she demanded that I give her all the discs from my camera."

"I'll be damned. I wonder why?"

"Well, she said it was a matter of National Security. Maybe I've been reading too many Agatha Christie novels, but I think she might be trying to hide something."

"And you have other pictures she doesn't know about."

"Is this phone secure?"

"My goodness, Mrs. Goldstein, you've been reading more than Agatha Christie. Tell you what, you sit tight. Lock your doors and if she returns don't let her in. We'll be right there. Ten minutes tops."

"Thank you."

Maretti paused. "Why do you trust me and not Agent Spears?"

"Call it woman's intuition. That and I think you're just too damned cantankerous to be crooked. I liked it when you kicked in Pettibone's door. I thought to myself, 'I wish I could do that. There's a man after my own heart.'"

Maretti hurried down the hallway, his shiny, well polished penny loafers slapping the highly waxed, but worn vinyl-tile flooring. Coat tail billowing like a parachute, he banged the door open and shouted, "Let's go, Grandfield," without breaking stride or looking to see if Detective Grandfield was behind him. "We got a hot tip."

A detective at a desk against the back wall looked up and hollered out, "You always got a hot tip, Gino. That's probably why your wives left." Maretti flew the squad room a generic single digit salute and kept walking.

A wave of laughter and catcalls chased Maretti out the door and down a hallway that led to a parking lot at the side of the building.

Maretti tossed Grandfield the car keys, and got in on the passenger side. "Take us back to Ruby Goldstein's place."

"Why am I all of a sudden doing all of the driving? You losing your sight, Gino?"

RUBY WAS WAITING ON THE FRONT porch when Grandfield pulled into her driveway. She was wearing designer jeans and a soft blue cashmere sweater. Maretti had a sudden, clear picture of long legs and painted toenails. He shook the picture away with a hard reminder to himself that she was a married woman. *End of story.*

She invited them in and ushered them down a short hallway to an airy kitchen and the smell of coffee. She pointed to four neat stacks of photos lying on the red and white checkerboard tablecloth. "These are duplicates. I have them all on my computer, but I also have a disc and as further protection, I've emailed these to a friend."

"And you need us, for what?" Maretti asked.

"I want you to take these away so if that nice lady agent comes back searching for more, I can honestly say I don't have more."

Grandfield moved to the table, sat down in a padded kitchen chair and started working his way through the stacks one photo at a time...looking for some anomaly or some familiar face. Maretti took the chair beside him and started working through the discards from Grandfield's stack. Ruby slid a mug of coffee quietly beside Maretti. He absent-mindedly sipped the coffee and continued to study each photo with a concentration that was almost physical in intensity.

Ruby, perched on a taller stool at the granite topped bar separating the dining area from the open kitchen, watched both men. She silently decided their ability to truly concentrate made them good detectives. And she felt drawn to Maretti's irascibility.

She wasn't sure why. Maybe it was the glint of intelligent humor lurking in his dark eyes. And maybe it was the fact he made things "move" in his world. He wasn't a pawn. He was a warrior, she decided. Yes. That was it.

The pictures, clear telephoto shots of license plates and faces, backyard parties, late evening trysts in Pettibone's gazebo, silhouettes against back-lighted curtains, were all shots that would have done credit to a trained watcher.

Maretti pushed that last of the photos into a pile and stared at Ruby's backyard through a pale yellow sheer before turning to Grandfield. "Well? See anybody you know?"

Grandfield shook his head. "No. Not one familiar face. No local bad guys. *Nada.*"

"Me either." Maretti added with a sigh. "Damn." He looked up at Ruby. "These are really good. You ever think about starting a private detective agency?"

Ruby smiled. "Thank you. Today's digital cameras make it easy. Even in low light. And, no...I hadn't thought about being a PI."

Maretti laughed, "Yeah, but cameras can't decide what pictures to shoot. Nice work. But I have to tell you, these" and he tapped the stack of photos with a blunt forefinger, "could be dangerous. Why don't you find someplace to hole up until we run this business to ground?"

"That dangerous?"

"Yeah. We have to share these photos with NCIS."

Grandfield looked at Maretti and shook his head, but Maretti ignored him and added, "I think NCIS has a mole. One of these people," he pointed to the photos, "could be that mole, and if the mole sees the pictures…" He let the sentence trail off.

"Look," he said to Ruby, "the photos will likely blow the lid off, and these types of people are big on revenge. We won't tell anyone who shot the pictures, but anyone familiar with Pettibone's house will take one look and know the shots were taken from here."

She nodded. "I thought of that. I have a cabin cruiser moored in Tacoma. I can go there for a few days."

"Okay. You got any cash?"

"Enough," she answered.

Grandfield nodded, knowing where Maretti was going with this, and added, "Don't use a credit card to make any purchases. Don't use a cell phone. Cash can't be traced." He stood up and headed for the front door. "I've got a cell phone in the car you can use to contact us." He opened the door and started to step out.

Grandfield didn't hear the shot that punched him back into the foyer. He didn't hear the shattered window glass in the kitchen either. But he retained enough consciousness to draw his weapon and roll out of the doorway just as another shot plowed into the tile of the entry way where his body had been. *Silencers,* he thought. He was having trouble breathing, but he didn't have any sense of blood. *Hit my vest,* he decided. *But damn it, it hurts.*

The windows in the kitchen continued to disintegrate from the fire of automatic weapons. Maretti had reacted, but too slowly to avoid a burning in his shoulder and a furrow down his left arm that left it useless. One slug punched his body armor and spun him sideways. He drew his 9mm Glock and stood facing the patio door to shield Ruby with his own body. "Down!" he shouted, backing into her and knocking her to the floor. They both scuttled behind the counter while bullets filled the air with disintegrating wallboard dust, pots and pans clanging as bullets smashed through the counters behind them.

He said, "Get the cell phone from my jacket pocket and call 911. Say, 'Officer down, shots fired,' and give them this address."

"You're bleeding!" she said.

"You think I don't know that?" he barked. "Get busy, woman!"

He listened while she called 911. Her voice was shaking, but she kept her composure and gave the 911 Operator the "Officer down" message and the street address. The operator told her to stay on the line, to remain calm, that the police and an ambulance were on the way. The firing slacked off, and then stopped altogether.

Maretti was startled when he heard Grandfield's pistol fire three times, the shots sounding like a canon after the fusillade of silenced rounds that had pounded the house. Then all was silent.

Ruby opened a drawer, pulled out a kitchen towel out and wrapped it tightly around the blood soaked sleeve of Maretti's jacket. "Are you going to check on Detective Grandfield?" she whispered.

Maretti, his lips clinched tight, his face a bit pale, showing the first signs of shock, just shook his head and whispered. "No. I can't. They'll be coming now. They'll want to make sure they killed us." He pointed to the cellar door. "Get down there."

"What about you?"

"I'm their worst nightmare," he growled. "A corpse that shoots back."

She crawled across the floor to the basement door, and slid through, trying to close the door without making any noise. He heard her lock the door behind her, and thought, *Good girl.*

The first sign of entry was a footstep crunching glass shards that had been blown into the hallway leading to the front door. That was his most vulnerable quarter and he braced the pistol against the corner of the cabinet—waiting for the shooter to show himself. He was banking on the granite counter top to protect him from anyone coming in through the kitchen door.

A bearded man peeked around the corner and then jerked back. Maretti simply fired two rounds through the corner of the wall and the man fell into the hallway, an airy film of plasterboard dust drifting in the sunlight slanting through the windows. Maretti could see the hole in the man's temple. "Game over, asshole," he whispered.

A crash of glass told him another shooter was coming at him from the patio. He reached up, held the pistol flat against the counter top and blazed away until the last round was fired. Holding the pistol under his left arm, he ejected the empty clip and struggled to dig another clip from his jacket pocket. Pushing a clip home, he then willed his left hand to hold the pistol while he jacked the slide to seat a round in the chamber.

Got to move, he thought and scooted back against the refrigerator just as a half dozen rounds punctured the cabinet he hid behind. He gave an exaggerated groan and banged the pistol on the floor. The broken glass betrayed the second shooter as he eased around the corner of the kitchen bar. Maretti rose and shot the man in the face three times, pulling the trigger as fast as he could. The fourth round missed as the man fell out of sight.

Maretti heard the distant wail of police cars, ambulance and fire trucks. "Here comes the cavalry," he whispered. He turned to the basement door to let Ruby know it was safe to come out, but his knees buckled, and despite his effort to concentrate, he just faded out.

Chapter 12

THOMPSON YELLED THROUGH THE OPEN DOOR and the computer-savvy Ms. Paige came in holding a small electronic notebook, complete with stylus. Dark curly hair framed a tanned face accented by a modest amount of make-up. A dark grey pantsuit accented a firm, gym-worked figure.

Thompson had to admit she was nice to look at and damned efficient.

"Yes?"

"I'm going home for the day."

She raised dark eyebrows that set off a magnetic pair of blue eyes. "What about your appointments? Captain MacDonald is scheduled for two. Denny wants some time with you at three, and there's a conference call this morning with D.C."

Denny was Dennis Moore, Thompson's Assistant SAC, a man forced on him by Thompson's boss in Washington, D.C. When told about the assignment, Thompson had bitched to the Director that he didn't need Denny, didn't want Denny no matter how good he was. And after the first month of watching Denny win the hearts and minds of Thompson's staff, he decided he didn't like the curly-haired, ass-kissing son-of-bitch.

The fact that Moore was twenty years younger, the fact that the women in the building found the good-looking asshole irresistible, and the fact that he was nearly six inches taller than the Thompson's five-ten didn't endear him to the SAC either.

When Thompson tried talking to his wife about Moore, she had scolded him. "You old reprobate, you're jealous. And maybe you're afraid of his popularity. Don't be so stuffy. Make friends. Be his mentor. You aren't going to be Springdale's SAC forever after all."

What Thompson heard loudest was the word "old."

To make matters worse, there weren't any real deficiencies in Moore's behavior or performance that he could put his finger on. He still didn't like him and his gut told him to keep Moore away from any really secret stuff, stuff that could endanger their counter- terrorism efforts.

Now Thompson stared up at his prim and proper secretary, and sighed. "Okay," he said, "Mr. Moore can sit in on the conference call. It's probably another Homeland Security alert. Reschedule Captain MacDonald for next week. And schedule Denny for tomorrow at nine."

She nodded, but he could tell by the tilt of her head and pursed lips she wasn't satisfied.

"Okay?" he asked.

"How long have I been working for you, Boss?"

He frowned and said, "About ten or twelve years, I guess. Why?"

"And I've been privy to secrets that no secretary could imagine as part of his or her job."

"Okay, Madeline, I admit that. And I admit to using people when it's called for. And you've never let me down. So what's the point you're making?"

She folded her arms across her chest, the tiny electronic notebook clutched in her right hand, and leaned forward in a challenging way. "You need to end this feud with Moore. It's not doing Silverdale any good."

"We're not feuding. I just don't like the guy."

"It's not necessary to like Denny, but it is necessary to partner with him. Stop pouting because you had to take him. Act like a manager for a change instead of a renegade agent."

"Damn it, Madeline, you sound like my wife."

"Doesn't make me wrong," she said stubbornly.

Months later he would still be pondering the question of whether it was her logic or the gleam of anger in her eyes that broke him.

Regardless, he pointed to a visitors chair and said, "Sit." He grabbed the phone and punched the speed dial. When Moore answered, Thompson said, "My office. Now," and slammed the receiver in the cradle.

Madeline and Thompson sat in silence except for the suddenly very loud ticking of a miniature electric grandfather clock mounted on one wall. A minute passed, the clock chimed the half hour, 9:30, and then Moore knocked.

"Come in," Thompson barked.

The tall, broad-shouldered Assistant SAC stopped just inside the door. "Ah...if I'm interrupting something..."

"You are the something, Mr. Moore. Have a seat. Madeline, get us each a cup of coffee, get somebody to man your desk and come back in here. I want you to sit in on this."

Madeline nodded stiffly and left the room, slamming the door shut on her way out. It wasn't getting the coffee that irritated her. It was the sense of being told to "fetch" like some hound dog.

Denny folded himself into an uncomfortable wood "easy" chair, and looked at Thompson without saying anything. Finally he nodded at the door and asked, "What do you suppose that was about?"

Thompson finally allowed himself a smile and said, "Woman talk. Says she's pissed at me. You can tell the degree of 'pissedoffedness' by the force of the slam. I'd say off-hand that was a ten-minute slam."

"Oh. I'm not too experienced with that."

Thompson frowned. "I thought you were married."

"Past tense, Chief, past tense. She couldn't take the Puget Sound rain, she missed her 'mommy' and she went home to Atlanta about a month after we moved here. So I haven't had a door slammed on me in over six months."

"Well, shit, Denny. You never let on anything was wrong. Is she coming back?"

Moore frowned and shook his head, jaw tight. "My phone calls go unanswered, my letters are returned, my emails are blocked, and my incoming snail mail is from her attorney. So...no, don't think she's coming back."

Thompson suddenly felt deflated. He turned his chair half away from Moore and then looked sideways, catching a sense of Moore's youth and of Moore's pain. He noted the clinched jaw, and then he surprised Moore when he got up out of his chair, walked around the desk and slid beside him into the only other visitor's chair, a scarred wooden monster scrounged from a navy surplus depot, "Thompson's rug," as it was referred to by those forced to sit on it while the SAC chewed ass.

By the time Madeline returned, almost exactly ten minutes later, Thompson had laid out a plan of daily briefings between him and Moore, had apologized for making Moore the target of his anger at D.C., instructed him to take the conference call from Homeland Security, and told Madeline not to cancel Captain MacDonald's appointment because Denny would be MacDonald's contact.

Thompson slid a letter lying on his desk over to Moore and said, "Sign this as my acting. That'll let the troops know we've smoked the peace pipe." Madeline nodded approval, and Thompson wondered again how Moore had gained the confidence and loyalty of so many people at Silverdale, especially Madeline's.

Thompson sighed, and said, "Okay, you two. Run this place for a couple of days. I have some personal things to attend to."

Moore sat back and almost whispered, "Are you going mole hunting?"

Thompson didn't answer. Moore looked at Madeline, shook his head, and said, "And I thought things were going so swimmingly there for a while."

Thompson just grunted, sat down behind his desk, and said, "You can both reach me on my cell phone. I'm giving myself two days to make this work. Now get out of here. I've got a call to make, and then I'm going home."

Moore reached across the desk and offered his hand. "Thanks, Boss. I can't tell you how much this helps. It'll be nice to have a real assignment for a change."

"As opposed to what?" Thompson asked.

"Well, as opposed to managing the coffee fund..." He left the statement hanging.

"That bad, huh?" Thompson asked.

Madeline waited until Moore left and then sidled up to her boss and placed a strong, lovely arm around his shoulder and gave him a sideways hug. Thompson was actually startled. In the ten or twelve years they had worked together, it was the first physical contact they'd ever had.

Madeline closed the door quietly this time, and it dawned on him he wasn't really mad at anyone except himself.

And he admitted for the first time his wife's purchase of the big house overlooking Lake Washington felt like a slap in the face. It was more than his salary would ever support. She had made the buy without asking him. It was her money. And he wound up with a commute of an hour plus each way—and that was only if he left about five in the morning to miss the worst of the commuter traffic and then waited until six-thirty or so to start home. There wasn't a damned thing good about it. He felt dismissed and a little emasculated.

"And then the Director suggests I need a deputy...like I'm slipping somehow," he grumbled and reached for the phone. "I'm getting paranoid."

Chapter 13

Nancy sat at the small table in her study, writing another of her weekly letters to her mother and half listening for the sound of a diesel pickup in her driveway. She already knew what Bud wanted to talk about. "Or at least what he thinks he wants to talk about," Nancy said quietly to herself.

Sliding glass doors brought early morning light, framing a view of the multitude of potted petunias, pansies, tall cosmos, snap dragons, sweet peas, marigolds, tulips, daffodils, and just about every succulent under the stars that she happily planted each spring. Hens-and-chicks were her mainstay. Because they are so tough, she thought. Two big flower pots were dedicated to a variety of beef steak tomatoes, and one to cherry tomatoes.

She sometimes laughed at herself for being so "optimistic." At an elevation of roughly 4,800 feet, Lakeview sometimes suffered a late August or early September freeze. "A product of global warming," she had grumbled cynically at last year's early frost.

Bookcases, a two-drawer oak filing cabinet, a wireless laptop, a printer, a Bose radio/CD player, and a swag lamp decorated the study. Two hardwood book ends guarded numerous, neatly organized, well-thumbed spiral notebooks, stacked against the wall behind the desk.

The sound of a diesel engine rumbled quietly in her driveway and then stopped. She sighed, pushed the letter aside and then hurried around the corner and through her plainly furnished living room with its never-used fireplace.

She opened the front door in time to see Bud lock the white four-door county pickup. She wrinkled her nose at the faint odor of diesel exhaust, and noted that Bud wasn't smiling.

There was a hint of wry amusement in her bright green eyes, and the small chandelier behind her lit the auburn highlights of her dark hair. He was amazed again by the fact that this bright, competent, beautiful woman claimed to love him. Him. Bud Blair. He shook his head slightly as she stepped back to invite him in. He noticed the suitcase sitting inside the door and grimaced.

"What?" she asked as she closed the door.

He reached for her and pulled her into his arms. "I'm beginning to dislike my job."

"Because??"

"Because I can't be gone right now. I'm sorry."

She hugged him and then pulled away to step back. She studied his sun-weathered, weary face, his slightly crooked nose, a perfect fit for his strength of character, a small scar that was somehow attractive running through his left eyebrow.

She took his hand and led him around the corner into the warmly lit breakfast nook. She pointed to a chair by the small table. "Sit, Bud Blair. We'll have some coffee and talk about what we are going to do, job or not."

Bud glanced at the titles in the book cases. He spotted a collection of writing about Lake County history, books on edible plants, geology, travel books, mystery novels, Carey's General History of Oregon, cookbooks, books on gardening, books on astronomy—all reflections of a curious wide-ranging mind.

And he was suddenly embarrassed by how little he really knew about this beautiful Yakima Indian woman.

She poured two cups of fresh brew, pushed a notebook aside and set them on the breakfast table. She sat down across from him, and took a deep breath. "I know that cops are bad risks when it comes to marriage."

He raised his hand and stopped her. "It occurred to me this is the first time I've been in your house. I like it," He frowned, "but the suitcase in the living room hit me like a ton of bricks. This whole cop business, being sheriff and jumping to do my duty, it isn't even about you and me. It's like an entity all of its own."

She interrupted, "When I worked dispatch in Yakima, I watched a number of cop marriages crumble under the pressure of the job." She looked at his hazel eyes. A slight frown on his forehead made her wonder if he was recalling his marriage to Linda Blair, ex-wife of nearly seven years ago.

"Is that what happened between you and Linda?"

He nodded slowly, and then said, "Yes. The job became my sole reason to get up in the morning. Linda and I became strangers. That's all there is to it. I didn't even notice her packed suitcase sitting in the hallway the night she told me she was leaving. Hell, her life didn't even touch on my daily life. I was the job."

And then he just stared out the slider door at the riot of colors that sat on her deck.

"Feeling sorry for your self, Bud?"

He shook his head. "No, just amazed at my own stupidity, or is it some kind of fanaticism? Could be, I guess.

"The first time I read Eric Hoffer's The True Believer, I was astounded at the stupidity of people who could surrender themselves to a fanatic belief, fanatic to the point of torture and mass slaughter, even suicide. Look at the Jones Town slaughter. How could parents actually kill their own children and then commit suicide simply because a charismatic leader said to?

"It's been a long time since I asked myself if law enforcement officers could reach the same point at some time in their careers."

She took a sip of her coffee and then said, "It's not the same thing. You have your own guiding principles. You don't need anyone to do your thinking. One person acts from a moral foundation; the other is a mindless fanatic." She paused, "What do you want from this life, Bud?"

"You know, I haven't thought about it for a long time, but what I wanted once-upon-a-time was a loving marriage, an ordinary job, and a house full of kids. Just a normal life, that's all." He stared at her eyes, not sure if the look in her eyes was pity or amusement.

She put the coffee cup down and reached across the table to lay her hand on top of his. "You know, Bud, until you came along, I had exactly two dates in the three years I've been here, and very little social life except for office parties, Christmas dinners, things like that. So," she pointed to her books, her notebooks and her flowers, "I had to create my own world. And you know what? I like my world. Or I did until you decided to notice me," she added with a frown.

"Except for trips to visit Mom and a hiking trip in the Olympics with my friend Edna and her husband Don, I haven't done anything exciting, but I've been content."

She pointed to the filing cabinet. "I've managed to become something of a gardener, a quasi expert on the history of the Oregon Territory, and almost an expert on the history of Lake County. Did you know I belong to the Lake County Historical Society?"

He shook his head.

"Well, now you know. It's been a pretty good life, and it's given me time to move beyond sorrow for the lost dreams of my first marriage. Would you like to know what they were?"

He nodded. "I would."

She smiled and withdrew her hand. "Well, I dreamed of finding a loving man to share a loving marriage, a home in a community that cherished children and the values of self-sufficiency, honesty, character and love. And I wanted…are you ready for this? I wanted a house filled with children of my own."

Bud looked at her, a grin tugging at his mouth, "And you don't think it's too late to have that."

"No. I intend to marry you, have at least three children, maybe four, and love your socks off. But you have to remember that I'm a complete human being…with or without you. I have a soul that needs to be fed right along with yours and our children."

He nodded. "I'd like that."

"And now?" she asked.

Bud put his Stetson on the floor and ran his hand through a thick crop of wavy brown hair, just a hint of grey starting to show at the temples. "Look, I tried to convince myself that a quick flight to Yakima and then right back was okay."

"And it's not," she interrupted.

"Can't make it work. I've got a body at Peel's Mortuary that needs a home. We need to find any relatives the guy might have had. He's the one Stone Fly killed when he shot down Crazy Charlie's little plane.

"We need to find out who killed Crazy Charlie. Somebody, someplace in the universe is pretty powerful and extremely well organized to pull that one off. I mean, substitute an ambulance and two EMTs and take Crazy right out from under our noses? In under an hour's time?

"We were all there, Maretti, Sheriff Redmond, Stone Fly, Michelle, Roger…me. And we never caught on to the fact they were imposters…not real EMTs. Hell! I even watched them give him the shot that killed him. Coolest customers I've ever seen…clucking about what a good job the field dressing was. Asking us to help load him in the ambulance. Putting Roger in the front seat to ride with the female driver. She was, how did Roger put it? 'A long, cool, woman in a black jumpsuit.'

"Even with a good description, Sheriff Redmond's BOLO hasn't so much as caught a whisper of those two. It takes good organization to go to ground and stay there.

"To be honest, I'm a bit spooked. Maretti tells me to watch my back. BB tells me the bad guys will come after me. And all I have to go on is a questionable ID made by those idiots in our jail of some bigwig Colombian drug dealer. Which reminds me that I need to contact the FBI, and I need to question Robert Clark, the guy we know as Cowboy. I want to know if he can corroborate the ID.

"I'm sorry, Nancy. I just can't go up there to Yakima right now."

After another thirty minutes, two cups of coffee, and a promise of dinner at the cabin that night, Nancy agreed to a small wedding in Lakeview.

"As soon as I find out who the bad guys are, and put a stop to this," Bud amended, then added the promise of a trip to Yakima for a formal introduction to Nancy's mother. "As soon as I put an end to the bad guys."

Nancy shook her head at that, and then smiled and reached across the table to take his hand. "I promised myself I would never marry a cop, but that was a promise made before I fell in love with one of those assholes. Well, here's to the dream. You finish up this business and then think about Nancy and her soon-to-be family."

"What's with soon-to-be family? You aren't pregnant?"

She gave him a devilish grin. "No, but I plan to work on it."

Bud got out of his chair and moved to stand beside her. She stood up and gave him a long, lingering kiss that promised something more—and then his cell phone rang.

Nancy laughed and pulled back. "See...the job always comes first."

He flipped open the phone and growled, "This better be good."

"Still happy, I hear," Michelle growled back. "We need to get you married pretty soon, or you won't have any friends left."

"So what's up," he said, ignoring her barb.

"Your friend, and now mine, Mr. Gar, that is Mr. NCIS Agent John Bernard, aka Stone Fly is here. Wants to talk to you."

"What about?"

"I'm not sure. He's not saying anything except he's been sent to watch your back."

And to look at the computer disc we stole from Cowboy's office. I haven't taken the time to look at it. I wonder what's on it? Anything important?

"Okay, I'm headed back to the station. Five minutes."

Bud shook his head, put on his Stetson, pulled the brim down low and took a deep breath. "And now I've got NCIS Agent John Bernard, aka Stone Fly down here 'to watch my back.'"

Nancy cocked her head back, nodded and said, "I'm glad that he is, Bud. You've scared me enough. I think I'll start carrying Daddy's .38."

"Might not be a bad idea. Maybe you better not hang around with me."

"I don't think I'll give you up. Can't let the bad guys mess up a good thing, now can we."

Chapter 14

SPECIAL AGENT IN CHARGE THOMPSON SWALLOWED his pride and called the limo service under contract to his wife, got an ETA of one hour and then he called his son, a graduate student at Stanford.

Thomas Thompson, so named by his maternal grandmother, was pursuing a bachelor's degree in computer science. This proud owner of a master's degree in Western Philosophy had persuaded his mother to finance the cost to study "something practical," as he said in a pleading letter home.

His father thought privately that his handsome son was turning into a professional student. He was tempted to say "leech," but Tommy held a sterling 3.8 GPA. And he worked evenings and weekends at a college pizza parlor to offset the expense of going to school.

Bill Thompson heard Tommy's deep baritone answer, "That you, Dad?"

"Yes. I need some help from my prodigal son."

Tommy said, "I'm neither lawyer nor priest, Dad. They're the only people who can help an old reprobate like you," And then he laughed before adding, "Good to hear from you, Dad. What's up?"

"Are you learning anything from those windjammer professors down there? Like, if I asked you to give me a list of all the top computer hardware and software I can buy off the shelf, you could do that?"

Tommy hesitated before asking, "How much are you willing to spend?"

"As much as it takes."

"In that case...let me crank up my laptop." Tommy put his cell phone on a table, and his father could hear the din of chattering voices in the background. When his son picked the phone back up, he asked, "You at work, son?"

"No. I'm in a coffee shop waiting for Sondra to get here?"

"Sondra?"

"Mom didn't tell you? Dad, I'm engaged."

Thompson said, "Well, I'll be damned. The perpetual bachelor is engaged. Congratulations. When do I get to meet her?" And then he idly wondered again why his wife of twenty-seven years didn't want any more children after Tommy was born. He liked being a father and often wished Tommy had chosen a university a little closer to home.

"We're flying up for Thanksgiving. You really need to talk to Mom once in a while, Dad."

Twenty minutes later, an email detailing an impressive list of computer hardware and software was on his laptop, including an e-mail address and phone number for the best computer supply store in Seattle. Thompson dialed the store number and placed an order for the items on the list, gave a credit card number and paid an extra fifty dollars for a rush delivery. The address he gave was for the brick mansion overlooking Lake Washington.

He thumbed the intercom between his desk and Madeline's and said, "I need you."

She came in almost immediately.

"Yes?"

"Find me the number for the Chief of Police for Bremerton, get him on the line for me."

He stopped, shook his slightly. "No...that won't do. I better do this myself. Just get me the number."

She answered, "You have it. It's on your monitor. You'll see an icon that looks like a telephone. That will take you to a directory of law enforcement agencies. Click on Bremerton and that's it."

"Yeah, I guess I did know that."

Ms. Green, Maretti's "arrogant asshole," answered in a strained voice on the first ring. "Chief's office. How can I help you?"

"This is Bill Thompson, Special Agent in Charge, NCIS, Springdale. I'd like to talk to your Chief."

"May I ask about what?"

"No, I don't think so. Just get him on the line."

"Hold please."

A deep male voice said, "Chief Homer. What can I do for you?"

"This is Special Agent Thompson, NCIS. I need a favor. I want to borrow one of your detectives for a couple of days, Detective Grandfield."

Chief Homer asked, "What's this about?"

The SAC took a breath, held it, let it out and said, "I read his report on the bomb incident in Oregon. It was an exceptional write-up. I think he could help me do some computer sleuthing for a couple of days."

"You know, you NCIS guys slam the door on my department every time there's a crime in Bremerton involving the Navy. It gets pretty damned insulting. And now you want to borrow one of our guys?

"Listen, Thompson. Grandfield was shot and killed this morning, and Maretti is shot up. We think he'll live, but that's not certain right now. And you know what I think? I think you have an NCIS asshole right in the middle of all this. And I also think your asshole is an agent named Spears. That's what I think."

Thompson swallowed hard, took a deep breath and swore quietly. "What happened?"

"According to an eye witness, your agent Spears went to the witness's house to get some photos the witness had taken...I'd call them surveillance photos if my witness had been trained in that field...good, clear photos of Basil Pettibone's guests. My witness says Agent Spears was agitated, mumbling about national security and wanting the camera, discs, and copies of every photo she..." he paused, knowing he had given away information he didn't want NCIS to have. "...my witness took. And there were a lot of them.

She didn't trust Spears, so she held out copies and called Detective Maretti. He and Detective Grandfield went to the house, and wound up in a firefight with four shooters. One got away. Our BOLO will be out in about five minutes."

"So your detectives killed three of the bad guys?"

"You're damned rights they did. Someone shot Grandfield as he was coming out the front door. We think the first bullet hit him in the chest. His body armor stopped the bullet, but it put him down. He managed to kill one of them as they came through the door, but the second guy killed Detective Grandfield.

"While this was going on, two guys with suppressed automatic weapons were hammering the kitchen where Maretti and our witness were sitting. Maretti took a round in the meaty part of his left shoulder, another that ploughed a groove in his left arm along the outside of the ulna, and another one in the side of his vest.

"According to our witness, he protected her with his own body and got her safely to the basement of the house where she locked herself in. Then he killed two of the shooters with head shots. We think the sirens chased the fourth man off before he could finish the job."

"Before the shooter could finish the job?" Thompson asked.

"No! Before Maretti could kill him!"

Thompson almost smiled at that, but it wasn't funny. "Okay, Chief. I'm really sorry about your detectives. Any help you need, you got. I'll have Spears arrested immediately and we'll get to the bottom of this."

"Okay. Tell you what, send me a forensics team to help my guys work the scene. The NCIS agent who was there gives you a damned good excuse to help.

"I've got a K-9 unit working the woods behind the house. The perp had to leave the van they drove to the house, so he's on foot. We have all of our units covering the area, we have a state police helicopter overhead, and we have the promise of helicopters from the Coast Guard.

"We also need a forensics examination of the vehicle. I have my guys running the plates, but we already know it was stolen from Sea-Tac." Chief Homer paused. "Can you think of anything we've missed?"

"Yeah, I'd like to know who the shooters were."

"Don't know. Early twenties, Black, no ID, and not too good at what they were trying to do. We're running fingerprints...or will be soon."

Thompson scratched information on a note pad, and said, "Give me an address. I'll get my forensics team on the way. They'll be there in fifteen minutes, max."

Chief Homer read off the address, and in a voice choked with emotion said, "And now the mayor and I have to give Mrs. Grandfield the grim news." He hung up without saying goodbye.

Madeline Paige hurried into the room holding a print out of the Bremerton City Police BOLO. "Boss, have you seen this?"

"No, but I just got off the phone with Chief Homer in Bremerton. Get me Abe on the phone. I want his team to arrest Agent Spears and Agent Warren...yesterday!" He handed her the scrap of notepaper and added, "And have the Bremerton forensics team head for this address."

Chapter 15

BB watched in amazement at the amount of food the young Cletus could put away.

"Don't you ever eat?" he asked?

Cletus looked up, a fork halfway between a diminishing mound of garlic mashed potatoes and his open mouth. "This be on you so I'm gonna get what I can," and then stuffed the potatoes in his mouth. "And I'm gonna want some strawberry cheesecake for desert, so you might as well order it now."

"Okay, Cletus. Did you find out anything? I want to know which of our local Muslim brethren planned to bomb my city, and I want to know who or what they planned to blow up. And now would be the best time for me to know all that."

Cletus looked up at his mentor, his father figure, his idol—and his tormentor. He put the fork down, leaned back in his chair.

"Don't know. Don't want to know. Those are scary dudes, man. I mean they kill people. Got some idea that you be for them or against them. If you be against, it's okay to kill you. No, no. I stay away from those dudes."

BB picked up his glass of beer and sipped while his eyes bored holes in Cletus. "Come on, Cletus. You're in the information business. You hear things, you sell what you hear. You're already taking chances. Just tell me what you know and go on about your business. No digging, no risky questions, no talk on the street. I just want to know what you know right now."

Cletus wiped his lips with a napkin, a by-product of BB's training in how to behave in public, put the napkin down and then reached into the inside pocket of his nice wool sports jacket. He shoved a birthday card across the table.

"Happy birthday," he said.

BB put the card in his pocket without comment.

"How's school going, Cletus? You pulling good grades?"

Cletus looked smug. "Straight As, my man, straight As."

"Don't you shuck-and-jive me, Cletus. You know I can check it out."

"Well, what you don't know, Mr. BB, is that I finished my AA degree in business administration, and now I'm going to Portland State. Gonna gets me a bachelor's, I am. Gonna move up."

BB eyed him and then when it was obvious Cletus wasn't going to say anything more, he asked, "What in?"

Cletus grinned, spread his arms expansively and said, "Well, my man, here's the plan. First I get a degree in criminology. I'm already sort of specialized that way, if you know what I mean. Then I gets me job as a big city detective. Have to take a cut in pay when I do that, but at least I won't have some ugly bad-ass detective peeking over my shoulder all the time."

BB was actually startled. It had never occurred to him that Cletus would ever do anything but hustle. He shook his head, tried to say something and finally just settled for reaching across the table and offering his hand to Cletus. The gesture knocked over his glass, and amber beer soaked into the white table cloth, but he ignored it and finally finding his voice, said, "Way to go Cletus. Way to go!"

Cletus looked smug. It was the first time he had ever managed to startle his closest and best friend. "Yeah," he said, "but you ain't heard it all. And then, while I rid the city of bad guys, I'm gonna go on to law school. Be a big time lawyer."

BB set his empty beer glass upright and grinned. "What does your mama think about all this?"

"She be proud of me. She says to tell Mr. BB he is a good man... been a good father to Cletus." He stopped because he was afraid he would start blubbering, and that wouldn't do, not for a hustler like Cletus Falls.

BB said, "You tell her she has been a good mother. And tell her you have a gravy spot on your new tie. See if she can get the stain out."

The tension broke and BB and Cletus both laughed.

BB tapped his jacket pocket. "Where'd you get this?"

"From one of my future clients. Gonna be a big time criminal before he's done. And he'll need my services. The way I see it, I'll have to arrest him, then I'll resign my position as a big time detective and be his lawyer. Make me lots of money that way." He laughed and grinned at BB. "Good plan, right? And speaking of money, it cost me a thousand to get that. You got that much?"

BB shook his head. "No...and I know it didn't cost you that much either." He reached into his back pocket and pulled out a dark brown leather wallet. He palmed a folded, limp five-hundred-dollar bill from a hideout on the inside flap of his wallet, and stood up. He reached across the table, shook hands and said loudly, "Congratulation, Cletus. I'm proud of you. Finish your meal. I've gotta get going." BB put a fifty-dollar bill on the table. "Pay with this."

Cletus watched his hero leave the dining room before slipping the folded five-hundred-dollar bill into his pants pocket. For the first time, he felt a little guilty about lying to BB. He really only had to pay two-fifty for the information in the birthday card. He shrugged.

BB knew that, he thought, and with his fork cut into a beautiful slice of strawberry topped cheesecake.

BB DUCKED INTO A REST ROOM on the main lobby, found an empty stall and locked the door. The birthday card contained a list of names, a North Portland address and a camera cartridge.

He put the list and the cartridge back, and returned the envelope to his inside jacket pocket. He stood on his tiptoes to look over the dividers and scanned the restroom. No one had followed him in.

The ten-minute walk back to his apartment took fifteen minutes of doubling back and checking for a tail he never spotted. The telltale over the door was still in place when he turned the key to his apartment.

The cartridge fit the cheaper of his two digital cameras and he turned it on. He scrolled the photos, amazed at the guts it took to get the pictures, and outraged at the contents.

He reached for his cell phone, dialed a number from memory and then killed the call. *No,* he thought. *Time to call in the cavalry.*

He dialed a new number and listened impatiently while the phone rang. A voice answered on the fourth ring. "Yeah?"

"Dutch, this is BB."

"Oh, hell. What do you want, BB? You gonna screw up another dinner? Barbara and I are dining. You know what dining is BB? It's where a loving couple enjoy a candle-lit dinner in a quiet, expensive four-star restaurant with a good bottle of wine, followed by a romantic climax."

"Need you Dutch. What I've got won't wait. Where you at?"

"Red Lion out on the river."

"That's not four-star, Dutch."

"Yeah, but I don't have far to go for the romance."

"Gimme a room number. This won't wait."

"You still on admin leave?"

BB grimaced and said, "Not relevant, Dutch. I should be out there in thirty minutes. Where do I find you?"

"Oh hell, BB. I'll be right here in the lounge drowning my sorrows and kissing my marriage goodbye."

"You do emote, Dutch. Tell Barbara I'm sorry, but it really is a matter of national security this time." And then he killed the call.

A SKINNY COLLEGE KID IN A red and grey Red Lion valet's uniform, the jacket sleeves too short for his long arms, watched as the classic red Corvette stopped at the front entrance. A big man unfolded from the driver's seat, slammed the door, tossed the keys at him and growled. "Back in thirty minutes. And there better not be any extra miles on the odometer or any bent fenders."

The skinny kid started to take offense until the big man handed him a twenty-dollar bill. "Take care of my baby, okay?"

The valet grinned and said, "Yessir. Thirty minutes?"

"Yeah. Thirty minutes."

BB pocketed the valet ticket and pushed through the heavy glass doors of the Red Lion. He spotted a "Lounge" sign and headed across the carpeted lobby.

Dutch Vanderlin, a broad shouldered man in his mid-fifties, salt-and-pepper crew-cut hinting at a military background, sat at a candle-lit table at the back of the lounge watching the wind whip white-caps on the Columbia River. An open bottle of wine and two glasses sat on the white table cloth.

BB slid into a chair opposite Dutch. "Where's Barbara?" he asked.

Dutch straightened his chair, cold steel in his blue eyes. "She decided she doesn't like you tonight, and went to her room. Do you know how long it's been since we've had a night alone?"

BB laughed. "Couldn't have anything to do with six kids and your mother-in-law, could it?"

Dutch gave BB a sour smile.

"Well," BB added, "don't try to con me that the job interferes. I know you Fibbies have a soft touch."

When Vanderlin continued to glare at him, BB added a little more softly, "I'm really sorry, Dutch. But I find myself a little out of my league with this one. And as you may know, I'm persona *non gratis* at work right now. Hell, I'm not even supposed to do any snooping. But this came my way," he held up the birthday card, "I had to find someone to share it with. And I couldn't think of anyone smarter than Elden J. Vanderlin, you being the FBI's Special Agent in Charge."

"Oh, hell." Dutch reached for the envelope, and said, "Give it to me and then get out of my life."

BB snatched the card back and said, "In the words of my source, I gots ta show you, man." He pulled a small, slim digital camera from his coat pocket.

BB opened the envelope, put the camera cartridge in the digital camera, and pushed the on-button. He handed the camera to Dutch, and said, "You won't believe this."

Dutch scrolled through the pictures slowly, absently sipped his wine, and then turned the camera off. He pushed the camera across the table, but not before ejecting the cartridge and slipping it in an inside pocket.

"Address?" he asked.

BB pushed the envelope across the table.

"Do you know this place?" Dutch asked.

"Yes…at least I know the address. I haven't been in the building. Don't plan on it. Might have to kill those son-of-bitches if I do."

Dutch nodded, caught the attention of a waiter and waved him over. "Whatever my friend wants."

"Coffee," BB ordered. When the waiter had walked away, BB looked out at the river, catching the reflected gleam of lights from the Vancouver side of the Columbia, and then said, "Do the pictures tell you anything?"

Dutch nodded. "We've been suspicious of these guys for quite a while, but we've never had any hard evidence to use. Where'd you get this?"

"From a reliable source who wishes to remain alive. I promised him anonymity."

Dutch shook his head, stared hard at BB, blue eyes angry. "I can't raid a mosque on an anonymous tip. I admit the pictures of the arms boxes, the explosives, the AK-47s look genuine, but I need the guy. I need your source. I promise we'll protect him."

BB weighed the pros and cons, winced at the lack of choices and pulled his cell phone from his pocket. When Cletus answered, BB said, "Don't say anything. Just answer yes or no. Did you look at the pictures?"

When he heard Cletus answer, "yes," he frowned and then asked, "Will you talk to the FBI?" There was along pause, and then he heard Cletus ask, "Can they protect me?"

BB shook his head before saying, "Sure. I know the head honcho here in Portland. He's one of my best friends. I'd trust him with my life. Now, little buddy, he's here with me now and he wants to talk to you. You okay with that?"

Cletus snorted. BB heard a weak laugh, and Cletus said, "I don't know what else I should have expected. But, hey, man, maybe I'll become a big time FBI agent instead of a big city detective. How would that be? Sure let me talk to the Man."

BB waved the coffee away and told the waiter to bring him a double Crown Royal on the rocks, no water. "And put it on that man's tab," he said pointing at Dutch who had the cell phone to his ear.

By the time the waiter returned, Dutch had ordered two agents to meet Cletus at an address specified by Cletus, and to take him to a safe house the FBI owned in the West Hills. He heard Dutch say, "Hold on a minute." He looked at BB and asked, "What does Cletus look like?"

BB sipped his drink, wondering if he was doing the right thing, and then answered, "He's Asian-Black, sixty-five inches tall, twenty-two years old, and my godson." BB didn't know why he lied about Cletus being his godson, but maybe it would get him better treatment from the FBI. He knew they could really bear down on people, even informants, especially paid informants. And BB felt certain the FBI would find that out.

Dutch shared the description with an agent and then said, "I'll be at the safe house in an hour. I have to take Barbara home first."

Dutch stood up, pointed at the dinner tab and said, "That's on you…for ruining Barbara's night out." Then he dropped two twenties on the table. "I'll buy the drinks."

BB watched him out the door and then turned to his double Crown Royal. He sipped at it and decided it didn't taste very good after all.

Chapter 16

Bud detected the faint smell of wood smoke when he punched in the code to the front door of the station. He looked to see if the place was on fire. What he saw was a disheveled-looking man in a blue sweat shirt standing at the counter, and Karen Highsmith grinning at something the man had said.

John Bernard turned as the latch clicked on the front door. Bud stopped, shook his head, and said, "Well, look what the cat drug in. Smelled you from outside. I won't ask what you're doing here."

John held out his hand, a big grin on his face. Even though they had spent no more than an hour together during the bomb incident, they shared a bond that neither bothered to examine. It was simple guy stuff. They trusted each other, and genuinely liked each other.

"How's the High Sheriff of Lake County?" John asked.

"Still alive."

"That's the idea. Amanda wants me to keep it that way."

Bud just grunted and shook his head.

John said, "I hope you're okay with that. I get the impression she never talked to you about it."

"No. She didn't. Kind of an imperious special agent, I think."

Bud had a fleeting memory of faint perfume and Special Agent Amanda Spears whispering "one-twenty" in his ear while he tried to estimate passenger weight for a helicopter trip to Fort Rock. He was still annoyed by that adventure. Dumb ass stunt, is what he thought of that incident.

John laughed. "I've known her for almost seven years, and I've never figured her out. At times she's as good as the best agents I ever worked with. And then, boom, she turns into a dragon lady, and then I think she's all about career. One thing is consistent. She's tough and she's smart as a whip. And that's all I'm going to say about my boss."

Bud raised his eyebrows. "Your boss?"

"Yeah, my boss. I'm a field agent. If I were in the spy business, you could say she was my handler. She orders up a mission, my team plans it and carries it out. It's compartmentalized. We don't know the other teams…or even if there are other teams.

"If a mission goes south, and, say we get caught, we truly don't know anything except what the mission was. Can't tell what you don't know. Anyway, Amanda backs us up logistically and politically."

Bud motioned John into his office, walked the short hallway to Michelle's cubby hole and poked his head in. Deputy Trivoli was on the phone, so he caught her eye and pointed back to his office.

Bud poured coffee and carried two cups back to his desk. Agent Bernard was standing in front of Bud's Lake County map, finger on Fort Rock, mentally retracing his night-time cross-country trip from his trailer in the Horse Ranch RV Park to Cowboy's ranch.

Bud stood in the doorway and watched before interrupting. "How long did it take you to get to Cowboy's ranch?"

"About three and a half hours. I was in position to watch the ranch just at half-light."

Bud looked at the map, estimated the distance and shrugged. Any man in good shape could make the trip in that time. It occurred to him he hadn't ever had a chance to debrief John Bernard. "What tipped you off about the hay truck?"

Michelle closed the door behind them and sat on one of Bud's wooden visitor's chair.

John frowned and then said, "A hunch."

"Just a hunch?" Michelle snapped. "We sent officers to check out a hunch?"

John moved from behind Bud's desk, picked up the coffee cup and took a sip while they waited. Bud knew there had to be more than a gut feeling behind the call.

"Well, when Crazy Charlie found the marker, he sort of went nuts…crazy like. And he…"

"Marker? What does that mean?' Bud interrupted.

"I left a small, smooth river rock on the front porch of bunkhouse. I wanted Crazy to know I'd found him."

"How would the stone tell him that?" Michelle asked.

"It was something we all did. It started during exercises. You know, sneak up on a guy…you can't kill your teammates…and let him know you could have…leave a marker. I started using small river stones, and pretty soon the whole team was doing it."

"Why did you want him to know you had found him?" Michelle asked.

"He is…was…prone to impetuous acts. Crazy stuff. That's why we called him Crazy. That and he talked all the time. Anyway, I thought I could goad him into confronting me. That way nobody would get hurt, and I could bring him in."

"Weren't you taking a lot for granted? What if he took you instead?" Michelle asked.

"Oh…I knew that wouldn't happen. Charlie was good, but not that good. His brains were gone. Drugs and anger do that."

"I get it," Bud said impatiently, "What about the hay?"

"Crazy was pounding on Cowboy's front door. I was about eight hundred meters away…too far to hear what was going on. Anyway, Crazy disappears into the house and after a few minutes Crazy and Cowboy came running out. They rousted a ranch hand out of the bunkhouse and had him back the truck into the hay barn. Cowboy and Charlie closed the doors, and I'm thinking, that's really lousy hay…some bales are almost black. I'm no cowboy, but even I know you'd kill a cow if they ate that moldy stuff.

"So I watch and in a few minutes the truck pulls out of the barn… still loaded with the same lousy hay. As it makes the corner, I catch a glimpse of a guy that looks Semitic. And again I think, 'Something is wrong here. Law enforcement needs to take a look at that load and at the passengers.' Cowboy was driving the truck, by the way.

"I knew your officers were too far away to make a stop, so I shot a front tire. They don't tumble to the fact that it isn't just a blown tire, so they get out and take a spare off the side rack, and start jacking the truck up. I've really got the range by then, so I fire a three-round burst and flatten the spare."

"At eight hundred meters?" Bud asked skeptically.

John just shrugged. "With a good rifle, the right load, and a decent rest, I'm good up to a thousand meters at a target that big."

Bud raised his eyebrows and shook his head. "Wow."

John started to say, "I could teach you how," but stopped himself.

"By then," John continued, "they are wise to what's happening. But they can't do anything about it because they haven't spotted my spider hole. I'm guessing they used some type of radio, because all of a sudden three quads come boiling around the corner of a loafing shed. One of the quads has an extra passenger, and he's kneeling on the rack behind the driver, holding a rifle in one hand. Through my scope it looks like an AK-47.

He's the one you found dead out in the sagebrush. The idiot driving the quad hit a boulder and shook his passenger loose. The passenger came flying off, arms wind-milling, trying to catch his balance. He didn't. Just tripped and slid headfirst into a big rock at about thirty miles an hour.

"Anyway, I decide it was time to boogie. So I started walking out through the sagebrush headed for the timber. One of them spotted me and banged away without even coming close. I could tell by the sound it was an AK-47. Good weapon, by the way.

"They were trying to execute a pincer movement. Not a bad idea unless someone nips off one of the pincers. Which is what I did. I pacified the guy on the south side and took him prisoner.

"And then Crazy came flying by in a small plane, a Super Cub maybe, really low and slow with a shooter who was trying to kill my prisoner. That irritated me, so I used my prisoner's AK to take out the shooter and disable the plane. Which as you know, Crazy somehow managed to land upright in Cowboy's alfalfa field. End of story."

"How did you entice Chase and Harley to follow you?" Bud asked.

"Oh that. I used a cowboy hat." And John chuckled.

"Cowboy hat?" Michelle asked.

"Sure. At a distance all you can see are silhouettes, so when I fired the AK-47 at the sagebrush in front of the quad and waved the prisoner's cowboy hat, Chase and Harley figured I was their bad guy buddy and followed me out to the timber. It was easy after that."

"I never asked how you took Crazy," Bud said.

John gave Bud a level look and said, "I lied to him. And that's all you get. Chase and Harley still here?"

Michelle looked at Bud and when he nodded, she said, "Yes."

"Mind if I talk to them. Won't take a second."

"What about?" Bud asked skeptically.

"I just want to reassure them they need to tell the truth, the whole truth and nothing but the truth, so help them God…and that I'm the only one other than God who can help them."

Michelle and Bud both chuckled. Michelle said, "I think they believed you the first time. They have been crying and talking and pleading and begging for someone, anyone, to save them. What does Chase keep saying? Oh yeah. She mimicked Chase's whining voice: 'We're dead. Just dead.'"

John and Bud both laughed.

Bud took a file from his top drawer and opened it. An FBI poster was the top sheet. He turned it and pushed it across the desk to John. "Anybody you know?"

John nodded. "Oh yeah. That's Raul Ortega. A really bad dude. We have good eye-witness evidence that he's a major player in the arms and drug trade. And he's a stone cold killer. Everybody wants this guy, FBI, CIA, NIA, NCIS, and every other alphabet agency in the free world."

Bud nodded. "Chase and Harley both identified him as the person who was giving Cowboy the what-for at Cowboy's ranch."

John stopped and looked around the room, at the sheet rock walls, at the soft dropped ceiling and then back at Bud. "No offense, but if Ortega finds out they're here, you are in big trouble. You can't stand much of a siege."

Bud started to take offense and then caught himself. John Bernard was a pro. But he felt obliged to defend his station anyway. "The windows are, quote, bullet proof, end quote. There is quarter-inch plate steel in the walls, the doors are steel…and we are shipping Chase and Harley to a more secure facility in Bend."

Michelle gave Bud a wry smile, and John Bernard laughed out loud. "Good call. The security you have is good enough for ordinary criminals and ordinary firearms. But these guys won't come after you with simple rifles. They'll use some really big guns that can punch a hole through your entire courthouse."

Bud glanced at Michelle and then said, "I don't think they'll come after me, but I can see them coming after Chase and Harley. We plan on taking them to the Justice Center in Bend. That's a bigger complex with a lot more security than we have here."

"How are you going to move them?' John asked.

"Deschutes County sheriff's vehicle."

John shook his head. "Not good. Think about it. If these guys can arrange in less than an hour to have fake EMTs snatch Crazy, they're more than capable of ambushing a county vehicle and taking Chase and Harley off your hands."

"Agreed," Bud said. "Any ideas?"

Michelle said, more to herself than to them, "I didn't study anything in school or at the Academy about subterfuge, but I read a lot of spy stories. What if we used a delivery truck? Something with Bud Lite or Mother's Cookies on the side."

They both nodded. "Sure. Good idea," Bud said, "and delivery drivers are early risers. Like o'dark hundred risers. And right now, I think I could use a 'Bud's Lite.'"

Michelle grinned at the pun and then said, "I'll bet Stallings Grocery has a delivery van. Want me to find out?"

Bud looked at John and then nodded. "I like it. We'll boogie out of here about 0400 and be in Bend before 0800. Straight up the highway, hiding in plain sight."

John stood up. "I'd like to tag along. And I'd like to question Cowboy. You did say he was at the Justice Center?"

"Yeah. I'd like the company. And I want to show him Ortega's picture. See if it rattles him. There's also a 'use of deadly force' review for Roger and Sonny tomorrow morning at 0900. I'd like to be there for that. I need my guys back on the job."

Michelle added quietly, "How about getting Deputy Holcomb something to do here in town. She's pretty exposed where she's at."

"Done," Bud added. "We can pick her up on our way back from Bend. Let her know. And ask Mrs. Davis to open up an upstairs apartment across the street for Larae. Pay Mrs. Davis whatever she wants. And tell her to keep quiet about it."

"I'm on it, Boss."

Bud looked at his watch and turned back to John, "How about something to eat?"

John shook his head, "What I'd like is a ride back to my trailer." He sniffed an armpit. I think I need a shower."

Bud grinned and said, "We can handle a little wood smoke. First I need to put a bulletin out about your buddy Raul, and then I'll give you a ride."

John said, "Good. I think I'll take a walk for a few minutes. Be back in ten."

A knock on the door announced Karen Highsmith who didn't wait for an invitation. "Bud," she said, holding out a printer copy of a bulletin, "you've got to see this." And her face crumpled and tears welled in here eyes.

Bud motioned to a chair, and handed her a tissue from a box in a bottom desk drawer. He had decided months earlier that a box of Kleenex was a requirement for the smooth operation of the Lake County Sheriff's Office.

His face paled as he read the bulletin. "Shit, shit, shit!" was all he could say.

He looked at John and then at Michelle with troubled eyes. They waited tensely for the bomb shell.

He cleared his throat twice and then read the bulletin aloud, his voice husky with emotion:

> Bremerton City Police Department, Bremerton, Washington Advisory: At approximately 0730 this morning, Detective Ronald G. Grandfield, Bremerton City Police, was shot and killed during a routine investigation at a private residence, and Detective Angelo M. Maretti was injured in a confrontation with four assailants. The assailants were armed with suppressed automatic rifles.
>
> Detective Maretti was treated at the scene by EMTs and transported to a local hospital. His condition is listed as serious. Three of the assailants were found dead at the scene by units of the Bremerton City Police. A search is underway for a fourth suspect who fled the scene on foot and is believed to be hiding in a heavily wooded neighborhood known locally as The Heights.
>
> Helicopters from the U.S. Coast Guard, the U.S. Navy, and the Washington State Police are coordinating the search with Bremerton City Police K-9 units, with patrol vehicles, and with elements of the Bremerton City Police SWAT team.
>
> Detective Angelo Maretti is credited with saving the life of a civilian who said Maretti shielded her with his own body and got her to safety even though he had suffered two gunshot wounds.
>
> End Bulletin:
>
> Harold H. Homer, Chief of Police

Bud let the paper drop to his side and stared into the past, remembering a disheveled Gino, penny loafers full of sand, Larae's blood on his white shirt, saying, "We ain't got not time for weepies."

Bud took a deep breath and almost whispered, "Way to go, Gino."

John looked at each of them carefully and said softly, "You know the detectives? Was Maretti at Cowboy's ranch when I brought Crazy in?"

Bud nodded and both Michelle and Karen said, "Yes," almost in unison.

Michelle heaved herself out of her chair, reached for one of Bud's tissues, and walked woodenly into the hallway, arms folded across her chest. She stopped at the door to the small conference room, remembering the efficient, tall, dark haired Grandfield. *A really decent guy*, she thought, and then she quit trying to stop the tears and just let them run down her face.

Karen sniffed and struggled unsuccessfully to hold back her tears, and her quiet sobs pulled tears from Bud's eyes.

John-Gar-Stone Fly-Bernard said quietly. "I'm sorry about your friends." He paused and added, "I've got a call to make."

Chapter 17

NCIS AGENTS DELBERT WINKLE, AKA DUDLEY Do-Right, and Abe McKenzie parked in front of Special Agent Amanda Spears' house. Flapping in the breeze, a hand written note pinned to the front door announced: "Come on back. I'm in the kitchen. A.S."

Weapons drawn, they cautiously threaded their way through living room furniture and down a hallway in the direction of fresh coffee aroma. They found her sitting on at her snack counter. Her badge wallet and her weapon lay on the kitchen table next to an attaché case.

She didn't say anything, just put her cup down, stood up and put her arms behind her to meet Dudley's handcuffs.

She looked at Abe with steely eyes and a clinched jaw. "Bring the briefcase," she said, "and my purse. Put my badge and my weapon in the purse. I'll want them back. And turn off the coffee pot."

They locked the door behind them, and helped her into the back of a dark blue Crown Vic that screamed "police," even without any obvious markings. A Plexiglas barrier separated the back seat from the driver's area. There were no window cranks or door handles in "the cage."

Abe took pity on her and moved the handcuffs to the front of her body before he snapped the seat belt in place. She shot him a grateful look.

She was stoic and silent and neither of her captors spoke during the ninety-minute ride to the carriage house. The only spoken words came later when Abe led them to a door at the back of the carriage house garage. He unlocked the door and flipped a switch that lit the concrete tunnel. "Holy, shit!" Dudley blurted.

Abe smiled grimly and Dudley nudged Amanda up the concrete steps while Abe closed and locked the door behind them. The two hundred-foot climb to the basement of the brick mansion above them took a little over three minutes. Amanda stumbled once, but shook off Dudley's hand and marched grimly up the concrete tunnel.

Abe pushed the strange cross-shaped key into the lock and turned. With an ominous hiss, the heavy metal door slowly opened.

Smoke eddied against the ceiling of the large basement room, overwhelming the room's exhaust system and filling the room with the stink of an acrid cigar.

Except for the long open racks of wine bottles, and six unopened cases from a winery in Oregon, there was little in the big concrete room except a step stool, obviously used to reach the higher racks, a padded folding chair, a small four-foot by six-foot wooden table, a small desk lamp, several Saran-wrapped wine flutes, and a dozen neatly stacked steno pads. The main source of light was a series of florescent tubes running down the center of the ceiling.

Abe set the brief case next to the spiral bound steno pads on the small table. He couldn't resist the temptation to open one. A woman's handwriting listed the history of each bottle: date of purchase, vineyard, vintage, type and quality, cost, and rack number. The SAC's wife was a true wine connoisseur. But the list had the feel of a lonely, solitary pursuit. Abe thought, *It's too bad the Chief doesn't like wine.*

Thompson pointed to the folding chair. "Sit," he barked at Amanda.

"I'll stand, thank you," she snapped back at him. "Take these damned things off me and put out that vile cigar. I'll cooperate, but you need to listen before you jump to conclusions. I'm not your mole, but I know who is."

Thompson clamped the cigar in his teeth, grabbed Amanda by the elbow and slammed her against the wall hard enough to bounce her head against cold concrete.

"Damn it, Agent Spears!" he yelled, "You got a good man killed this morning! I should shoot you right here and now."

Abe barked, "Chief," and Dudley started forward, but the SAC stepped back before they had to restrain him.

Abe thought about Amanda's orders to bring her badge and her weapon because she was going to need them back. "Sir," he said, "maybe we should hear what she has to say before we send her off to special agent heaven."

He picked up a white plastic step stool, used, he supposed, by Thompson's wife to reach the higher shelves of wine, and placed it against the wall next to the table. He motioned to the stool and quietly told Amanda to sit.

She took it better from Abe than from Thompson, sensing empathy in Abe, not exactly empathy maybe, but at least neutrality. He hadn't yet condemned her as the agency's mole. She grimaced as she sat down and knew her back would carry bruises tomorrow.

Thompson stopped his pacing and stood towering over her, cigar clamped in his teeth, the tip cherry red from his furious puffing. Dudley and Abe had never seen the SAC so angry, and they flanked the pair, poised to intercede if Thompson's anger led him to violence this time.

She spoke before her angry boss could say anything. "This is what I think. Someone listening to our conversations about the bomb blast in Fort Rock told the bad guys what was going on. The bad guys snatched Crazy and killed him. It was a nice, neat professional job. I don't know why they wanted him dead, but I can imagine they thought he knew too much about Cowboy's operation."

She stopped and asked, "How am I doing?"

"Great," Thompson growled, "Keep digging your grave."

"There's a certain logic in suspecting Warren or me...or even both of us...but only because we were on the scene. And even that assumes we're both stupid.

"Since I know Warren isn't stupid, and since I know I'm not the mole…and you should know that, sir," she said with venom in her voice, "and since it's absurd to think Toby Warren, the son of Congressman Warren from Montana is a mole, it's a more logical assumption to look at those people who were listening to our phone calls.

"If you think it through, Boss, it makes more sense to suspect you than Toby or me. But I know who the mole is, so that let's you off the hook. I think I was disappointed it wasn't you." She glared at him in defiance.

He glowered back at her and said through gritted teeth, "Your behavior says otherwise. You led the bad guys right to Ruby Goldstein's this morning. After you left, she called Detective Maretti about your visit, and when Detectives Maretti and Grandfield went to her house to get the duplicates of the photos you wanted, four armed men tried to kill her. They would have, except for Maretti and Grandfield.

"And now Grandfield is dead and Maretti is shot up. So who in the hell knew you were going to Ruby Goldstein's place?"

Her eyes widened in shock at the news and she started to rise, but Thompson put both hands and on her shoulders and pushed her back down. Abe started to intervene, but Dudley shook his head "no."

Amanda heaved herself upright, handcuffed arms shooting up, missing Thompson's nose by a hair, knocking the cherry from the cigar, showering them both with hot ash, but knocking his arms free from her shoulders. Her angry spittle sprayed Thompson's face as she shouted, "I went back to the Goldstein place to see if she had any more photos! Look in the briefcase, damn you, before you go any further! And take these things off my wrists! I've got work to do." She patted at the small cigar embers that melted black craters in her white silk blouse.

From Amanda's purse, cell phone music announced a call. They all ignored it.

Thompson took a deep breath, coughed once, then slowly unclenched his fists, and took the mangled cigar from his jaw. He nodded in the direction of the briefcase. Abe held it up and with raised eyebrows silently asked Amanda for the combination.

She hesitated and then said, "282." Abe turned the tumblers on the front of the black briefcase and snapped the catches open. "Look at the top photo," she said, "It was taken by Ruby Goldstein. That's the front door of Pettibone's house. There are others that show the same people going into Pettibone's house. Different parties, different times, but the same people."

Abe gave a slow whistle, and handed the photo to Thompson. Then he fumbled a key from his pocket and unlocked the handcuffs. She rubbed her wrists.

Amanda took a deep breath to slow her breathing and said quietly and directly to Thompson, "I went to see Ruby Goldstein to see if she had any more pictures of our person going into Pettibone's house... not," she emphasized, "to destroy evidence, as you apparently assumed. I'm sorry as hell about Detective Grandfield. He was a good cop. But I don't think I did more than beat the shooters to her place. I don't think anyone followed me. But it's a good thing Grandfield and Maretti got there when they did. Because otherwise, she would be dead."

Thompson stared at the photo and said, "Crap. Who would ever suspect." He handed the photo to Dudley who groaned, "Oh, no."

Thompson said, "Yeah. I guess I should have looked at something other than her big tits."

Abe asked, "You want us to pick her up?"

Thompson shook his head. "No. I've got an idea."

Chapter 18

THE NURSING STAFF HAD KEPT RUBY out of Maretti's recovery room until Chief Homer talked to the shift supervisor. "What's the harm? He saved her life, so she probably feels grateful. We can shoo her out when his brother gets here. The brother lives in Steubenville, Ohio. So…it's going to be a while."

The doctor looked at Chief Homer and shrugged. "Okay. I'll tell the nurses she's cleared to be in his room."

"How's he doing?" Chief Homer asked.

"Considering blood loss and two-hours of surgery to repair his arm, he's doing great. The bullet clipped the end of his elbow."

He touched the point of the chief's elbow. "Right there, that 'knob.' We had to remove a lot of bone splinters and bullet fragments. He's going to feel a lot of pain when he wakes up. But given the messy nature of the wound, I think our surgeons did a darned good job on your detective's arm."

MARETTI'S FIRST LUCID MEMORY WAS WAKING up in a hospital room. Ruby Goldstein was napping on a small recliner squeezed into a corner between the bed and a curtained window. Someone had covered her with a blanket. His limited view of the sky told him it was late afternoon.

I must have been out for hours, he thought. He tried to move his left arm, but it was strapped to his chest, a bulky cast hiding the work of the surgeons.

He raised his head and studied Ruby, watching the steady rise and fall of the blanket she had pulled up to her chin. There was an adhesive bandage on her cheek and one on her forehead. He worked hard to recall what had happened, but his memory was fragmented. He vaguely recalled two young paramedics cutting his jacket away with scissors, and a young woman, who kept saying, "Don't move."

He also remembered hearing Ruby talking to someone beyond the bullet-riddled counter. He hadn't understood what she was saying, but the name Grandfield penetrated his fog and he tried to sit up, couldn't, and lay back looking up at the EMTs. "Where's my partner?"

He remembered the glance between the senior paramedic and the young woman, the one with the ponytail. He knew it wasn't good. He had looked Ponytail straight in the eye. "Tell me."

Ponytail couldn't hold his gaze and looked at the senior EMT who shook his head. She said, "He was badly hurt, but he was still alive when we found him. He's on his way to the hospital right now."

Maretti remembered thinking, "She's lying."

"You're going to be all right now. What's your name?" She found a vein in the back of his right hand and started an IV drip.

AT FIRST, DURING THOSE INTERMITTENT WAKING periods, Maretti pretended to sleep if he heard someone enter his room. He knew he wouldn't be able to keep his tears at bay, tears of grief and rage at Ron's death. *What kind of person simply orders up someone's death*, he thought, *And how do I tell Ron's wife he won't be coming home?*

He also knew the Chief wanted to debrief him, and he didn't feel like talking to anyone right now, not even Ruby, although it was somehow comforting to find her there when he was awake. But by dinner time he was thirsty.

Chief Homer, flanked by FBI Agents Hoosier and Payne caught him drinking tea. They shooed Ruby out of the room.

FBI Agent Ed Hoosier bleakly said, "I'm sorry about Grandfield."

Chief Homer said, "I know it's not much help, but we cornered the fourth guy in a garage. He tried to shoot it out with our SWAT team and then turned the gun on himself. He's in critical condition, but still alive. I hope he pulls through so we can question him."

Maretti nodded and growled in a weak voice, working hard to keep tears from breaking through his tough-guy façade. "Unless I kill him first."

Agent Payne chuckled. "Oh, I think you've done enough of that for one day. Want to tell us what you remember?"

Maretti looked steadily at Chief Homer and asked, "Does Ron's wife know?"

The chief nodded. "Toughest thing I've done in a long time."

"Did Ron get any of those son-a-bitches?"

"One for sure," Homer answered. "And it looks like you took care of two others…and possibly wounded the fourth. We found a blood trail leading from the back deck. The K-9 units cornered the guy about fifteen minutes after we got there."

"Why did you go back to the Goldstein house?" Agent Hoosier asked.

And so Maretti told them about the phone call, about NCIS Agent Amanda Spears going back to the house, demanding all of the pictures Ruby Goldstein had taken, about Ruby calling him and about the bad guys opening up on them with suppressed automatic rifle fire.

"What was in the pictures?"

Maretti sipped at his tea and shook his head. "I don't know. Ron and I looked at them, but they didn't mean anything to either of us." He looked at Chief Homer. "Did you find the pictures?"

"Yeah, we found them. Every detective in the shop looked at them and didn't see anything useful. Our friends here," he pointed at the two FBI agents, "are running a facial recognition program on Pettibone's guests, but so far there isn't anything to tie any of them to anything evil…unless being a member of Bremerton's elite social set is evil."

"Money and power," Maretti whispered.

The Chief's cell phone rang. He glanced at the number and then answered. "Chief Homer."

A man said, "Chief, this is Bill Thompson, NCIS. We were wondering how Maretti's doing."

"Well, he appears to be his usual grumpy self, so I think the Good Lord has further mischief in mind for him."

"Good. Tell him we are thinking about him. And tell him we are damned sorry about Grandfield."

"I'll do that. Anything else?"

"Yeah. Did you find any photos at the Goldstein house?"

The chief nodded and said, "We did, but they don't mean anything to us. The FBI is looking at them now. What do you know?"

Thompson hesitated and then thought, *What the hell. I can always retire.*

"Chief," he said, "we found one of our employees in the photos, a person who works in our Analysis section. My deputy has a surveillance team watching her right now. We want to see who she contacts."

"So you have a mole?"

"It'll probably cost me my career when this comes out, but, yes we have a mole. Someone fairly close to me, someone I would never suspect of betrayal. The hell of it is, it isn't against the law to attend a party, so…" Thompson left the statement hanging. "So you found more photos?"

"I don't know about more, duplicates certainly. You want copies?"

"Please."

"Okay. Who gets them?"

Thompson thought about it and said, "I want them delivered to Springdale, and personally handed to Dennis Moore, my deputy. I'll let him know."

The Chief of Police for the city of Bremerton simply asked, "Can you use this mole to bait bigger fish?"

"That's the plan. By the way, did you see the bulletin from the sheriff of Lake County, Oregon?"

"Haven't been in the office for hours. What's it say?"

"It ties a Colombian by the name of Raul Ortega to the smuggling operation in Christmas Valley…you know, where the bomb was detonated."

"Wow. That'll blow the lid off things. Either that or get the sheriff killed."

"My thoughts exactly."

"Where does Agent Spears fit in all of this?" Chief Homer asked.

"Fishing, are you?"

"Ruby Goldstein told me Spears was in a sweat about the photographs, threatened Mrs. Goldstein with arrest if she didn't cooperate, which she didn't as it turns out because I have a full set of the photos she took."

Thompson said, "Agent Spears recognized one of the people in the photos as an NCIS employee. She was merely trying to see if we could tie our person to more than one visit to Pettibone's house."

"I think she got Detective Grandfield killed," Homer growled.

Thompson's voice was emphatic, "No. No she didn't. We think our mole got wind of the pictures and told someone, Pettibone maybe, who ordered Goldstein killed."

Chief Homer said, "Okay. The mole angle makes sense. And that would explain the four one-gallon cans of gas we found in the van the shooters drove. We think they intended to kill her and torch the house to destroy any remaining photos. So what do we do now?"

"We bait the trap."

"With whom? The sheriff?"

"You know, Chief, I don't know you well enough to share that information. In fact I've probably said too much already."

"I don't like that very much, Thompson. It suggests we can't be trusted."

Thompson snorted, "Who can be? That's what we're trying to figure out."

"Where does the Bremerton city police fit in the picture?"

"You don't. This is just a heads up. I just don't want you arresting Agent Spears."

Chief Homer cut the call without answering.

Maretti and the two FBI agents had been listening to the Chief's side of the call. Maretti said, "I take it that NCIS is going to use Bud Blair to bring some Colombian bad-ass out into the open?"

Homer nodded. "He didn't say so, but it looks that way. If NCIS is going to try and bring Raul Ortega out in the open, Sheriff Blair might just be the bait to use. But don't you tip Blair off. I'll have your badge if you do."

Maretti looked at the FBI agents. "You heard him, threatening a wounded man, a man who is delirious from a high level of painkillers, a man who isn't even aware of his surroundings."

Detective Payne caught Maretti's eyes and winked. "Got it, Gino. I will bear witness."

Chief Homer started to bark at Maretti, and then shrugged. "Go back to sleep, Gino. You done good today. I don't think anyone could have done better."

In the hallway, Hoosier and Payne stopped the chief. "The forensics teams found fingerprints all over the van," Payne said, "we have dozens of shell casings, and we think we know where the perps bought the gas cans. There was a gas receipt in the van. We'll check that."

"Phone records?"

"None of the shooters had a cell phone, but the finger prints gave us an address. We have agents armed with a search warrant headed there now. If we find anything, I'll keep you posted."

"Do that," Chief Homer said, and walked down the hallway, fuming at the snub from Thompson.

Chapter 19

BUD'S DESK PHONE BEGAN RINGING MINUTES after his bulletin went racing through cyber space. John watched with a wry smile while the sheriff stonewalled all requests for information about his sources.

The sheriff listened as patiently as he could to half-veiled threats from the FBI, Homeland Security, CIA, and other agencies he didn't really know any thing about, each demanding the name of his source, "or else."

Disgusted, he finally left a message on his answering machine which bluntly said, "If you are calling about the Lake County Sheriff's Bulletin regarding Raul Ortega, you know everything I know. When I know more I'll tell you."

Bud shook his head and said to John Bernard, "Let's get out of here."

John grinned and said, "You're in the soup, now, Bud. Welcome to the world of cover-your-ass law enforcement."

"Karen," Bud called as they headed to the front door, "make sure Asa Connor gets a copy of the bulletin. And email him a copy of Ortega's picture."

She looked up over the booking counter, a phone to her ear, her curly hair bobbing as she nodded and mouthed, "Will do."

John slid into the passenger seat of Bud's pickup, and as soon as they were headed through town to Hunter's RV Park, he asked, "Asa, as in Asa Connor of the Lake County News?"

"Yeah, that's right. You talked to him before, didn't you." It was statement of fact, not a question. "Asa told me some well-informed anonymous caller gave him all kinds of good information about

Cowboy's operation. I can add two plus two, John. The information had to come from you."

John looked out the windshield at the hills in the distance and said nothing.

Bud hadn't expected an answer, so he continued. "I want him to run Ortega's picture and a copy of the original bulletin. We have a watcher system in place...for druggies, mainly."

"And the picture will give them someone to look for, right?"

"That's the idea."

"Isn't that dangerous?"

"I don't think so. At least I hope not. They all run small stores that pump gas, sell beer...that sort of thing. It's just normal contact for small businesses. All they're supposed to do is wait until any suspicious person leaves and then call us."

"So...all the main routes into Lakeview are watched?"

"Yeah."

John looked at Bud and said, "Your watchers must trust you a lot."

Bud turned left into the RV park and then said, "I don't know if they trust me personally, but they have a lot of confidence in my officers."

The Dodge pickup stopped in front of John's decrepit-looking trailer, and without shutting down the engine, Bud said, "I'll pick you up at 0400 for our trip to Bend."

John stepped out and shut the door. He watched the county pickup on around the loop and thought, I like him. Now to keep him alive.

Marvin Goodnough flagged Bud as the pickup neared the office of the RV park. Bud powered down the window. "Sheriff, is everything all right?"

"Yeah, Marv. John's a friend of mine."

"John? He gave his name as Justin Beaver. I thought that was odd. And he paid cash."

Bud shifted mental gears and said, "Beaver...yeah, that was his mother's maiden name, I think. And he never liked the name Justin, so we've always called him John...like in John the Baptist."

"Christian guy?" Marvin asked.

Bud could barely keep his face straight. "Yes Marvin, you could say that. He often reads to people from the Good Book, and holds 'Come to Jesus' meetings every chance he gets. But, Marv, only his closest friends call him John. So you just stick with Justin, okay? And I wouldn't mention this conversation to anyone."

Marvin was sure the sheriff was pulling his leg, but he nodded and said, "Okay. As long as he pays his rent, I don't care if he calls himself Moses."

"Thanks. Do you drink beer? I'd like to buy you a beer later and have a chat."

"No," Marvin shook his head, "I don't drink beer. But I like a little Johnny Walker now and again."

"If I didn't know better, Marv, I'd say you were trying to hold me up. You wouldn't do that, would you?"

The owner, manager, bookkeeper, and all-around handy man for the park just grinned.

Bud grinned back, and said, "Okay, Johnny Walker it'll be. And take care of my friend, you hear?"

Bud put the pickup in gear and eased on up the paved lane to the main highway.

Marvin Goodnough turned back in time to see "Justin," towel and canvas tote in hand, head for the shower room.

Or is that John the Baptist? Marv thought. He was grinning as he walked into the office. "Clyde is gonna love this." He picked up the phone and hit a speed dial for Clyde Whittaker, owner of the Valley Falls mini mart, RV park and gas station.

Bud knew that Marv would be telling the story about John the Baptist to his friends. He just hoped they would buy his spur of the moment story, and then thought, Well, Justin is a common enough name, but 'Beaver'?

Bud turned north up Highway 395 to his small two bedroom house, a gray-green rambler that guarded the east side of the highway, along with a dozen or so attractive, tree shaded single-story ranch-style homes. There was enough elevation to give each house a view of irrigated hay fields, willow-lined creeks, pastures dotted with cattle and horses, scattered barns and ranch yards, some marked by old Lombardi Poplars and cottonwood trees, and the pine-timbered mountains that sheltered the valley on the west. Cougar Mountain held center stage in Bud's vista.

In his first year as undersheriff, Bud made it his business to get acquainted with the people and the country. He would stop on a Saturday afternoon at one of the local watering holes in small places like Adel or Silver Lake to sip a cold beer and listen to tales, getting to know the people of Lake County—characters like Clyde Whitaker at the Valley Falls store, Buffalo Boggs, self-styled "Inn Keeper" in Paisley, Amy O'Fallon in Adel.

When the snow melted and when he had time, he and Molly drove into the high country to see the old lookout sites like Abert Rim, Dog Mountain, Fish Hole, Crane Mountain, Slide Mountain, and Drakes Peak. He and Molly hiked into the Gearhart Wilderness, fished Dairy Creek, or walked the dike at the Summer Lake Wildlife Refuge to shoot bird pictures, just poking around and falling in love with a place that claimed his heart.

They were all "favorite" places, but if pushed he would admit that Drakes Peak in the North Warner Mountains would be near the top of the list. There was no tower, never had been, just a ground cabin sitting on top of a big bald knob. The cabin stared at the world through windows on all four sides, with a bed, a small wood-burning stove, a cupboard-counter, propane-powered lights, and a small refrigerator for comforts. The old viewfinder still sat in the middle of the cabin floor. And the view was—what? Bud disliked words like "tremendous" or "fabulous," but where else could you see Mount Shasta to the southwest on a clear day, and then turn and look behind you at the broken fault scarps of Hart Mountain to the east? And if you were there on a late afternoon, you might watch the shadows grow and turn a landscape flattened and muted by the mid-day sun into sharp contours of meandering streams, bluffs and canyons.

BUD'S CELL PHONE RANG AS HE pulled into his driveway. He scanned the number, a Washington, D.C. 202 prefix, and grimly ignored it. Molly barked and tried to jump up and lick his face when he opened the gate to the fenced backyard.

He poured dry dog food in her dish, and put the sack back in the black metal cabinet that stood like a sentry on the small back porch. He opened the faucet and filled her drinking dish with fresh water.

The small black lab wagged her tail and looked up at him before digging in. She ate like she hadn't been fed in weeks, big crunchy gulps that scattered food pellets all over the deck. He laughed and said, "Molly, you can be a prissy lady some of the time, but you eat just like a hound."

His cell phone rang again, and he started to ignore the call until BB's number scrolled across the screen.

"That you BB?"

"Hey, Honky, how you hanging? I hear you don't answer your phone anymore."

"What? Did you call my office?"

"Yeah, and I listened to the message. Got on my computer and looked up Raul Ortega. And then I called Dutch Vanderlin. He wants you to call him back. Says it's important. Actually he said some unkind things about you in words that I'd be happy to share."

"So why would I want to talk to Dutch? All I get from the Feds is a hard time."

"Honky, you know he's one of the good guys. Talk to him. Please."

Bud hesitated before saying, "Okay, but I don't have anything new to share. It's all in the bulletin."

"Hanging up now, Honky. Stay by the phone."

Bud pulled the drapes back from his front window, and stood in the unlit living room, watching the highway. A trailer load of small logs, what Bud's logger father would call "pecker poles," pulled by a dusty, blue Kenworth diesel, passed the house, headed south to the lone surviving sawmill in Lake County.

It was Dutch Vanderlin on the line when the cell phone rang again. "Bud, how you doing, old friend?"

"Staying busy," Bud answered in tone that was too sharp to be friendly.

"Yeah, you have. For the moment you are one of the most famous men in America. But don't let it go to your head. People have short memories." And then he laughed.

"What do you want, Dutch?"

"Got a little problem with the Seattle SAC and also with a Deputy Assistant Secretary for Homeland Security. They looked in their little black books and remembered that fracas you and I had years ago with Portland's Organized Crime division. Remember that?"

Bud remained silent.

"Anyway," Dutch continued, "the boys in D.C. say you aren't answering your phone. They ordered me to get in touch with you… to arrest you if necessary. Which I will gladly do if I have to. They want your source."

Bud said, "No" and then remembered that Dutch really was one of the good guys. He sighed and then relented. "Okay, Dutch. Tell you what. Meet me at the Justice Center in Bend at 0800 tomorrow morning. I'll give you a chance to talk to my sources. But I want them protected. And for an added bonus, you and I will question one Robert Clark, aka Cowboy. I think the Bureau should be interested in this guy…gun running, explosives, smuggling illegal aliens…that kind of thing."

"Tell me," Dutch said, "is your source Mid-Eastern or Mexican?"

"Why?"

"I'm trying to tie the explosives and the guys who detonated the bomb to a mosque here in Portland."

"Wow. That's hot, Dutch," Bud said, forgetting for the moment that he was mad at the FBI, at all Federal agencies for that matter. "That might give us a new angle when we question Cowboy. It makes sense if you think about it. Cowboy has been protesting his innocence, but I think…hell, I know…I can tie him to gun running, people smuggling, and drugs. I don't know if we can tie him to the

Portland end of things. Let me think about it. And keep those D.C. assholes off my back."

"Okay, Bud," Dutch said. "I'll tell them I have a chance to meet your source, but I can't guarantee more than twenty-four hours before they send somebody after you."

"Goodbye, Dutch," Bud growled and hung up.

He dialed BB's number. "Okay," he said when BB answered. "Here's the deal. Dutch is going to meet me in Bend tomorrow morning...at the Justice Center. I'll give him a chance to talk to my source. Good enough?"

BB laughed, "That'll keep you out of jail for a while at any rate. See you tomorrow."

"You're not invited, BB."

"The hell I'm not," BB snorted, "I am officially working for the FBI as liaison with the sheriff of Lake County."

"Bullshit," Bud snapped.

"See you tomorrow, Honky."

IN THE WEST HILLS, HIGH ABOVE the city of Portland, a late-generation tracking device emitted a microburst signal that carried an encrypted recording of the conversation between Detective Dell BeBe and Sheriff Henry (Bud) Blair.

In Springdale, Washington, a buxom young woman, called "Buttons" behind her back—especially by her male colleagues— stored an electronic copy in an appropriate file. And then, within standard protocol, she printed a copy for her supervisor. But she "accidentally" made two copies. She knew her friend would want one.

She slipped both copies into a file folder marked "Witherspoon" and carried the folder back to her desk. Her colleagues were all concentrating on monitors, reading intercepts or typing, oblivious to her clandestine activity.

In the SAC's private conference room, Dennis Moore and a member of Abe's team, call sign "Bambi," watched a flat-screen monitor fed by a surveillance camera as Buttons slid a copy of the intercept into the top drawer of her desk.

Dennis looked at Bambi and nodded at the big, wall-mounted screen. "Follow her. Find her contact."

Bambi, a lean, forty-one-year-old brunette with a runner's build, nodded, and asked, "And when we do?"

"We leave Buttons in place, but we follow her contact. I want the big bad wolf."

Bambi nodded and left the room.

Assistant SAC Dennis Moore thumbed a number on his cell phone and waited until Thompson answered. Without preamble Dennis said, "Our mole is…"

Thompson supplied, "Buttons."

"Yes. How did you know that?"

"We SACs are omniscient. When you take my job, you'll have new and amazing skills like omniscience, omnipresence, and the ability to see through solid objects."

"You sound happy."

"I am, Dennis." He paused and then added, "I'm happy as hell that Agents Spears and Warren are in the clear. I can put 'em back to work. And then again I'm not happy. Who in the hell would ever think that Buttons was a mole?"

"Evidence?" Moore asked.

"Photos. Who you got on Buttons?"

"Bambi. Abe and Dudley will hook up with her as soon as you turn them loose."

"Already on the way."

Chapter 20

NCIS AGENTS BAMBI AND DUDLEY SPENT an evening hour watching the front door to Button's apartment building, while their partner, Abe talked Assistant SAC Dennis Moore into getting a search warrant. Moore insisted they include NCIS agents Spears and Warren in any search. Abe replied, "Why not invite the whole damned world?"

Denny had simply grinned and said, "Not the whole world. Just NCIS. The Good Guys. And I don't want her apartment searched while she's still there. We'll monitor her phone calls and wait until she makes contact with…her contact…whoever in the hell that is. Your team follows Buttons. Spears and Warren search the apartment."

Abe fumed at the delay and held an internal debate about calling Thompson, and reluctantly abandoned the notion.

A light rain on the windows of Dudley's dark blue 4x4 Toyota pickup worked in harmony with tinted side and back windows to make it difficult for anyone on the street to identify the occupants. So they parked a short half-block from the front entrance to Buttons' apartment building, a three-story, red brick structure with small individual patios for each unit, and underground parking. A gold-lettered sign on the glass of the entrance door read "A Secure Facility for Single Women." The brass plaque that carried the name of the building was obscured by dense Irish yews that stood like green sentinels on either side of the walkway.

Bambi said, "You know, Dud, this place has to be expensive. Where would a GS-9 analyst get that kind of money?"

"Family?"

"No. I checked. Her parents paid taxes on about $60,000 last year. She's an only child, so no big brothers or sisters helping her out. Wrap that up with her expensive Acura, and we have someone living well beyond her means."

"So maybe baby Carlotta Mayes, our very own "Buttons," grows up spoiled and pampered, but wants more than her parents can give her?"

"I don't know. Maybe she's just in love. Love does funny things to some people."

"Uh, oh," Dudley said. "Here comes a cab."

Bambi jumped out of the pickup and walked across the street for a closer look at the front door. Her jogging gear didn't earn her a second glance as she propped a leg on a low retaining wall and stretched.

Buttons, dressed in jeans, boat shoes, a blue hooded windbreaker, and carrying a bulky red daypack, hurried out the door not thirty seconds after the cab stopped. Bambi heard her say "Poulsbo" as the taxi door slammed.

Dudley started the pickup and did a mid-street U-turn and then Bambi jumped in the passenger's seat. His hands-free cell was ringing as she slammed the door and reached for the seatbelt.

She heard "Call Center," and then Dudley was calmly and smoothly relaying information about the cab: license number, company, cab number, direction, and passenger. Bambi added, "Headed for Poulsbo. Notify Special Agent McKenzie."

The cabbie drove within the speed limit on the expressway that ran north from Springdale, and kept to the right lane. Dudley stayed a dozen car lengths back. When a faster car moved into the right lane in front of Dudley's pickup, he figured it was a perfect tail. And it helped to have a destination. The cab stayed in the right lane of the expressway for all of seven minutes, and then took the Poulsbo exit. The street ran along the north side of the Poulsbo harbor, a backwater bay connected to Puget Sound to the east.

The car in front of Dudley followed the cab and a short distance later signaled a left turn into a private driveway.

Bambi's cell vibrated and she flipped it open. "Yeah?" she answered.

Abe asked, "Location?"

"We're a mile or so from Poulsbo, not too far behind a Silverdale cab. I saw Buttons get in the cab. What do you know?"

"We traced a call from her apartment to a cell phone. We don't have an ID on the person she called."

"Hold on. The cab is turning into the boat basin."

Dudley pulled into the curb on the right and got out, heading in the direction of a café-mini mart across the street. He pulled the hood of his sweatshirt up over his head, and hurried, like he was wanting out of the light drizzle.

Bambi watched through binoculars as Buttons closed the cab door and walked through the small park on the south side of the street to a gate guarding the boat dock. All the slips were occupied, lights showing in a half-dozen cabin cruisers. And a few boats were tied to anchor buoys out in the harbor.

Buttons punched four numbers into the key pad and opened the gate. The late evening sky was dark enough for the lights lining the dock to have automatically turned on, and Bambi had a clear sight of Buttons walking to the far end of the dock, and climbing a short set of steps onto a white boat. *Yacht*, Bambi thought.

A Seattle native, Bambi loved boats and loved the Puget Sound area. It was too rainy and too far to see the name on the boat, but she knew it was a Cobalt 46.

She reached behind the seat for her daypack and pulled a small laptop from the case. A quick search gave her what she was looking for. The Cobalt 46 was powered by twin Cummins engines that came standard at 425 horsepower each, or with option "monster" Cummins delivering up to 540 horsepower each. Fuel capacity: 350 gallons.

"Fairly long legs…at ten knots," she murmured. "Not so long at high speeds." There was no mention of top speed, but she'd bet her bottom dollar it was capable of thirty-plus knots. "Fast…really fast for a boat that size."

Dudley slid back into the pickup just as Bambi dialed Abe's cell. Dudley said, "Uh-oh. He's casting off."

"Hold a minute," she said when Abe answered. She lowered the window and then took a long look through a large telephoto lens attached to a late generation digital camera. She held the trigger down and heard the camera snapping rapid fire pictures as a tall blond man untied the lines and jumped back on board. She could hear the rumble of diesel engines and saw the Cobalt swing away from the dock and slide quietly out into the bay.

She picked her cell phone back up and said, "He's doing a runner on us, Abe. We need to get the Coast Guard involved. And right now," she added as the Cobalt's bow rose into the air and then leveled out as it got up on the step. "I don't have a name, but it's a Cobalt 46 and faster than hell."

Dudley sprinted to the harbor master's office and banged on the door. A short dumpy-looking man came to the locked door and hollered, "We're closed. What do you want?"

Dudley produced his credentials and flattened them against the glass in the door. Two minutes later he had the name of the boat: the *Might As Well* out of Anacortes, Washington.

The Cobalt was around the point and out of sight before Dudley slid back into the pickup. He just started to say, "The boat's called The..." when there was a bright flash of light from beyond the point, followed a good ten seconds later by the muted sound of an explosion that rolled up the bay like thunder from a lightning storm.

Dudley stopped and then shook his head. "I think the bad guys are closing shop."

Bambi nodded and said, "Shit. Damned waste of a nice boat."

"That's a little cold blooded, don't you think?"

"Dud, I like boats a hell of a lot more than traitors. I don't know who got 'em, and I don't care."

Dudley thumbed 911 into his cell and waited to report an explosion. The 911 operator assured him it had already been reported and wanted to know if he had seen the explosion. He said, "No, but tell the Coast Guard to look for a yacht called the *Might As Well*." The operator wanted his name, but Dudley ended the call without answering.

Bambi was talking to Abe when Dudley started the pickup, did a U-turn in front of a "No U-turn" sign and headed back to Silverdale.

A LATE EVENING FISHERMAN, DRESSED IN forest-green rain gear, watched as scattered debris from the *Might As Well* rode the surface swells. A life jacket here, a floating picnic cooler there, and lots of paper scraps, money hidden in another cooler, now scattered across the water like confetti. The big cooler holding the money was the one in which she had hidden the bomb.

The woman known to her employer simply as "Miz Kay" threw the remote detonator as far out in the bay as she could. She cut the monofilament just above the reel, folded her stool and picked up the empty bait bucket. As she slogged her way through the muck of the shoreline and back to the car, she thought, *All that lovely money... gone...except what I took to make room for the bomb.* She thought she might have as much a three or four hundred thousand dollars in the trunk of her car. She smiled and whispered, "Time to retire."

She popped the trunk, and carefully stowed the fishing gear, folded her rain gear and her muddy boots in a plastic bag and then closed the trunk lid.

She noticed a man walking a dog at the far side of the parking lot. He looked and waved and then walked on. She waved back and then settled into the front seat. Doors locked, she slipped a disc with opera music into the player. She snapped her seat belt in place and then turned the key to start the engine. For a second time that evening an explosion ripped the air of Poulsbo bay, town, and harbor. This time money rained from the sky like confetti.

Chapter 21

Bud's pickup rolled up beside John's trailer at 4:00 a.m. In the headlights, the trailer sat like a sad refugee from a salvage yard, but through the open door Bud saw a spit-and-polish interior that looked new. John came around from the back of the trailer with an oversized canvas duffle bag. He waved a greeting to Bud, and then reached into the open door of his trailer and killed the interior lights. He pushed the door shut, twisted a key in the lock, and wiggled the knob to make sure he had it right.

When John opened the passenger door and pushed the duffle bag onto the floor boards, Bud smelled fresh-cut alfalfa in the cool air and heard the faint, rhythmic "chuck…chuck…chuck," of a big irrigation system working slowly around a pivot in a 360-degree arc. It felt somehow comforting to Bud. In spite of the terrorists, the drugs, and the murder that had invaded Lake County, some normal living went on. *Thanks to law enforcement*, he thought.

"Morning, Sheriff."

"Morning, John. Sleep well?"

"I never sleep well the night before a mission."

"Mission, huh? I don't know if this qualifies as a mission, but I didn't sleep well either. Too much on my mind, I guess."

Bud slipped the automatic transmission into drive and nudged the pickup on around the loop and out to the highway. He turned right, heading back to town.

"You know," Bud said, "I liked Michelle's suggestion to use an anonymous delivery van to get Chase and Harley to Bend. That was yesterday. Today…I've changed my mind. In the first place, there's no way really to secure Chase and Harley in a van, and in the second place, it just doesn't feel right. I'll be damned if I'll hide in my own county!"

John studied Bud and then gave him a smile. Bud caught the look from the lights of the instrument dash. "What are you smiling at?"

"Well. You'll accomplish two things with an attitude like that. You'll get shot at. That's one. And you'll either get shot or shoot someone else. That's two."

"So you think I should hide?"

"Hell, no. That won't work either. But a little subterfuge wouldn't hurt."

Bud pulled up to the intersection of highways 395 and 140, the highway to Klamath Falls and stopped. He looked both ways and then turned left on Lakeview's main street, deserted at this early hour except for a log truck idling in front of Jerry's Café, the driver heading out the restaurant door with a Styrofoam cup in his hand.

"They start early, don't they," John observed.

Bud didn't answer, just drove three blocks, turned left past the courthouse, then right into a parking slot in front of the station.

Bud used his pass key to open the front door and called, "Naomi, it's me, Bud."

The auto switch lit up the small foyer and the booking area behind the public counter. A sleepy looking Naomi Peel, wife of the town's mortician and Karen's night matron, heard Bud and unlocked the door to the cell block.

"What are you doing back there, Naomi?" Bud asked as the chunky, middle-aged woman closed the cell block door behind her.

"Michelle and Karen both told me to sleep in the cell block. We have an empty cell, and they said it might be safer to keep the place locked down."

"Okay. Maybe they're right. Get Chase and Harley up, and get them dressed. Send Chase down here first. I'm taking them to Bend."

"Now?"

"Yes, right now. And make sure they pee before you let them out. We aren't making any stops."

She looked puzzled, but unlocked the cell block and walked down the concrete hallway to Chase's cell while Bud kept the door ajar.

Ten minutes later, the sleep-befuddled prisoners, wearing handcuffs, waist chains and leg irons were strapped in the back of Bud's crew cab pickup behind the heavy Plexiglas divider—the "cage." Bud pointed the pickup north up 395 towards the Valley Falls junction with Highway 31.

Chase was whispering, "Harley, where they takin' us? This ain't good, Harley. They gonna kill us for sure. That there is that special forces guy who took Crazy down. Them guys is stone-cold killers."

Harley just said, "Shut up, Chase. If he was gonna kill us he'd a done it before now, so quit your whining."

"What you gonna do, Harley? Spit on me? Head butt me?"

"Yeah...all of that, so shut up."

Bud didn't say anything until they were in the little valley threaded by Crooked Creek. Bud slowed for three mule deer that froze in the right-hand ditch and then bolted across the highway and into the pasture on the west side.

He chuckled and said, "We don't want to hit one of those."

Then he said, "John, there's a laptop in a soft case behind your seat. Dig that out and turn it on. The disc we found at Cowboy's house is in the laptop. I looked at it last night. It got interesting. Did your cryptologists ever break Cowboy's code?"

John said, "I don't know. Until yesterday morning I was camped out on Timothy Lake trying my best to ignore the rest of the world."

"I think you'd better find out," Bud said.

John pushed a button on the side of his watch and lit the face. "Hmmm. Four forty-five. I guess we'll have to wake somebody up."

When the phone stopped ringing, a sleepy voice said, "That you, John?"

"The one and only, Amanda. Sorry to wake you up. Had a question. Two actually. Question number one: Are you in the clear?"

"Yes. Thompson knows I'm not the mole. I'm back in harness."

"Good. Who is it?"

Amanda paused, and then said, "Not on the phone."

"Okay. I won't even hazard a guess, but it if isn't Warren, I'll be disappointed."

"Then you will be. What else do you want?"

"Did our analysts get Cowboy's code worked out?"

"I don't know, but I think they would have told me. Why?"

"Well, Amanda, I think Sheriff Blair might have beat them to it. Why don't you put the coffee on and wake up. I'll be back." He snapped the cell phone shut.

Bud was grinning like a school boy and nodding. They rounded the last curve in Crooked Creek canyon and rolled into a moonlit landscape, the trees sheltering Clyde's little RV-park visible a couple miles ahead. East of the highway, Abert Rim, black with night shadows, rose some 2,000 feet above the farm fields that surrounded Valley Falls. Bud goosed the pickup to seventy, reasonably confident they were through the worse of the deer country.

He glanced in the rearview mirror at his prisoners. Chase was asleep with his head on Harley's shoulder. Harley was awake, sitting upright, stone-faced. He caught Bud looking at him and tried to figure out what was going on. But lack of sleep and a history of drugs and alcohol abuse had diminished his already limited IQ. So he just scowled at Bud's reflection and took another mental step in the direction of absolute fatalism.

John opened the laptop and turned it on. The laptop booted up and glared at the dark cab with a bluish light.

Bud said, "Go to Microsoft Word and type in JOHN."

"Okay," John said, "I did that."

"Highlight it and then go to Font."

"Okay. Now what?"

"Now scroll through the font choices until you find MS Reference Specialty. Got it?"

"Yeah. I got it."

"Go ahead and select OK." Bud said. "And voilà—what do you see?"

John turned the laptop so Bud could see the font: **SSHS**

Bud looked smug. "And there you have it."

"Cowboy simply hid his messages by changing the font?"

"Yep, and I have to tell you I'm not really that smart, just lucky. I was typing my weekly letter to my dad and thought I'd dress it up a little, make it more interesting. So I kept trying new font types and found that. Something about the MS Reference Specialty font starting tugging at my brain. I knew I had seen something like it someplace earlier. And then I got to thinking about Cowboy's disc. And the rest is history."

"So you simply highlighted and selected a more normal font and there it was?"

"Yep. Look for 'Cowboy' in documents."

Bud instinctively slowed as they passed the Valley Falls junction of highways 395 and 30 and then resumed speed on the straight.

John found the document "Cowboy," worked the keys of the laptop for a few seconds, paused and read a list of activities: dates, names, shipments, products, amounts, payments, collections, phone numbers, aliases, employees.

"Wow," John said quietly. "The whole nine yards. All we have to figure out is who RO and BP are and we can roll up this whole pipeline and shut it down."

"I already know who they are. "RO" is Raul Ortega, and "BP" is Basil Pettibone. Has to be. I'm thinking you should email that document to our buddy Amanda along with what I've figured out. She can start unraveling things from that end."

John Bernard, Special Agent, NCIS stared at Bud with an almost incredulous look on his face. "You know, Bud, you are damned-near brilliant. Not quite, but close. I'll bet our cryptologists are still working on this. How do you work with three squares and a circle with an arrow on top? I can hardly wait to rub it in."

"Don't do that. I just got lucky. And we might need them again."

The big crew cab pickup crossed the Chewaucan River and a short thirty seconds later Bud negotiated a lazy curve that took them almost due west and onto a flat five-mile straight that simply cried for speed. Bud goosed the pickup to eighty-five and settled in the seat hoping to miss the jackrabbits that haunted the highway at night. He caught the faint glimpse of a small coyote streaking across the highway at the extreme edge of the pickup's high beam headlights. He grinned and said, "You're gonna get yourself killed, Mr. Coyote."

John added, "My sort of animal. They're tough and they're smart."

"True survivors," Bud added. *Like us, I hope.*

Chapter 22

For Amanda it had been a long day and a short night. The confrontation with Thompson had been draining even though he had finally conceded her innocence. Without apology he had simply said, "Abe. Give her badge and her weapon back."

Assistant SAC Dennis Moore's phone call had started a chain of events that kept them all busy until after midnight. First came the late-afternoon ride back to Silverdale. At least that had been in the comfort of Thompson's private limo and not in handcuffs in the back seat of a police car.

Agent Warren had not been returned to duty because the issue of "his" off-shore account had yet to be resolved. It was a formality, but one that had to be observed.

Amanda and Abe McKenzie had searched Button's apartment, but found nothing of interest. "I get this sense of a lonely person," she had said to Abe. No family photos, no group photos, just one picture of a smiling Basil Pettibone at the wheel of a boat. It sat on her bedside table.

Abe said, "That looks like she used her cell phone. I wonder if he knows she took this shot?"

Sadness for Buttons eased into Amanda's soul, and then she thought of her own life. She had trusted teammates. But she didn't have anyone close, anyone to love. A fleeting picture of Bud Blair's rugged face and his wry smile slipped through her mind. She shrugged the feeling away.

All business again, she placed the snapshot into a baggie, dated and signed it and said, "I don't see anything else except her computer. Do you?"

"*Nada,*" Abe replied. He unplugged her computer and picked it up. "I'm done. We'll let the nerds look through this. See what they find."

They sealed the door with crime-scene tape over the objection of the apartment manager, a tough-looking crew-cut woman in an expensive pantsuit, complete with a white shirt and a tie. The manager kept saying, "I have to consider the reputation of Arnold Arms. You can't leave that there."

Amanda patiently explained the need to preserve evidence and the penalty for interfering with an investigation. The building manager turned and stalked away, but not before growling, "Bullshit. You'll be hearing from my attorney."

Amanda said to a retreating back, "Have at it, lady."

Abe grinned and walked to the elevator. "And you were so polite, Agent Spears."

Curbside, Amanda hit the key lock and popped the trunk on the dark blue Dodge Charger. She moved her kit to make room for the computer, put the snapshot in a brown paper bag, sealed it with scotch tape, dated and signed the bag, and then slipped it inside the cargo net. She slammed the deck lid and said, "Well, there you have it. Let's head for the barn."

As they settled in the front seat, Amanda at the wheel, Abe said, "About this afternoon…"

"Over and done," she snapped.

Abe's cell phone buzzed before he could say more. Amanda could faintly hear Bambi on the speaker.

And then they were headed for Poulsbo, red light pulsing on the dash.

The NCIS team, led by Agent Amanda Spears, including Abe, Dudley, and Bambi, investigated the car explosion. The scene was lit by headlights and spotlights from four Poulsbo city police cars. Six police officers, including the chief of police, were keeping a curious crowd away. Orange pylons supported yellow crime scene ribbon strung in a wide circle around the charred wreckage.

Amanda thanked the Chief for a good job and turned her team loose to work the scene.

The badly mangled remains of a woman were gathered piece by piece and placed in a body bag. Abe and Bambi zipped the bag, slid it onto a stretcher and loaded it into an NCIS van which arrived five minutes behind Amanda's team.

The vehicle VIN number was photographed and the number called to headquarters. Abe found a scorched H&K .40 caliber handgun in the wreckage along with four extra clips. Bambi scrapped sooty residue from the trunk lid lying a good twenty feet from the burned-out car. Dudley took dozens of photos and then helped Abe, Bambi and Amanda gather as many soggy bills as they could on the rain slick pavement of the parking lot. Judging by the paucity of bills, scavengers had already made off with a lot of the money.

Abe said, "I'll bet some will be buying rounds in the local water holes tonight. Want us to work it?"

Amanda nodded and said, "You and Dudley make the rounds. But I'm less interested in the money than I am in finding out what people saw." She nodded to a crowd being kept back by the Poulsbo city police.

Bambi saw her staring at a dozen or so people with camp lanterns working the area beyond the crime scene perimeter, stooping to pick up pieces of paper that had to be US currency. "Want it stopped?"

Amanda said, "Yeah. Go run those idiots off."

She handed a soft case containing the forensics evidence and the handgun to a young assistant forensics pathologist, had him sign for it, and told him to scoot back to the lab.

"Bambi," Amanda called, "Let's work the crowd and then work the neighborhood." She saw the dozen or so camp lanterns leaving the scene, carried by a crowd who decided they didn't want anything to do with an angry police officer. Besides, they had pockets already stuffed with large denomination bills.

Bambi walked over to the chief of Poulsbo's city police and asked, "Do you want to arrest those assholes?"

The Chief grinned and said, "Nope. I'd have to arrest half the community. I think I'll leave that to you Feds. In the meantime, I keep thinking of all that money feeding back into our local economy."

Bambi shrugged. "Your funeral."

It didn't take long to produce a witness. They flashed their credentials as they approached the police line and asked, "Anybody see anything useful?"

An older man said, "I saw a guy fishing out on the point. I thought it was a bit odd given the rain and the ebb tide."

They pulled him away from the crowd and he identified himself as Nolan Crawford. Said he was a retired Seattle homicide detective. He winced when Bambi shined her flashlight on his face. "Get that out of my eyes," he snapped, and Amanda had an impression of a man used to giving orders and having them obeyed.

"Is there someplace dry we can talk?" Amanda asked.

"My house is over beyond the point. We could have coffee and talk there."

Amanda nodded and said, "Okay. I'll leave my partner here to wait for the wrecker."

SEATED ON A TALL STOOL, AMANDA leaned her elbows on Nolan's coffee bar dividing the kitchen from the breakfast nook, and sipped a welcome cup of coffee.

"You had anything to eat today?" Crawford asked.

She grinned and said, "You know how it is."

He brought a cookie jar to the counter and said, "Help yourself."

She munched a soft peanut butter cookie and took a sip of coffee. "Okay, what did you see?"

Crawford described a small man in rain gear, fishing where no one in his right mind would fish, on a mean low tide that meant walking through muck to get to the water.

He told about seeing the boat explode and just disappear. About watching through binoculars as the fisherman threw something out into the bay. He said he lost sight of the guy when he went to find his cell phone and call 911.

"Think you could pinpoint the spot where the guy threw whatever-in-the-hell-it-was in the bay?"

"I could." Crawford reached into his shirt pocket and slid two folded pieces of notepaper across the table. "My report."

Amanda unfolded the notepaper, college ruled, and deciphered Crawford's handwriting. It was a good report. All of it was there, and Crawford had dated and signed it.

"Thank you, Mr. Crawford."

He smiled and said, "You're welcome. Nice to feel useful again. And before you ask, I made a copy for myself." He paused, "Now. I'm betting the two explosions are connected. Want to speculate?'

She shook her head. "Can't. Not yet. But when we know, I'll call you. Got a cell phone?"

He took a business card out of his wallet and handed it to her. It read "Nolan Crawford, Private Investigations, Skip Trace, Missing Persons." It had a cell phone number and fax number.

"You get much business?"

He smiled and shook his head, "In Poulsbo? Not much. But I like to keep my hand in the game."

Crawford glanced out the windows facing the bay and saw the bright lights of a Coast Guard cutter coming slowly up the channel. The cutter's search lights steadied on an object floating on the water.

"Looks like the Coast Guard found something," Crawford said as he grabbed his binoculars and walked out on his deck. He focused the binoculars and yelled back at Amanda who was still sitting, eating cookies and drinking coffee. "It looks to be a life jacket," he called back.

AT MIDNIGHT, AFTER A QUICK DEBRIEF at NCIS headquarters in Springdale, Moore sent them all home to get some rest.

Chapter 23

WHEN THE DARK BLUE SUBURBAN PULLED to the curb in a NE Portland neighborhood, Cletus was standing in the shadow of an alley running the length of a residential block. He waited until a tall man in a windbreaker opened the passenger door and stepped out onto the sidewalk, dimly visible in the rain damp glow of a street lamp.

"Mr. Falls," the agent spoke softly. "FBI. It's safe. Come on out."

Hand tucked in the belly pocket of a Blazer sweatshirt, Cletus slipped out of the alley and into the edge of the pool of light.

"I needs to see some ID," he said.

The agent reached inside his windbreaker and pulled a badge wallet and flipped it open. He held it in front of him while Cletus tried to see it at a distance of twenty feet.

"Ah, hell," he said. "I can't read it from there. You bring it over here."

The Agent walked slowly over, holding badge out like a shield.

When the tall man was within five feet, Cletus said, "That's close enough."

The agent said, "Satisfied, Mr. Falls?"

"Yeah, I guess so," Cletus answered. "How'd you see me? Night vision?"

The tall man nodded. "Let's get out of here. You armed?"

Cletus took his hand from the belly pocket and grinned. "Bluffing."

From the back seat Cletus asked, as the Suburban pulled away from the curb, "Where we going?"

The driver looked at his partner and then said, "To a safe house."

The narrow, two-lane road in the west hills wound its way through lanes of fir, alder, and maple, past houses perched on piling driven into tree-covered side slopes that might—or might not—be stable. Every few years *The Oregonian* carried pictures of a house that had gone sliding down the hill and into someone's back yard.

The FBI safe house wasn't really a house. It was a late nineteenth-century mansion built high atop Portland's west hills by an early entrepreneur grown wealthy from interests in shipping, lumber, land, and politics. Century-old Douglas fir choked the view and hid all but the turret tower.

The driver turned down a narrow, winding paved lane and stopped in front of an iron gate flanked by brick-faced gate posts about twelve-feet tall. Beyond the gate, the vehicle headlights lit up ugly metal teeth protruding from the driveway, just waiting to eat soft rubber tires, metal cords and all.

How the hell did I get into this? Cletus wondered.

The driver reached from the window and punched a series of numbers into a keypad. A few seconds later, the trap sank back into the pavement and the heavy gate swung silently open.

The Suburban followed a circle drive counter clockwise and stopped just beyond the front entrance under a tall breezeway that protected a narrow brick walk. The tall agent in the front passenger seat jumped out and opened the door for Cletus. The agent pointed and said, "Just follow the walk," and then got back in the vehicle and shut the door.

No front door for this boy, Cletus thought as the Suburban drove around the circle drive and back down the lane. He finally just shrugged his thin shoulders and followed the walk around the left corner of the building to a door inset in the thick walls of the house. He was reaching out to knock when the door swung open and a slender Black woman not two inches taller than Cletus opened the door and said, "Come in Mr. Falls. We've been expecting you."

Cletus wasn't sure what lambs felt when being led to slaughter, but he had a hunch it wasn't a lot different than he was feeling right now. He swallowed hard and stepped into a brightly lit hallway. He heard the lock click behind him.

"Relax Mr. Falls. We keep our doors locked. Discourages intruders. Would you like some coffee?"

An hour later Cletus was in love. Her name was Sarah, she was beautiful, and she was an FBI agent. He sat at a kitchen table, drinking coffee and eating Dutch apple pie, and he forgot to worry about Cletus for a change. He was thinking maybe he should go to work for the FBI.

He also knew he'd been sweetly sucker punched. But when Sarah smiled, he didn't care. He worked overtime to impress Sarah. She asked few questions, and basically just let him talk…and talk.

He told her everything he could about the photos from the NE Portland mosque, how he had gotten them…who had taken the pictures…his belief the photos were real.

"He's one of my main men," he said of the photographer. "If he says something is so, then it is."

She pulled from him the story of his long relationship with BB and how BB kept him straight. Cletus laughed and said, "He kicked me in the butt the first time he caught…I mean, the first time we met."

Sarah smiled and said, "He must have liked you."

Cletus would have done nearly anything to keep her talking, to hear her soft slightly husky voice, and to see her smile. "Mama thinks he is one fine man. Keeps Old Cletus on the straight and narrow."

"You have an import business?"

And suddenly the old Cletus warning signals went off in his head like alarm bells and he put his pie fork down on the plate and stared hard at her.

"Whatcha ask that for?"

She shrugged and the motion pulled her teal blue blouse tight across her chest. He almost forgot where he was again—almost. She smiled, and then said, "We can talk about that some other time. Excuse me a minute, Cletus."

She pushed into the hallway and walked quickly to a door just beyond the kitchen. Sitting in a room just slightly bigger than a broom closet, crowded by two chairs at a low desk were the agents who escorted Cletus to the safe house. Skulls wrapped in head phones, they had listened patiently to Sarah's interrogation of Cletus and watched the monitor to observe Cletus's physical behavior—looking for telltale signs of lying or withholding information.

FBI Agent Sarah Watkins pushed the door open and said, "What do you think?"

The taller agent grinned and said, "I think he's in love."

She smiled and shook her head, "I mean about his information?"

The shorter agent said, "He's legit. At least his information is legit. Let's call the SAC and get things moving."

Sarah frowned and asked, "Do we have enough?"

Both of the men nodded an affirmative.

Sarah walked back to the kitchen and said, "We want to thank you, Mr. Falls. You have been extremely helpful. We'd like you to stay here with us for a couple of days."

"Why?"

"For your safety."

He cocked his head to the side and grinned. "You gonna keep me locked up, Agent Watkins?"

"You'll have free run of the study, the swimming pool, and the gym. And your suite, of course."

"Don't trust old Cletus, do you?"

She shrugged. "It could get people killed if you got cold feet and tipped off the bad guys."

"I ain't about to do that. It ain't good for business to have people messing things up. 'Sides, blowing people up is unpatriotic and unconstitutional."

Chapter 24

AMANDA'S TIRED BRAIN REJECTED THE INSISTENT ring of the cell phone by doing what human brains do: incorporating the sound into a dream that swirled and eddied around the dark waters of Puget Sound. She was on a Coast Guard Cutter, her cell phone was ringing, she was stumbling, falling overboard, and John caught her and pulled her back. She watched her cell phone hit the water and sink.

And then she was awake, disoriented, breathing hard, sweating—and wondering what the hell was going on. The cell phone was buzzing on her bedside table and she picked it up on the last ring. She glanced at the caller ID and flipped open the phone. "John, is that you?"

John's news that Sheriff Bud Blair had deciphered Cowboy's code sent adrenalin surging through her veins and she was instantly awake. She slipped into a robe and ran barefoot to her study. She watched her computer boot up and then realized she had left her cell phone in the bedroom.

"Steady, girl, steady," she lectured. Cell phone in hand she hurried back to the kitchen and started a pot of coffee. The coffee was trickling into the pot when her computer said, "You've Got Mail."

"Wouldn't you know it," she grumbled, "I have a long day, and then John calls me at 4:30 A.M." But she knew why he had called. If Bud Blair had it right, John's email could break open one of the most important cases she had ever worked.

She turned on her desk lamp, sat in her chair, brow wrinkled in concentration as the first pages slid into the print tray. She read the first page. She reached for and read the second page. As the third page came sliding out of the printer, she thumbed a speed-dial number and waited impatiently for an answer.

A sleepy sounding Abe McKenzie said, "This better be good, Amanda."

"It is. Get your team up and have them rendezvous at my place. ASAP."

"You in trouble?"

She stopped and thought about the two explosions in Poulsbo. "I don't know. Probably not."

"I'll be there in five minutes," Abe said and hung up.

Amanda's second call woke Dennis Moore. He sounded more alert than Abe had when he answered the phone. "Good morning, Amanda. What's up?"

"I have information you need to see right now."

Moore didn't ask what it was. He simply said, "I'll be in the office in twenty minutes."

The printer ran through the last twenty pages of Cowboy's records and stopped. She saved the file to disc and then emailed a copy to her work computer. The disc and the printed pages went into her brief case. Then she deleted the message from her computer and turned it off.

She slopped coffee into her favorite mug, killed the kitchen lights, and turned on her yard lights. She retreated to her bedroom, coffee in one hand, briefcase in the other. She opened the top drawer to her side table, lifted her Glock onto the comforter, and killed the light, waiting for Abe to arrive.

Five minutes later she heard a soft rap on her front door. Pistol in her right hand, she edged down the hallway to the living room. She used the peep hole to make sure it was Abe and then slid the safety chain from the slide, twisted the deadbolt and unlocked the door.

He stepped in and she reversed the sequence of locks, deadbolts and safety chain. "Boy, am I glad to see you," she said.

"What's up?"

A vehicle pulled up to the curb and Abe watched as Bambi and Dudley started up the walk. "Team's here," he told Amanda.

Dudley, dressed in blue jeans, a black hooded sweatshirt and dark running shoes followed Bambi up the walk. If Abe's call hadn't sounded so urgent, Dudley would have enjoyed following Bambi's tight fitting jeans up the steps to Amanda's house.

Yellow light from a street lamp dimly lit the living room and Bambi noted Amanda's robe, her sleep disheveled hair, and the pistol in her hand.

"And?" Bambi demanded.

"I need you for back up."

Without a word, Dudley walked through the dark kitchen, scanned the floodlit patio and the small backyard, and said *"Nada."*

She led them to her bedroom, turned the lock tumblers on her briefcase, and handed the Cowboy file to Abe. "You guys read this while I get dressed. I think I'm a bit paranoid, but I didn't want to use the bathroom until I had some back-up. We're to meet Dennis at the office in fifteen minutes."

Abe pushed the switch on the bedside lamp and spread the file on Amanda's bed. Dudley and Bambi leaned over each shoulder and read the file with him. Two pages into the file, Bambi said, "Holy crap. This is a gold mine."

They were still reading when Amanda came back out of the master bath wearing navy blue slacks, black jogging shoes, and a black cable knit sweater. Her hair was casually brushed and Abe caught the faint perfume of toothpaste.

"Ready?" Amanda asked.

MOORE WAS IMPATIENTLY WAITING WHEN THE team arrived twenty-five minutes after Amanda's phone call. His impatience was immediately forgotten when Amanda slipped the Cowboy disc into her computer and lit up a big screen on the wall.

Moore read the document without comment through the first six pages, and then said, "And some cowboy sheriff decoded this?"

Amanda hesitated and then answered almost defensively. "He's not a country-bumpkin. In a former life he was a detective in

Portland, and a good one from what I hear. He's also good friends with Maretti."

"It doesn't matter who decoded it, does it?" Thompson's voice said from directly behind them. "Let's get busy. Amanda, contact your friends in the FBI. I think they'll want to get here ASAP. Denny, get Judge Waltrip out of bed. We'll need some search warrants. Where's John?"

Amanda said, "I put him with Sheriff Blair. Told him to cover Bud's back."

Nobody asked how Thompson had gotten to the office so quickly, but he decided they needed to know. "The drive to Seattle takes too damned long. Denny briefed me on yesterday's events. So I drove down last night and stayed at the Oxford Inn."

Chapter 25

"How would you set up an ambush, John?" Bud asked as the big pickup wound up the lazy curves beyond Summer Lake, heading for Picture Rock Pass.

John said, "Car wreck. You're a cop. You have to stop. So a car wreck gets you stopped, and a couple of flankers come at you from both sides. A third person is made up to look like a bloody victim. Not hard to do in the dark. Headlights would be all the special effects needed. Boom. You're had."

Bud nodded and asked, "How else?"

"Okay. Three cars...or big pickups. They box you, force you off the road and you're surrounded. Boom. Same story."

"Any other good ideas?" Bud asked dryly. "How about a tree across the road?"

"Not likely," John said. "Not unless they know exactly where you are and when you're going to be there. They won't want to draw attention to what they plan to do. Traffic might back up. Too many witnesses."

"Okay," Bud said. "A wreck, then. If there is a real wreck, we stop short and light the scene with our headlights and use the spotlight. Agreed?"

"I'd add one other detail. If it's still dark, you let me out about a hundred yards short of the scene and I'll flank them." He patted the duffel. "I can see in the dark."

"Okay. It's a plan."

"Right," John said, "but remember, with the first shot most plans...maybe all plans...go to shit."

But there was no ambush, and fifteen minutes after the Lake Country sheriff's pickup pulled into the sally-port at the Justice Center in Bend, Chase and Harley belonged to Dutch Vanderlin and the FBI.

Dutch, BB, John, and Bud watched a big Deschutes County deputy lead Chase and Harley to a holding cell. The heavy outer door to the cell block closed and Dutch offered a big grin and a big meaty hand to Bud, and Bud found himself grinning in spite of himself. He actually liked Dutch. It was just that he didn't like Feds in general. Rule number one: Never talk to the press. Rule number two: Don't trust the Feds.

"I owe you one, Bud."

"Yes you do, and you're going to owe me another one. He turned and gave BB a big bear hug. "You ugly bastard. I told you to stay home."

"Couldn't, Honky. I knew you were in too deep to swim out by yourself."

Bud looked at Dutch and asked, "What the hell is he doing here? Is he really working for you guys?"

Dutch nodded, and BB smirked and said, "Special Assistant to the SAC, Portland FBI, as liaison with the sheriff of Lake County."

John stepped forward. "You're Detective Dell BeBe, Portland city police."

BB offered his hand. "Mr. Stone Fly, I presume."

"Not today," John said, "just John Bernard."

Bud said, "Forgot my manners." He pointed at Dutch. "John, this is Dutch Vanderlin, FBI, Portland. Dutch, this is Special Agent Bernard, NCIS."

"NCIS?" Dutch said. "You're kinda off the reservation."

John shrugged and said, "I work counter-terrorism. NCIS tracked a sailor to Christmas Valley. We suspected him of arms and people smuggling." *And discovered we have a mole.*

"And now?" Dutch asked.

John gave Dutch a hard stare and then shrugged. "And now, nothing. I've been ordered to protect the high sheriff of Lake County is all."

BB said, "The bad guys are coming after him, aren't they."

"NCIS thinks so," John answered.

Bud interrupted, "Let's find a cup of coffee. John has something to show you that'll perk up your morning."

Deschutes County Sheriff Cal Redmond came barging through a side door, hat in hand, red hair askew. "Howdy boys. Who's who?"

Introductions made, Redmond led them to a small conference room and the smell of fresh coffee. A dozen donuts sat on a counter between a big stainless steel coffee pot and a dozen Justice Center mugs upended on a layer of paper towels. Cal poured and they each carried a cup and a donut to the Formica-topped folding table. They scraped metal folding chairs back and sat down.

"Thanks, Cal," Bud said. "Now hang on to your hat. All hell's about to break loose."

"Again?" BB asked.

"It never really stopped," Bud said. "Have faith and all will be revealed. John?"

Special Agent Bernard placed the laptop on the table and booted it up. "What we have is a testament to Bud's modesty" he said. "Bud and I searched Cowboy's house after the big blast north of Fort Rock and found a coded file on his computer. We downloaded it to disc and stole away into the sunset."

"Who knew about the file?" Dutch asked. "I know NCIS didn't share it with the FBI or Homeland Security."

John looked at Bud who just shrugged. Finally Bud said, "In all honesty, we didn't know who to trust after Crazy was killed, so we just sort of kept it hidden. I think NCIS Special Agent Spears may have a copy, but I don't know that for sure."

"She does now," John added.

"And?" Sheriff Redmond prompted.

John turned the laptop to Dutch and said, "Take a look."

After page three Redmond walked to a wall mounted phone and rang his office. Bud heard him bark, "Get a portable printer down here. Don't forget to bring some paper this time." He turned and looked at Bud. "How in the hell did you figure it out? The code, I mean."

Bud smiled and said, "I just sort of stumbled on to it. It's a clear message, but Cowboy turned it into a jumble by changing it to a weird font. All you do to turn it back into a readable form is highlight the sucker and change the font. Simple."

Dutch was off in the corner of the room talking on a cell phone. Bud overheard something that sounded like "mosque," but the door to the conference room swung open and a small woman whom Bud gauged to be about fifty—maybe fifty-five—and hair just starting to show gray streaks, plunked a printer on the table and strung a cord to a wall outlet. She was clad in a tight-fitting khaki Deschutes County sheriff uniform, and she was glaring at Cal Redmond. "What do you mean by 'this time'?"

Cal looked sheepish. "I'm sorry Carol. I thought you were Brenda. She always forgets something…like printer paper."

"Well, I don't," she tossed over a retreating shoulder. The walls rattled when she slammed the door behind her.

Dutch folded his cell phone and grinned at Cal. "I'll trade you. Yours for mine. Mine blackmails me with tears."

They all chuckled. And then Dutch took charge. "Here's what going to happen. I just got off the phone with our Seattle office. There will be a coordinated, simultaneous raid on two mosques, one in Seattle and one in Portland. We're good to go this afternoon.

"Two agents and an assistant federal prosecutor from our Portland office will fly into the Bend airport in about an hour. They'll take our prisoners to Portland for processing and subsequent trial.

"I have a question for you, Sheriff Redmond. Is Cowboy in good enough shape for us to take him out of here?"

"Cowboy? Yeah. He looked to be in pretty good shape the last time I saw him. But our doctor will be in about 8:30. You can ask her."

"Good enough," Dutch answered. "If she okay's it, then Robert-the-cowboy-Clark goes with us."

Bud interrupted. "Dutch. Just slow it down a bit. I need to talk to Cowboy before you steal him away. I want him to confirm his connection to Raul Ortega. And I need to find the connection between Cowboy's operation and the murder of Crazy Charlie. As I recall, he's still my prisoner."

"Never was," Dutch retorted.

"Well, he's sure as hell mine," Redmond growled. "If Bud wants to talk to him before you steal him away, he gets his turn. Understood?"

Dutch took a deep breath and said, "I feel some urgency here, but I'll give Bud a chance to talk to Cowboy."

"That includes NCIS, as well," John said.

"Yes. Okay," Dutch Agreed.

Bud looked at his watch. "I think we'll go find some breakfast. I'll be back in an hour…say 7:30 to question Cowboy. And then there's a use-of-deadly-force hearing for two of my officers at 9:00."

The cell phone in Dutch's pocket chimed. He flipped it open and said, "Dutch." The longer he listened the deeper the frown on his face. He finally said, "Hold on a minute." He looked at Bud and said, "Go on without me."

Bud softened and asked, "You want us to bring you something back?"

Dutch shook his head and put the phone back to his ear.

Cal asked, "That invitation for breakfast include me?"

"Damned right, it does," Bud said.

They got themselves a booth in a back corner of a Shari's restaurant. A sleepy-looking waitress took their orders and poured coffee. As she walked away, Bud said, "So tell me BB. How did you come to be mixed up in this?"

BB was a good story teller and they all laughed as he took them through his story about a little guy selling fake Blazer gear, and selling the same information to multiple agencies. Cal started to ask who his snitch was, but BB's hard stare cut the question off in mid-sentence. BB decided he didn't like Cal Redmond. *You don't ask the identity of a snitch,* he thought.

Midway through hash brown potatoes, toast, one egg and coffee, Bud set his fork on the edge of the plate, wiped his mouth with a napkin and said, "John. Something is bothering me. Were you really sent to protect me, or am I just bait? I think NCIS wants Raul Ortega to come after me so you guys can grab him."

John frowned and thought carefully before answering. "No one said anything to me. All Amanda said was to watch your back. No one mentioned Ortega. But I wouldn't put it past our SAC to think along that line. Why?"

"Because Gino Maretti called last night and said he was damned sure the FBI and NCIS were using me for bait. He said he was threatened with his job if he warned me." And then he grinned at the memory of the expletives Gino had used.

BB growled, "Those double-dealing shitheads."

John nodded. "I agree, but I don't think it matters. Ortega will send someone after Bud, regardless of what NCIS or the FBI does. And if Bud's in the soup, so am I."

Cal eyeballed the two of them, and then nudged BB. "Let me out of here. I need to make a call." Cal Redmond stood up, ran his fingers through his wiry red hair and put his brown Stetson on. He looked at Bud, his green eyes hard and calculating. "How would you like an escort home?"

Bud glanced through the restaurant window at the parking lot and then up at Redmond. "No…I think we'll handle it…whatever comes our way."

Cal fished in his wallet and dropped two twenty dollar bills on the table. "See you back at the office."

Bud, John, and BB watched Cal walk to his Deschutes County Suburban, back out and drive around the building.

BB broke the silence. "How well do you know that guy, Bud?"

Bud shrugged. "Not well. I see him at the Annual County Sheriff's Conference. When my officers got hurt, he personally called for medevac. He took Chase and Harley to Lakeview for me. And he offered a couple deputies to patrol the north county country while we're shorthanded."

Bud stopped talking and sipped his coffee. Something was tickling the back of his mind, and then his face turned blank as bits of information—words spoken, actions taken, sequential events—starting lining up, falling into place.

BB said, "Bud, I've seen that look before. You just put something together, didn't you?"

Bud blinked, took a deep breath and gave BB a tight smile. "It's thin, but it might tie up some loose ends."

John Bernard watched the exchange and said, "Want to clue me in?"

Bud looked at John, not saying anything, brain racing, sorting, putting pieces in place "You want to clue me in?" John asked again.

Bud nodded. "I don't have any solid evidence. But there has been one person at each scene, someone with the means to set up the hit on Crazy." He gave John a questioning look. "Other than you, I mean. I've got that much nailed down."

"You think I did it? Or Amanda?"

"No. I know you didn't do it. Why bring in Crazy and then have him killed? If you intended to kill him, you would have done that before you brought him in. And according to Agent Spears, she's been cleared. Have you checked with anyone else in Springdale to confirm that?"

John nodded and slid across the seat. "Good point, Sheriff. Maybe I'm too trusting. I'll be back."

BB looked at Bud. "It all hinges on knowing who you can trust, doesn't it?"

"Yes it does, my friend, yes it does."

"And you trust John?"

Bud looked through the big window and watched John pace the walk, a cell phone to his ear.

Bud hesitated and then said, "Yeah. I do."

"So who don't you trust?"

"I'll let you know along about noon today."

The ring of BB's cell phone interrupted his next question. BB unzipped the side pocket of his windbreaker and fished the phone out. The caller ID told him it was his friend T. J. Wildish. "Hey, Wildman. You up kinda early for a preacher man."

Bud heard a faint voice in the tiny speaker, and what he thought might be "I told you not to call me that."

BB said, "Okay, okay, Reverend. What you got?" He fished a small pocket sized notebook from his shirt pocket and patted various other pockets, fumbling for a pen. Bud shook his head and slid a pen across the table.

Reverend T. J. Wildish sounded excited, and BB said, "Slow down. I'm taking notes." When the voice stopped, BB said, "I owe you one. Thank you, T. J." Bud heard the voice again, and BB groaned and said, "Really? Okay, I promise. Gotta go."

"Well, hell, Bud, now I have to go to church…four Sundays in row. That was Reverend T. J. Wildman's price. But I got a name for Dutch: Akeem. I don't know if that's a last name or a first name, but he's a terrorist son-of-a-bitch tied to a mosque in Portland." He looked around to make sure no one was within earshot. "You remember me telling you about Cletus?"

Bud nodded.

"I didn't want to mention his name to Redmond or your buddy John, but one of Cletus's informants sells some pictures to Cletus, who sells them back to me. The pictures show the front of the mosque, street address and all, and shots of all types of weapons and explosives in the basement of the mosque. It took cast iron *cajones* to get those shots. Probably used a cell phone. Anyway, that's the evidence the FBI took to a judge to get search warrants. But they didn't have a name for any arrests. T. J., whom I know you remember, did some fishing inside the Portland Ministerial Association. He found out the big bad wolf in the Portland Muslim community is someone named Akeem."

BB dialed Dutch's phone, and Bud slid out of the booth and headed for the restroom.

BB was telling John stories of being partners with Bud in an earlier time when Bud walked back to the booth, but he didn't sit down. And he didn't like the story.

"So Bud tries to talk this young hood into giving up. But the idiot child just shoots Bud instead. Right in the chest. The body armor stopped the slug, but it broke some ribs and knocked Henry out."

"Henry?" John asked.

"Yeah. That's what I call him when I'm pissed. Anyway, I shot the kid and an ambulance took Bud to the hospital."

"And your point, Detective BeBe?" Bud growled.

Ignoring Bud, BB said, "My point is this: My old partner is a nice, compassionate guy. Maybe too nice. So you remember this story when it comes time to shoot the bad guys."

"Enough," Bud warned. "Did you tell him I whipped your ass the last time you told this story?"

BB looked at him, and then a grin tugged at the corners of his mouth. "Ain't the way I remember it, Honky. I think I'm the one who put you in a cab and sent you home."

Bud's shoulders slumped and he sat down. He looked at John, "He's right. I play it back every once in a while. And I wonder how it would have turned out if I had drawn my gun instead of trying to talk the kid down. It was not my finest hour."

John shrugged. "Shit happens."

Bud picked up his coffee cup. "You mentioned subterfuge coming up here. So here's what I'm thinking. We don't take the main road back. I'm assuming Roger and Sonny will be released for duty, so we'll have two vehicles: one to spring the trap and one for backup."

"They didn't hit us coming up. Why would they hit us going back?"

"Because I'm going to tell the person I believe is dirty, and no one else. If they hit us going back, I'll have the proof I need to bring him down."

"If we survive," John said dryly.

"We will because they'll have to improvise and they'll make a mistake."

"You sure about this?" John asked.

"I think so. It might be risky, but I don't know a better way to find out."

A young waitress asked if they wanted any more coffee. No one did, and she put the ticket on the table. Bud piled Redmond's two twenty-dollar bills on the ticket and nudged John with his elbow. "Let's get out of here. Roger and Sonny should be here pretty soon. By the way, what does Silverdale say about Agent Spears?"

"She's clean," John answered.

Chapter 26

MARETTI WOKE TO THE SOUND OF people arguing in the hallway outside his hospital room. He glanced at the wall clock and frowned. It was nearly 8:00 a.m. A food tray with cold oatmeal, cold toast, and lukewarm juice sat untouched on a service tray. The recliner in the corner held a rumpled hospital blanket, but no Ruby Goldstein.

He reached for the coffee cup and sipped. He grimaced at the taste of the cold bitter brew and set the cup back.

A red-faced doctor pushed in followed by an equally red-faced Chief Harold Homer, Bremerton City Police. A uniformed officer peered around the corner and then pulled the door shut and stepped back out into the hallway.

The doctor turned to Chief Homer and said, "I strongly advise against moving him. We need to monitor his recovery for another twenty-four hours."

Homer nodded. "I agree, but I can't guarantee his safety here. And if he stays here, he could pull some very, very dangerous people into your hospital, people who don't care about innocent bystanders. As far as they're concerned, the more the merrier."

Gino said, "What's the fuss about?"

Homer threw a blue gym bag on the foot of the bed. "Can you walk?"

"I made ten minutes in the hallway last night."

"Good. Brought you some clothes. We're gonna get you dressed and out of here. Someone blabbed...or bragged...about you at O'toole's last night. That same someone is now on administrative leave from the Bremerton Police Department."

Maretti said, "Chief. It was in the papers."

"I know. But the papers didn't say anything about terrorists. Our idiot child did. Just blurted the whole sad story out in front of a dozen people. Paddy tried to get him to shut up, but he was too drunk to pay attention.

"Paddy called me this morning. Said he knows all of his customers by name. But there was a stranger in the bar last night. A small dark-haired man, pale faced like he had just shaved off a beard. Paddy thought it was odd, and when our idiot child finished his story, Paddy said the stranger put some money on the bar and walked away.

"Oh. And another thing. Our idiot child told his audience which hospital you were in. That's been guarded information until last night."

Gino swung his legs over the side of the bed and asked. "Who's the idiot child?"

"Manny."

"Judas," Gino exploded. "I thought he was going to AA."

"Well...I guess he fell off the wagon last night. Paddy said he was really in the bag."

Gino said, "You guys get out of here and let me get dressed."

The doctor shook his head. "Mind if I help?"

Gino considered the request for a long five seconds and then relented. "I can get my pants on by myself. But I might need help with my socks and shoes." He glanced at the cast on his left arm. "And maybe with my shirt."

Ten minutes later, after a hypodermically-administered painkiller, Gino rode a wheelchair to a "Medical Staff Only" elevator which hummed and creaked down three levels before the door slid open. Chief Homer pushed the chair while a uniformed hospital security guard led the way. An alert uniformed police officer trailed Homer and Gino. The security guard punched a key pad at the inner door to the ER, turned down a short hallway and opened a side door to a waiting police van. An unmarked police car blocked the ambulance ramp, and another idled at the curb. Gino couldn't see who was driving either car.

Chief Homer climbed in the back with Gino. "So here's what's going down. Your buddy Basil Pettibone was blown out of his socks...and out of his yacht last night. Coast Guard divers found his body at first light this morning. His girl friend, Ms. Carlotta Mayes was on the boat, but no body yet. Last word I had was divers are searching the wreck. A Cobalt 46."

"Wow," Gino said, "Too bad about the boat."

The Chief smiled, the light coming on in his brown eyes, creases lining his tanned face. "Yeah, too bad," he agreed dryly. "But it gets more interesting. NCIS is convinced someone planted a bomb on board, and then detonated the bomb by remote when the yacht reached the ship's channel outside the Poulsbo harbor.

"They also have human remains from a second explosion in a car parked near the harbor. And a witness who said he saw a fisherman throw something in the bay...like maybe a remote, as in detonator...right after the explosion. Divers are searching for that now."

Gino winced as centrifugal force pushed him into the arm rest of the seat. He noted a left turn. South, he thought. "So, the bad guys hire an assassin to take Pettibone out of the picture, and then they eliminate the assassin to hide their tracks."

The Chief nodded. "Looks that way."

"And you think they'll come after me next." It wasn't a question.

Homer nodded. "It's a possibility. These guys are big on revenge."

Gino was quiet for about thirty seconds before he asked. "Where's my weapon?"

"Forensics. Standard procedure."

"I'll need a piece."

Homer reached into his jacket pocket and handed Maretti a brand new H&K .40 along with three twelve-round clips. "Shoot straight. It's all the ammo I had at the house."

"Badge?"

Homer slipped Maretti's badge wallet from an inside jacket pocket. "Here. I'll put this all in the gym bag. Nice and tidy."

"I feel better already. Where we going?"

"Your place. We like your dead-end street. No close neighbors. Fairly open front and back yard. We plan to keep you company for a couple of days. FBI says they'll have the bad guys neutralized within the next twenty-four hours."

"What about Ruby?"

"Your nice-looking girlfriend? She'll be staying with you until this is over. Her place is shot to hell. And by the way, she lied about being married. No husband. He died three years ago. Left her a big insurance policy, some solid investments, and that nice house all paid for."

Maretti shook his head and said, "Not my type." Chief Homer thought Gino didn't sound very convincing.

The lead police car stopped at the curb in front of the last house on a dead-end street, Maretti's single-story rambler, a 1970s structure from a housing boom that demanded cookie cutter construction, complete with attached garage. Bachelor Gino Maretti had done nothing to improve the structure except to add a covered patio off the back porch and to paint the house when it was needed.

The front yard was simply a lawn. No shrubs, no flowers—just grass. The narrow side strips and the back yard reflected the same Spartan tastes. It faced east and was surrounded on three sides by a Northwest rain forest jungle—vine maple, ferns, devil's club, mossy fir, spruce and cedar trees. It was possible to crawl and climb through the rotten tangle of tree roots and decaying trees felled long ago by Pacific storms. But it wasn't easy. Chief Homer thought just getting to Gino's house through the timber made the trip unlikely. City boys would come by road.

Ruby waved out the picture window, and Sergeant Milo Jackson, Bremerton City Police, opened the entry door.

"Hey, Gino. How you hanging? Me and Brandt are your babysitters."

Gino smelled fresh-baked cookies and the aroma of coffee when he walked into his small living room. He also noted two

AR-15s propped in a corner. Ruby gave him a tearful hug and led him by the right hand to the kitchen and into a chair.

"Home sweet home," Gino said with a thin smile. "Chief, where's my car?"

"Impound parking garage. Not a prayer they can get at it."

"Thanks. When's Ron's service."

"I don't know yet. The Masons are helping Ron's wife with the funeral."

"I didn't know Ron was a Mason. Never said a word about it." He suddenly felt light-headed and nearly fell off the chair before Milo caught him. Milo put a strong arm around his waist and said, "Let's get you to something softer than that." With Milo on one side and Chief Homer on the other trying hard to keep Gino upright without hurting his left arm, they helped him shuffle down a short hallway and into a back bedroom. "Maybe you better lie down for a bit."

A concerned Ruby hovered in the doorway while Milo eased Gino down on his bed. He started to unlace Gino's shoes when she said, "Here. Let me do that."

A drowsy Gino tried to wave her away, but suddenly he was too tired to resist. Chief Homer said, "Goodbye, Gino. See you tomorrow." But Maretti was already asleep.

To say NCIS Analyst Witherspoon was irritated would be the understatement of the year. He was livid when he saw Cowboy's "decoded" disc.

"Judas Priest! All of you overpaid nerds can't crack a simple code, so a cowboy sheriff does it for us. Shit! This is too embarrassing. I'm gonna go have a smoke while you smart asses tie names to the all of the initials on the list. We don't go home until that's done. Got it?"

Chapter 27

Early the next morning a team of Navy divers found the remains of a woman in what was left of the forward stateroom of the *Might As Well*. A metal rescue stretcher was lowered from the dive tender and the body was pulled from the wreckage while a slowly circling twenty-five-foot Defender Class Coast Guard boat kept a flotilla of small boats away from the dive area.

A Coast Guard lieutenant watched through binoculars as scavenger boats worked the surface with long handled dip nets, skimming scraps of soggy money from the flat, rain dimpled surface of the channel, racing from one "school" of money to the next. Angry shouts and raised fists marked the competition.

A white eighteen-foot Boston Whaler pushed by twin 115-horsepower Honda four-cycle engines came roaring down the channel from the direction of the Poulsbo Harbor. The slap-slap of the hull carried across the water as the Whaler crested small waves and slammed back into the water. As it approached the dozens of money scavengers, a deputy sheriff throttled back and then idled up to a small cabin boat.

The lieutenant couldn't make out the words, but the raised voices carried an angry defiant message.

"Scooping contraband from the water must not be legal," he laughed and then said to the helmsman, "Better the sheriff than us. Well," he pointed south as a black nosed, red and white Coast Guard Jayhawk roared around the headland, "let's get her loaded. We're on station until a salvage ship gets here. ETA twenty minutes."

Wearing life jackets and hearing protection, two crew members carried a rescue litter to the edge of the raised helipad and then turned faces away from the prop wash as the big helicopter settled on the deck. The noise of the jet engines drove the lieutenant back into the wheel house.

Less than two minutes later, the Jayhawk was airborne and screaming down the sound towards Silverdale. "I wonder what the rush is?" he said aloud to no one in particular.

The senior diver, hair still wet from the shower, dressed in dark blue khakis and a hooded sweatshirt knocked and entered the wheelhouse. He handed the lieutenant a small metal canister.

"Pictures?"

"Yes sir. It's definitely a Cobalt 46. Was…" he corrected.

NOLAN CRAWFORD, RETIRED DETECTIVE, SEATTLE POLICE Department, was excited and pleased when Amanda and Abe knocked on his door. "Welcome," he said as he swung the door open. "Coffee?"

Amanda, eyes red from lack of sleep, shook her head. "Thanks. Later maybe? A couple of navy divers will be here in about five minutes. Do you think you can show us where they should look?"

Crawford nodded and snagged a Mariner's baseball cap and a dark green North Face rain jacket from a coat rack by the front door. He led them around the corner of his house down to the beach and to a small rock cairn on the bank. "I built this last night. I'd say the object the fisherman threw in the water is about a hundred and fifty feet out. Tide was out last night, so it's a wee bit further from the bank this morning than it was last night. I took a rough compass bearing of about a hundred and eighty-five degrees."

The divers spent less than five minutes in the cold water before slogging back up the beach, a weed-covered remote in a small net bag clipped to a weight belt. Amanda Spears and Abe Mackenzie thanked them profusely, tagged and bagged the remote and locked it in an evidence box.

Nolan Crawford was grinning from ear to ear. "I told you," he said to the divers as they started stripping their wet suits. "I knew you would find it."

One of the divers, a blond-headed young man about twenty-two years old, grinned back and said, "Yeah, but your bearing was off. It was more like a hundred and ninety degrees." And they all laughed.

"I got the coffee on. You all want some? I got some bear claws and cinnamon rolls. Best in the West. Came fresh this morning from my favorite bakery in Poulsbo."

The divers looked at each other and shrugged. "Why not," the senior diver said.

Amanda asked, "Does that include us?"

"Darn right it does. Haven't had this much fun in the past five years. Come on. Let's get in out of the rain."

Chapter 28

A SECOND CUP OF BILLIE'S FREE coffee sat steaming on the counter of the Christmas Valley Lodge. Wally and Billie were swapping "I-remember-when" stories.

"Mama didn't have electricity in her house until I was seven years old," Billie said. "When I was little, we used coal oil lamps. Water came down off the hill in a flume. I don't suppose anyone even thought to have it tested. Anyway, when we lived in the mill camp, Thursday night was bath night at the shower house for the women. Saturday night was the men's night."

Wally laughed, "Yep. I don't know if people actually believed the old saw that too much bathing was dangerous to one's health, but a real bath was hard to come by.

"I remember one winter back in Montana. Mother ran out of chopped firewood, so she just pulled a long skinny pole through the back door and stuck the end of it in the fire box on the wood cook stove. She'd feed it a little at a time into the fire box. I was pretty little, but I remember thinking we were letting in as much cold air as we were warming up. I guess my dad got snowed in at the mill. Couldn't get home for a couple of days, so we were in sort of a fix."

"You know," Billie said, "I remember one winter when…"

A loud bang on the door between the restaurant and the living quarters, followed by some mild cussing, interrupted the story. Larae backed awkwardly through the door, a daypack and her equipment belt in one hand, and a small suitcase in the other. She was better at getting around on her walking cast. Better, but she wouldn't be dancing anytime soon.

"Where do you think you're going?" Billie asked. "And what are you doing in uniform?"

Wally stood up and said, "Here let me help."

Larae shook her head. "I'm fine." She set the equipment belt, complete with pistol, spare clips, handcuffs, quick ties, flashlight, and portable radio on a table in the corner. The pack went into one chair and the suitcase into another.

"You leaving?" Wally asked.

Larae stumped over to the counter and sat down next to Wally. "Officer Trivoli called and said to get packed because she was pulling me out. Said I was too exposed out here. So sometime this morning, someone will pick me up. That's all I know."

Her cell phone buzzed and she opened the phone. "Hello?"

"Good morning, Larae. This is Bud. Did Michelle contact you?"

"Yes. I'm packed. What's going on?"

"I'm pulling you out. I think you'll be safer in Lakeview."

"Are they coming after me?" she asked.

"I don't know," he said. He sounded frustrated, but she knew he wasn't frustrated with her. "Let's just call it a hunch. Roger or I will be by to get you sometime around 1100, the Lord willing and the creek don't rise. Whatever you do, don't go with anyone driving a Deschutes County police vehicle."

"Good lord," she almost whispered. "Are you on to something?"

"Supposition backed by some mighty thin soup," he answered. "Stay alert and carry your weapon. Might be a good idea to wear your body armor, too."

"You're scaring me, Bud."

"Good. That'll keep you awake. Gotta go."

Wally watched a little bead of sweat form on Larae's forehead. "You hurting, Sweet Mama?" He pointed at the walking cast on her left leg.

She shook he head to help clear her thoughts. "What?"

"You hurting?"

"Oh," she said, "it's not that."

Wally ran a hand through his thinning gray hair and then set his glasses on the counter. There was steel in his blue eyes. "The sheriff told you something, didn't he."

Billie placed a cup in front of Larae and poured coffee without saying anything, worry etched in her forehead.

Larae looked at her friends, struck by how much she had grown to love them in the short two months since she started working for Billie as an undercover bartender. Impulsively she wrapped her right arm around Wally's shoulders and gave him a hug. She looked up at motherly Billie and winked.

"Okay, here's the deal." She said, "Bud thinks the bad guys, whoever in the hell they are, might come after me. It wouldn't be the first time, but here's the clinker. He said I was not…let me repeat that…not to go anywhere with anyone from Deschutes County."

Wally swore quietly and Billie said, "Not even with that nice young Deputy? The one who stopped by yesterday?"

"No. Not with anyone from Deschutes County."

"Good heavens," Billie said.

Wally nodded at Billie and slid off the stool. "Thanks for the coffee. I've got some things to do."

The women watched him walk out the door and turn right down the gravel lane towards his small house. Billie raised her eyebrows at Larae, who just shrugged and shook her head.

"Well, if you're traveling, you better have some breakfast first," Billie said and headed for the kitchen.

LARAE WAS CHEWING A STRIP OF bacon when a tan Deschutes County sheriff's four-door pickup wheeled into the gravel parking lot. A lanky deputy Larae didn't know stepped down from the driver's seat, slammed the door, and came legging it up the walk. Without really knowing why, Larae pulled her back-up weapon, a small .380 from a holster strapped to her right ankle. She held it along her hip, and turned slightly to keep it out of sight.

The Deputy barged through the door and stopped at the sight of Larae in uniform. "Morning," he said. "I'm looking for Larae Holcomb."

"Well, you found her," Larae said. "What do you want?"

"Sheriff Redmond said I was to take you into protective custody."

She shook her head. "No. I don't need protective custody, so you just run along and tell your boss that."

"I don't think you understand," he said. "If you don't cooperate, I'll have to arrest you."

She noticed he wasn't wearing a name tag. "How long you been on the job, Deputy?"

"I don't think that's relevant. Is that your stuff in the corner?" He could see her semi-automatic pistol in the holster of her equipment belt. "Let's see what you have there." He started for Larae's belongings.

Larae shook her head. "No. Don't touch those. Billie," she said without taking her eyes from the deputy, "why don't you go back to the kitchen. I think I smell something burning."

"There's nothing burn... Oh. Okay. I better tend to it."

"Now, Deputy," her voice dripping with sarcasm, Larae said, "why don't you just have a cup of coffee and we'll talk about what's going to happen here."

The bully in him showing itself, the man just grinned. "No, I'm taking you in." He started to pull his weapon, but Larae lifted the .380 and pointed it at the bridge of his nose.

"And you'd be wrong. Put your hands on top of your head and turn around. If you are going to play cop, you should study more. Where's your name tag?"

"Musta forgot it."

"In a pig's eye. No cop would forget his identification. Not done, ever."

"Doesn't matter. You wouldn't shoot me, and you know it," he grinned.

"No," Wally said as he racked a shell into the chamber of a short-barreled shotgun and stepped out of the doorway to the bar, "she might not. But I will, so do what she tells you. I don't know if a slug will go through your Kevlar or not. But go ahead and pull your pistol if you want to find out. I do know a big slug will knock you down and break some ribs. Might even stop your heart if I put my shot in the right place."

The chilling, metallic rack of a lever-action rifle drained MacNabb's last ebbing thoughts of resistance. White-faced, he turned and saw an angry Billie Thompson pointing a .30-.30 Winchester at his crotch from about fifteen feet away.

"You shoot him in the head, Wally, and I'll shoot his man parts."

The deputy fainted dead away—just swooned and peed his pants. Wally leaned the shotgun in a corner and with expert proficiency, flipped the deputy over on his stomach, pulled handcuffs from the man's equipment belt and snapped them around his big wrists.

Larae holstered her pistol and stumped over to her equipment belt. She dug in a pouch and fished out a quick tie. She watched Wally snug the plastic restraints around the man's ankles.

"You've done this before, haven't you?"

Wally grinned and said, "Nah. Saw it in the movies once."

"Bull feathers."

When he revived, MacNabb rolled up on his side. The first thing he saw was Wally sitting in a chair about six feet away, the shotgun pointed generally at the deputy's crotch. Wally wrinkled his nose and said, "Whew, you smell bad, boy. Now what we want to know is who told you to arrest Ms. Holcomb, and where were you to take her? And don't hold back. I don't know if I can keep Billie from separating you from your manhood."

"Let's start with your real name," Larae said. She clumped over and pulled a wallet from the man's back pocket.

He blustered and said, "I'm Officer MacNabb with the Deschutes County Sheriff's Office and you are under arrest."

"That's interesting." She held up the driver's license. "This says you are Lawrence Smith."

He had nothing to say after that. Larae read him his rights and told him he was under arrest for impersonating an officer, for attempted kidnapping, for assault of a police officer, and public indecency.

Wally prodded him with the shotgun and said, "Let's start over. Why are you here? Who sent you?"

A quick phone call to acting undersheriff Michelle Trivoli started an electronic search of public records. While she waited for Michelle to call back, Larae just sat on a counter stool and watched. She had every confidence Wally wouldn't shoot Lawrence Smith or whoever he was, but she was still sorting her reactions to the sudden appearance of Wally and his shotgun, and to the angry determination of Billie.

She was even more interested in Wally's background. His use of the handcuffs and the quick tie was fast and proficient. But that would have to wait for another time.

Chapter 29

Roger Hildebrand squeezed the Lake County pickup into a narrow slot between two black and brown Oregon state police cruisers in the Justice Center parking lot. He grinned when Sonny Sixkiller parked his highly polished gold Lexus in the empty end of the parking lot, as far from any other vehicles as possible. It didn't matter that the Lexus was nearly ten years old. Sonny didn't want any careless s.o.b. dinging his doors.

They slid picture ID into a depression under a thick window to an unsmiling police officer. She scrutinized them both, longer than necessary in Roger's opinion, and then smiled as she pushed their licenses back through the slot under the window.

"Nice job down there in the desert, guys. Welcome to the Justice Center. Your boss is straight down the hallway, left at the first corridor, third door on the right." A metallic click signaled the door was unlatched.

A grim-faced Bud Blair had his cell phone to his ear when Roger and Sonny opened the door to a small office. John Bernard was sitting on a loveseat pushed back against the wall of the office, keen eyes watching, listening to Bud's side of a phone call.

Bud pointed Sonny and Roger to a couple of visitor chairs. As they sat down, Bud swore softly and asked, "Is he for real?"

Then he said, "Hold on, Larae. I'll be right back." He turned to Roger and Sonny and said, "You two go find out if Deschutes County has a MacNabb working as a deputy. And don't let Redmond know you asked."

He watched until the door closed behind Roger and Sonny and then put the phone back to his ear. "Roger and Sonny are here. I sent them to check and see if there really is a MacNabb. Keep your phone handy." He killed the call and searched through recent calls until he was satisfied he had the right number and hit the Send button.

Outside in the hallway, Sonny said, "I wonder what's up? I don't think Bud has ever ordered us to do anything. He always asks first."

Roger nodded. "Something big, I think. How we gonna do this?"

"We'll pretend that MacNabb is an old friend we haven't seen in a while. Want to look him up while we're in town. Maybe she'll know," Sonny said and nodded at a nice looking young woman walking towards them.

When Roger asked her if she knew his old buddy MacNabb, she said, "Yes. I know Deputy MacNabb. I think he's in the squad room. Go down this hallway and take a right at the first corridor. Ring the bell."

"Thank you."

Sonny rang the bell and when he identified himself as the Lake County undersheriff, the door made an audible click and Roger and Sonny pushed into the squad room. The real MacNabb, a lean, medium-sized man, maybe five-nine, red hair askew, was indeed in the squad room, geared up, and pissed off. He glared at another officer and then said, "Who the hell took my pickup?"

He also glared at Roger and Sonny and said, "What the hell do you two want?"

"Officer MacNabb?" Roger asked.

"Who wants to know?"

Sonny tried to keep his irritation under control, and Roger said, "Temper, temper, Officer MacNabb."

Sonny snickered, and MacNabb's shift supervisor laughed out loud.

MacNabb glared at Roger for a long three seconds, and then started to grin. He stuck out his hand, read Roger's name tag and said, "MacNabb, Officer Hildebrand. And some son-of-a-bitch took my pickup, so I'm a wee bit irritated this morning. Why are you looking for me?"

"I don't really know," Roger admitted. "For some reason, our boss wanted to make sure there really was a MacNabb on the Deschutes county force."

"Hello?" Dutch said into the cell phone.

"Dutch, this is Bud. Special Agent Bernard and I are in an office off the main hallway. Third door on the right. Got that? Main hallway, left at the first corridor. Third office on the right. We have to talk. Like right now."

Dutch said, "I'm interviewing your friends Harley and Chase. Can this wait?"

"No, and those two don't know any more they haven't told us already."

Dutch stood up and looked at BB. "Finish this up. I'll be back in a minute," and walked out the door. "Where's the front door?" he asked the jailer. "I got lost in here."

Two minutes later Dutch knocked and opened the door to the empty office Bud had confiscated. Dutch closed the door, looked at John, and gave Bud a questioning look.

Without preamble, Bud said, "I'll vouch for John. We have a leak. You need to move your raid up…like go right now. If you wait until this evening, you won't find anything in the mosque. It'll all be gone."

"How do you know?" Dutch asked.

"Just do it, Dutch. And don't mention it to anyone here."

"Who's the leak?"

"I'll give him to you on a platter before the day is out."

"Bring us in, Bud. Let the FBI handle it."

"There isn't enough time. And I think you should get BB back to Portland to take care of Cle…his snitch."

"I know who Cletus is. We have him in protective custody. We'll take care of him."

Bud took a deep breath. "Dell BeBe is one of my closest friends and one of the smartest people I know. In his world, he's the finest detective I know. He's street smart, he's tough, and he knows which rocks to turn over to get at the truth. But out here in the high desert, I'm afraid he's out of his element. Take him home, Dutch. Let him babysit Cletus. Please."

"You really love that big lug, don't you?"

Bud grinned and said, "No. He's a pain in the ass."

"Okay. I'm going back on the plane. I'll send somebody back for the car later. He can ride with me."

"Thanks, Dutch."

"What are you going to do, Bud?"

"Just call me Cheese," Bud grinned.

Dutch looked at John. "Have you figured this out?"

John nodded. "I can add as well as our fine sheriff. And I was there for the main action, just like our traitor."

"Well, don't you both get yourselves killed. At least not until I know who to come after."

"We'll try not to," Bud said. "Besides, if we figured it out, you can, too."

Chapter 30

TWO BURLY GUARDS PUSHED COWBOY'S WHEELCHAIR into the interview room. He was handcuffed to the arms of the chair, wore leg irons and a thin hospital robe over clean, blue scrubs. Bud motioned the guards to push the chair to the edge of a small table. He said, "Thanks, we'll take it from here." The guards looked disappointed, but nodded and left the room.

Dutch and Bud stood across the table from Cowboy, and John walked around and stood behind him. Cowboy craned his neck and glared at John. "You again. Who the hell are you?"

"Special Agent John Bernard, NCIS counterterrorism unit."

"Sucker punched me, you asshole. I'd like to see you try it again."

John frowned and said, "I debated with myself if I should keep you alive or feed you to the coyotes. Once upon a time we executed rapists."

"I ain't no rapist," Cowboy protested.

"So you just intended to kill Larae Holcomb? Not rape her?"

"Snotty bitch had it coming."

"Enough," Dutch interrupted. "Let me introduce myself. I'm Special Agent in Charge Elden Vanderlin, FBI, Portland. "I'm here to take you to Portland where you will be held in a Federal facility pending prosecution for conspiring with foreign nationals to commit acts of terrorism, for treason, for drug running, for people smuggling, for assaulting a federal officer, for assaulting sworn peace officers, for arson, and for being an all around threat to public safety.

"You will be convicted, and if we can keep you alive long enough to strap you to a table, you will be given a lethal injection. Your cold body will then be given to your family to dispose of as they choose."

"I want my lawyer."

"Is Pettibone your lawyer?" Bud asked.

"Yeah. And I'm not saying another damned word until he gets here."

John put his hands on Cowboy's shoulder and pinched the muscles on the side of his neck. "He won't be coming. Someone killed him. Blew his boat out of the water. Besides, under the Patriot Act I don't have to give you access to a lawyer."

Cowboy squirmed and tried to shake loose from John's hands. "Quit hurting me. You assholes always got some fancy grip."

"So that's it, then." Dutch said. "We just wanted to see what you looked like. You were Mirandized earlier and you said you didn't want a lawyer, so we are what you get." He started for the door. "See you in Portland."

"Wait," Cowboy said. "What do you want? I'll make a deal. I can give you the top dog."

Bud slid a picture of Raul Ortega across the table. "This guy?"

"You already know that. Otherwise you wouldn't have his picture."

Bud slapped the table with both hands, the sound echoed like a shot in the concrete room. Cowboy flinched and John increased the pressure on his neck. "Is this the top dog?"

"Yessir. And I can give him to you. But I want a deal. I want witness protection."

"What's this guy's name?" Bud asked.

"I don't know. He uses code names. Calls himself *Jefe* or something like that. I only saw him one time. Came to the ranch to impress me about how important the next job was. Promised me $250,000 at the end of it." He looked up at Bud and said, "And he also promised to kill anybody who messed it up."

"Did he tell you what the job was?" Dutch asked Cowboy.

"I'm not saying another word unless we have a deal. I want witness protection. I have it all written down. Names, dates, places, shipments, the whole enchilada. But you ain't getting it until we have a deal."

Dutch slammed a briefcase on the table, lifted the lid, and turned the case toward Cowboy. "You mean this?"

Cowboy blanched. The big man looked afraid for the first time. "Where did you get that?"

John leaned forward and said quietly in Cowboy's ear, "You idiot. Did you actually think to purge your computer files? We have all of your records."

"They're encrypted. You can't bust my code, so you still need me."

"Wrong. The sheriff deciphered your quaint code. So we got it all." John said.

Cowboy sat still, mind racing, trying to find some leverage he could bargain with. The three men waited, not saying a word.

Finally Cowboy said, "I can bring Ortega to you. I know you can't get close to him unless I bring him to you."

"How can you do that?" Dutch asked.

"I'll tell him I captured the sheriff. Ask him if he wants me to kill the sheriff or would he like to do it himself."

"What makes you think he'll sucker for that?" Dutch asked.

"Revenge. He sends people to take care of the small fry. But he'll go after the sheriff personally. Besides, the Muslim brotherhood will pay him big bucks." He looked away from Dutch and glared at Bud. "You made the hit list, Hot Shot."

Bud glared back. "And then he'll kill you, sure as hell. Think about it. We're your only chance to stay alive."

"Make me a deal."

Dutch said, "I'll tell you what. You bring us Ortega, and we'll talk deal. Until then the charges stand."

Bud leaned over the table and gave Cowboy a hard look. "You can start showing us what a good boy you plan to be right now. I want to know who killed Crazy Charlie."

"I don't know. Had to be someone local."

"Anyone we might know?"

Cowboy looked nervous and turned to John. "I'm sorry about your old buddy Crazy, but I don't know who killed him." Then he whispered, "The walls have ears."

Chapter 31

THE HEARINGS OFFICER, A LAWYER FROM the State's Attorney General's office intoned, "This hearing is now open. Is Officer Roger Hildebrand, Lake County, Oregon, present?"

Roger rose and said, "Here."

"Is Officer Sonny Sixkiller, Lake County, Oregon, present?"

Sixkiller rose and said, "Here."

"Please be seated."

The hearings officer nodded at Captain Delbert Delaware, Oregon State Police. "Have you concluded your investigation into the shooting death of a 'John Doe' on...," he glanced at a file on the table in front of him and read the date of the bomb blast north of Fort Rock.

"I have," Delaware answered in a deep voice that matched his height.

The hearings office, whose name neither Roger nor Sonny managed to capture during the entire hearing, swore in Delaware who promised to tell the truth.

"It is my understanding this matter has been before the Grand Jury. Is that correct?"

"Yes," Delaware answered.

"And the result was...?"

"The Grand Jury did not find grounds for criminal prosecution," Delaware answered.

"So we have the matter of an administrative review to resolve," the hearings officer said. "And you were the chief investigator."

"Correct," Captain Delaware answered.

"Please tell us what your investigation discovered."

When Delaware finished his report, the hearing's officer said, "So it was a justifiable shooting."

"In my opinion, yes," Delaware answered. "The man was assaulting…"

"Thank you, Captain. I want the officers to speak for themselves."

The hearings officer said, "Officers Hildebrand and Sixkiller, please rise. Raise your right hand. Do you solemnly swear to tell the truth, the whole truth and nothing but the truth?"

Each said, "I do," and impulsively Sonny added, "So help me God."

Roger restrained a smile and echoed, "So help me God."

The hearings officer, whom Roger decided to call "Sour Puss," ignored the addendum and said, "Please be seated. Officer Hildebrand, did you shoot an armed assailant on the date described in the affidavit?"

"Yes."

"And did the assailant die?"

Roger was beginning to wonder what Lemon Puss was up to, but he said, "I don't know. He went down. I think I hit him."

"Hit him?"

"Yes…with a bullet."

"I see. And what was the assailant doing?"

"He was shooting at me with an AK-47."

"So he was shooting at you?"

Impatiently, Roger answered, "Exactly."

"How do you know it was an AK-47?"

"The AK has a very distinct sound," Roger answered.

Sour Puss raised his eyebrows. "And how would you know that?"

"I spent some time around people who were shooting at me with AK-47s."

"Were you in the Gulf?"

"I can't answer that, and you know it, or you wouldn't have asked," Roger growled.

For the first time, Sour Puss smiled. "Thank you. It isn't often I get to meet a hero. That'll be all, Officer Hildebrand."

John and Bud who were seated in hard folding chairs at the back of the conference room turned hearings room, looked at each other. Bud shrugged. "I don't know what he's talking about," he whispered.

"Officer Sixkiller, did you shoot at the John Doe who was found dead at the scene?"

Sonny face was deadpan when he answered, "Yes."

"Did you hit the man?"

"I don't know, but I think it was likely."

"Why did you shoot at him. Wasn't he already down?"

"I could only see his boots. I was afraid he would get back up or try to sneak up on Roger. I mean Officer Hildebrand. So I shot at him."

The hearings officer closed the file suddenly and said, "It is my finding that the death of a John Doe by gunfire at the hands of Officers Hildebrand and Sixkiller was self-defense. I order them returned to duty. The hearing is closed."

The attorney Roger named Sour Puss rose and walked around the table. He was a close second to Captain Delaware who had his hand out and said, "Congratulations. You guys did a hell of a job. Anytime you want to work for me, give me a call."

Sheriff Blair walked up to Captain Delaware and shook his hand. "Thanks. That was quick service."

"Don't mention it. The Governor made it high priority. Contrary to rumor, we can move quickly when we need to."

Sour Puss was dwarfed standing beside the tall, state police captain. But he was grinning at Roger. "Sorry about that," he said, and held out his hand. "We have to observe the formalities of the hearing or the press will gut-shoot us, and you boys will look guilty regardless. I hope we put that to rest. The Attorney General's office will issue a press release that says you have been investigated and exonerated. No hard feelings?"

"No, I guess not," Roger said, "but you shouldn't have mentioned the Gulf."

"Yes, I should have. You are much too modest, Officer Hildebrand."

Roger looked grim. "How do you have access to classified information?"

"What you did is still classified, but the citations are not. We were just trying to be thorough."

Bud started to say something, but John caught his sleeve and mouthed, "No."

JOHN, BUD, SONNY, AND ROGER CONGREGATED in the parking lot beside Bud's pickup for a post mortem of the hearing. Bud held out his hand to Sonny and Roger and said warmly, "Nice to have you guys back. How's the head, Sonny?"

"I'm good," Sonny said.

"It's bullshit," Roger said and leaned back against the bed of the pickup, arms crossed. Sonny nodded agreement.

"No," Bud said firmly, "it's not. It serves to remind our customers, John Q. Public, we're in a high risk business that may call for the use of deadly force. And it reminds criminals it isn't safe to threaten police officers."

John nodded, "And it tells the public you don't shoot people just because you got pissed off."

He gave Roger a long steady look. "Seal?"

Roger nodded and patted his belly "A bit thinner in those times. You? You got the look."

"Not a Seal."

Bud looked over at Sonny and raised his eyebrows. Sonny just grinned, shrugged, and shook his head as if to say, Don't ask.

Bud nodded "Well, let's get you all up to speed."

In terse sentences he told them about Larae's encounter—and capture—of a man masquerading as a Deschutes County Deputy. "She has him in custody at the Christmas Valley Lodge."

"So that's what that business with MacNabb was about," Sonny said. "Right," Bud said. "The way I see it, if anyone bothered to check, they'd find there really is a MacNabb working for Deschutes County. Only he wasn't in Christmas Valley this morning."

"So there's a leak in the Deschutes County Sheriff's Office?" Roger asked. Bud nodded, but said, "Maybe. With any luck we'll find out who it is before noon today. I told one person, and one person only our route home. Said we were going to take the back way home...the old Fort Rock road through the Deschutes National Forest to Christmas Valley, take the cutoff north to Highway 30 east of Silver Lake, and then on home.

"If anybody hits us going home, we'll know my suspect is the leak."

"Want to share?" Sonny asked.

Bud shook his head. "For now, it doesn't matter. Roger, you bring your county rig?"

"Yes. And it's loaded for bear."

"Sonny?" Bud asked.

"My Lexus, since my rig is out of service for the time being. But I can leave it here and ride shotgun with Roger."

"Okay. We'll stop at that mini mart a couple blocks down the street, gas up, get a cup of coffee and stall just long enough to give our suspect a short head start. He will have to improvise, so I'm hoping he'll make a mistake. John and I will take the lead. You two lay back a few hundred yards, but come fogging if we run into any trouble. And keep your eyes open. They might try to hit you first."

Sonny and Roger were almost to Roger's pickup when Sonny's cell phone buzzed. He glanced at the caller ID and frowned. He answered, "Is that you, Sis?"

Nancy said, "Yes. I've got some bad news, Sonny. Mama is in the hospital in Yakima. Verna called and said it looks like she's had a stroke. I'm at home, just about packed, and then I'm going to drive up."

"Not good, Nancy. And I'm not sure I can leave right now. Let me call you back."

Roger asked, "What's up?"

"My mother is in the hospital. She had a stroke."

Roger pointed at the Lexus at the back of the parking lot. "So go. We'll be okay."

"I don't know, Roger." He paused and then said, "We better tell Bud."

Bud wasn't happy at the news, but when Sonny said, "I can ride shotgun to Lakeview and then go up," Bud said, "No. We know your mother had a stroke, but we only think we might be ambushed going home. So you saddle up and head north. We'll be fine."

Sonny turned and started trotting in the direction of his car when Roger hollered, "And don't get a ticket." Sonny changed out of his uniform shirt and slipped on a slightly wrinkled blue short-sleeved sport shirt. He put on his Honkers baseball cap, adjusted his Polaroid sunglasses, and turned the key. They watched him ease out of the parking lot and a few seconds later heard the bark of tuned mufflers as he accelerated up Highway 97.

"Well," Bud said, "that leaves the three of us. John, you ride with Roger. Same plan, just a small change in numbers."

Chapter 32

DUTCH AND A DOZEN FBI AGENTS set up a command post in the North Portland Precinct. A ten-member FBI anti-terrorist team, clad in dark Kevlar crowded around a chalkboard as their unit commander sketched the layout of a mosque a short dozen blocks from the station. The plan called for a simultaneous assault on the front and rear doors.

A Portland city police SWAT team was already in place, snipers hidden in buildings and on rooftops with a clear view of all four sides of the mosque, the rest in a van parked in a garage a block away, ready to sprint down an alley and surround the perimeter of the building when they got the "go" signal.

The unit commander said, "We secure the building, and these fine gentlemen," he pointed to the agents behind the team, "will follow to arrest these guys." He pointed to a row of seven photos taped to the chalk board, "We want to take these guys alive, but if they fire on us, don't hesitate. They may be ready for us, so do it as we trained. Shock and awe, guys."

"Anything to add, Agent Vanderlin?"

Dutch said, "Yeah," and pushed his way to the chalk board. He pointed at the photo in the center. The picture was a basement shot of a bearded man standing in front of stack of weapons, holding an automatic rifle aloft in one hand, and grinning at the camera. "This guy is new to us. His name is Akeem. We think he's the stud duck in this pond. We want to take him alive if at all possible. We have an arrest warrant for all of seven of these guys. That's the good news. The bad news… they may have been tipped off a couple hours ago, so expect them to be prepared and look for IEDs."

He glanced at his watch. "We go in twenty minutes. Any questions?"

One member of the team, a short burly guy Dutch didn't know by name asked, "Why not go now?"

"What we hope to do is catch these guys at prayer. If all goes well, we walk in the front door and nobody gets hurt. We also want to time our raid to coincide with another operation in Seattle. We don't want these guys grabbing cell phones and tipping their friends off." He turned to the precinct commander. "Are your units ready to block the streets?"

"We're good to go."

"Okay. We'll run communications from here. All radios will be set to the TAC channel, and we'll have a National Guard helicopter and one city police helicopter overhead when we hit these guys. The City will coordinate air operations."

Dutch turned to his Deputy SAC, Dave Sutherlin, a tall young man who specialized in tactical operations. "Anything we forgot, Dave?"

Sutherlin scanned the screen of his small laptop, ran through his checklist and looked back up. "It's all in place: transport, communications, bomb squad, medical, public relations. And food and water," he added with a smile. "Plus a small team scheduled to arrive here in thirty minutes to process those we detain…do the fingerprints, facial scans, background checks, the whole nine yards."

TWENTY MINUTES LATER A NATIONAL GUARD Helicopter and a Portland city police helicopter zipped into view as Portland's finest SWAT team sprinted down the alley and fanned out to secure the perimeter of the mosque.

Two five-man FBI assault teams tossed stun grenades through the front and rear doors of the mosque and charged through the smoke, weapons ready, shouting, "Hands in the air! You are under arrest! Stay down! Don't move!"

The stunned worshippers all did as ordered—all, that is, but one young man kneeling on a prayer rug. He yelped and tried to run to a side door only to be slammed to the floor. "Stay down, asshole, and stay alive," a short burly man in black Kevlar shouted. He wrenched the young man's hands behind his back and snapped handcuffs on his wrist, ignoring a cry of pain as the cuffs cut into the man's flesh.

Dutch and eight other agents flooded into the room, guns drawn, black vests proclaiming FBI. They worked quickly to pull hands behind backs and pull plastic quick ties around unwilling wrists. When the situation was stabilized and secure, four members of the assault team broke off and trotted to a door that led to the basement of the mosque. They carefully opened it and shone flashlights down the dark stairs. One found a light switch and illuminated the stairwell.

"Watch it," the leader said. "Trip wire. Fourth step." He thumbed his lapel mike and said, "We got an IED. Get Bomb Disposal in here."

THE RAID IN SEATTLE DIDN'T GO as smoothly, even though it was nearly identical in plan and style to the Portland takedown. The difference was a man coming out of a restroom in a side hallway. The flash-bangs didn't stun or disorient him. Instead he ran down the hallway to a locked room, punched a number code into a key pad and pushed through a heavy metal door. He then locked the door behind him. When the "infidels" finally pounded the lock into submission and rushed through the door, he opened fire with an automatic rifle. Two heavy slugs punched the team leader back out the door and onto his butt in the hallway. A second FBI agent swore and emptied thirty rounds of high-velocity ammunition into the room. A third agent took a quick peek around the doorjamb and said, "You got him." He pulled a stun grenade from a side pocket and tossed it into the room.

It proved redundant. The shooter was lying in a spreading pool of blood that seeped from several bullet holes.

When the smoke cleared the first man through the door stopped and stared. Almost in awe he said, "Guys, look at that. We almost bought the farm." He pointed at a dozen cartons of explosives stacked in a corner. Both Catholics on the team crossed themselves. One said, "Thank you, Sweet Jesus."

The designated number two on the team thumbed a lapel mike and said, "We need medical, ground floor, north east corner of the building. And get Bomb Disposal here ASAP." He walked back to the hallway and found his team leader sitting propped up against the wall, assault rifle across his knees, trying to unstrap his vest. "What the hell were you thinking? That isn't how we rehearsed it."

IN PORTLAND AN FBI FORENSICS TEAM, accompanied by a bomb disposal squad from the Oregon State Police descended the stairwell into the basement and started work. "Get me fingerprints," Dutch ordered.

Dutch was sitting on the front steps of the Mosque smoking a cigarette bummed from the only smoker on his team when a Dish-mounted van roared around a corner and screeched to a stop. The side door of the van slid open and two people jumped out and trotted up to the barrier. The woman carried a microphone. The tall man, ponytail flapping as he jogged, carried a camera on his shoulder.

They were stopped at the street barrier by uniformed Portland city police. A helicopter from a local TV station hovered overhead. Shaking his head, Dutch tossed the cigarette aside and thumbed his lapel mike. "Dave?" When the Deputy SAC answered, Dutch said, "The vultures are circling. Get our public information people here right now." He recognized the young reporter, a beautiful Asian woman from one of Portland's TV stations.

He watched in wry amusement as she insisted she be allowed beyond the barrier. The two officers at the barrier kept shaking their heads. Dutch heard her say, "I'll go to the mayor if you don't let me in."

Dutch walked down the steps and hurried to the barrier. "Ms. Chou," he said. "If you will just be patient for another ten minutes, I think you'll have the biggest story of your career."

"And you are?"

"Special Agent Vanderlin, Portland FBI. We'll have a statement for you in just a few minutes. And as soon as the site is secure, I'll let the press film a rather impressive cache of arms, ammunition, and explosives found in the basement of the mosque."

"The ones you planted, you mean."

Oh shit. His steely blue eyes bored into hers and then prudence beat back an overwhelming desire to simply punch her in the mouth. He stomped off and found his team leader. "Tell our people to search these guys for cell phones. Somebody already told the press we planted the weapons."

IN PORTLAND, SEVENTY-THREE MEN WERE DETAINED. In Seattle, the number was eighty-three. Processing of suspects would last two days. After processing, seven men were detained in Portland, and fifteen were detained in Seattle. National radio and television stations would echo daily reports of the outrage for the next month. Most overlooked the arms cache in each mosque. And the ACLU looked forward to years of litigation.

Chapter 33

Bud drove the old Fort Rock road that wound casually in a roughly southeast direction from Bend through sun-dappled ponderosa pine, seasoned by an occasional thicket of lodge pole.

He had a casual knowledge of the big bang theory and he owned a William Orr's Geology of Oregon which detailed tectonic plate movement and the vulcanization of the Western U.S. and Canada. But somehow that information about constant change—information he believed—didn't affect his sense of the permanence of the natural world, or the spiritual lift he felt in wild places.

He drove slowly around a corner and thought, *I don't know if I could ever go back to asphalt and concrete again.*

Forty-five minutes into the drive he was beginning to wonder if his hunch was wrong. The only vehicle he had seen was a pickup backed off the road in a lodge pole thicket. He powered down the window and was blessed by the smell of fresh cut firewood. The drone of a power saw greeted his ears. "Just a wood cutter," he decided.

As he neared the National Forest boundary, the pine trees grew shorter, darker barked and scattered, sharing space with a few junipers that marked the margin between the forest and the open sagebrush country of the Fort Rock-Christmas Valley basin. The road climbed a lazy hill and as he topped the rise, he spotted a vehicle parked alongside the road in the bottom of the dip. The vehicle hood was up, and a tall woman stood ready to flag him down. He slowed and grabbed his mike. "County Three, this is County One. Close up. There's an older brown and yellow Jeep stopped by the road. A Cherokee it looks like. Hood up. I think we're about to identify the leak."

Bud heard Roger answer, the sound of a racing engine in the background, "We're coming. Watch yourself."

Adrenalin pumped through Bud's system. He tensed as he pulled a ten-gauge semi-automatic shotgun up on the seat, barrel pointed at the passenger door, and eased on down the road. When he was about thirty feet from the Cherokee, the woman looked up and Bud recognized her as one of the EMTs that carted Crazy Charlie away.

He floored the accelerator and shot past her. He was about seventy-five feet beyond the Jeep when the first bullet punched through the rear window and starred the windscreen. He slammed on the brakes and cranked the pickup to the right, spun the wheel counter clockwise and backed up, blocking the road. Without taking time to shut the ignition off, he jammed the gear shift in neutral. He swung the door open, aware of sharp pinging sounds from rounds hammering the bed and cab of the pickup. He took a quick peek over the bed of the pickup, shouldered the shotgun, and fired two quick rounds at the tall woman as she walked down the road calmly shooting at him with some kind of machine pistol.

He steadied his aim and fired at her head. At a distance of fifty feet the double-ought buckshot punched her back and down. Without thinking, he fed three shells into the magazine of the shotgun and looked around trying to spot any other shooters. An anguished cry helped him locate a second shooter. The man's cry sounded like, "Aimee!!"

Bud crouched, ran to his right, and took cover behind a big ponderosa. Bullets chewed chunks of bark from the trunk of the tree. He heard the shots this time. It gave him an aiming point.

"Somewhere left of the Jeep," he decided. He took a deep breath, dove behind a small pine and rolled to his right. A pink-faced man peeked around the trunk of a big yellow pine, and Bud fired six rounds as fast as he could pull the trigger, bark chip showering the air. The man swore and ran diagonally through the timber. Bud peppered him twice with double-ought buckshot and had the satisfaction of watching the man fall. Bud aimed and pulled the trigger again. No recoil punched his shoulder. The shotgun was empty. He fished in his jacket pocket for another round and found the pocket riding empty.

The short man got to his feet, fired another burst in Bud's direction and then hobbled out of sight behind a thicket of young pine. Bud got to his knees, pulled his pistol and fired a full clip blindly into the thicket. He popped the empty clip and slapped another one home. Cursing grimly he curbed his anger and reluctantly held his fire.

Pistol ready, he walked back to the road and looked at the still figure of the woman lying face up in the dust. He kicked the machine pistol away from her dead hand, and then found himself breathing hard, his hands trembling slightly.

Roger's pickup slid to a halt about thirty feet from the Cherokee. He backed across the road, and the cork was in the bottle. Unless the Cherokee took off across country, it was effectively out of the game.

Pistol ready, Roger jumped out, door ajar, and walked up to Bud, looking beyond him at the body in the dusty road and at Bud's bullet pocked vehicle. John Bernard walked away from Roger's pickup in a wide arc, scanning the scattered trees for shooters, rifle at the ready.

"What took you so long?" Bud growled.

Roger shook his head in disgust. "Damned cows got in the road and wouldn't get out of the way. Chased two yearling calves for half a mile before they understood it was possible to leave the roadway." He paused, "What happened?"

"I recognized her," he said pointing at the dead woman. "She was one of the fake EMTs who hauled Charlie off. Her partner is out there," he pointed west of the road, "in the timber, so keep your eyes open. He's armed with some kind of machine pistol."

"So you just shot her?"

"Hell no, I didn't! When I saw her I accelerated and got by before she opened up on me. Damnedest thing. She just came walking down the road firing at me. So I shot back."

John came hurrying back. "Found a set of man tracks. And some blood. It looks like you hit him, Bud."

"I was trying to," Bud said.

"Looks like he hit you, too," John offered. "You got blood on your left arm."

Bud looked at his bloody sleeve and shook his head. "I'll be damned." Suddenly his knees felt weak and he felt light headed. He walked gingerly over to the ditch and plopped his butt on a small cutbank. "I better sit down."

Roger hurried to his pickup and began talking on the radio. Bud couldn't make out the words, and he wondered who Roger was calling.

John cussed the Lake County Sheriff's Department while he tended to Bud's wound. "You gotta do something about this, Sheriff. Your first-aid kits suck." He helped Bud out of his blood soaked jacket and then slipped on a pair of white surgical gloves. He dug through the kit and found a pair of scissors. "Let's see what we have here." The scissors chewed reluctantly at the heavy material of Bud's khaki sleeve. John muttered to himself as if Bud wasn't really there, "Missed the bone. Didn't chop any arteries. Cross grain, but not too deep. Good Purple Heart wound."

He tore a gauze pad from its wrap and slapped it on the wound, a bleeding gouge a half-inch deep and about two inches long on the outside of Bud's upper arm, just below his shoulder.

"Hold that," John ordered. Bud kept the pad in place with his right hand while John unwound a roll of cloth tape.

"Okay, raise your arm so I can get the tape around the pad." Bud winced when he lifted his arm, but he bit back a groan and was patient while John wound the tape over the ends of the pad and around Bud's arm. "That'll have to do."

Roger walked up and said, "You look like you've done that before."

"Maybe once or twice."

Bud stared at the dead woman, blue bottle flies congregating to feed on the blood, and to lay thousands of tiny eggs. The buzzing bothered him, but he failed to find in his soul even a hint of compassion. A cold-blooded killer who got what she deserved.

Bud said, "Cover that up, Roger."

"No, Boss. We leave her right there until the state police get here. ETA, forty minutes."

Bud nodded compliance and stared at the bullet holes in his vehicle, the engine still idling. "I'm thinking we need to get John to Christmas Valley...give Larae some backup. What do you think, John?"

"I think it's a good idea, but what are you going to do about the shooter out in the forest?"

"Well...I'm going to track him down and make him tell me who he works for."

"Boss," Roger said, "want to tell us who the leak is now?"

"Sure...the only person I told about our back road route...Cal Redmond."

"Shit. If it wasn't for this ambush, I'd find it hard to believe. Can you prove it?"

"No," Bud answered, " But I'm convinced of it. That's why I need a prisoner."

"Well, we'll get one for you. Boss," Roger said, "I have an ambulance in route. They'll take you to Saint Charles and get you stitched up."

"Not yet, they won't," Bud snapped. "I told you I'm gonna track this guy down. You get that ambulance turned around. My arm will keep for now."

John shook his head, a hint of a smile on his face when he said to Roger, "Stubborn son-of-a-bitch, isn't he?"

Bud shook his head. "Doesn't anybody do what I say? John, take my rig and head for Christmas Valley. Take Larae and her prisoner...MacNabb...to Lakeview and lock him up. You," he pointed at Roger, "fall a tree the other side of your pickup and block the road.

Hang some crime scene ribbon on it." He fished his phone from a shirt pocket and checked cell coverage.

"And then call Bobcat Larson. If he's home, go get him and bring him back here. His place is the first house on the right past the Horse Ranch as you head toward Silver Lake."

"You sure that's what you want, Boss? I think it would be better if *you* took Larae and MacNabb to Lakeview and let me and John track this guy."

"No...I mean, yes...that's the way I want it. Let's just keep this manhunt in the family. No state police, no Deschutes County...just you and me. Okay?"

Roger shook his head in disgust, but he trotted back to his rig and pulled a small chainsaw from the big steel tool box bolted to the bed of the pickup. He walked up the road sizing up the trees. He stopped at a twelve-inch diameter pine that was already leaning west across the road. The saw coughed and sputtered on the second pull of the starter rope and then snarled to life on the third. He put in an undercut, lined up his back cut, and fell the tree. Roger hit the kill switch and silence filled the forest.

THEY LEFT BUD SITTING ON THE side of the road, two Aleve dissolving sourly in his stomach, and a fully loaded AR-15 across his lap. They also left a water bottle, two power bars and a roll of bright orange plastic flagging. Bud didn't feel like eating anything, but he drank half a liter of water.

He took a deep breath and then pushed himself up. He walked across the road and started a slow, cautious circle around the thicket of small pine, the last place he'd seen the man he'd shot at. *I wonder if he'll try to circle around and get back to his vehicle. What would I do? Depends on how bad I was hurt, I guess.*

He found the blood trail and followed it about fifty yards into the timber. The injured man was going in roughly a straight line away from the jeep. Bud pulled a strip of flagging and tied it to a limb so he could find the trail again. He glanced at his watch. Almost eleven.

He had been scouting the timber for about ten minutes when the rumble of an engine caught his ears. It sounded like the vehicle wasn't traveling fast, just sort of idling down the road. Bud backed up against a tree at the edge of the pine thicket and waited, watching. A Deschutes County sheriff's pickup topped the rise and stopped. Bud thought he recognized Cal Redmond, but the reflected light on the windshield made it hard to tell.

A good two minutes passed before the pickup eased quietly down off the rise and stopped by the downed pine. Bud almost smiled. *He's wondering what's going on. No police vehicles. Just a Jeep with its hood up. A dead woman in the road. A tree deliberately fallen across the road. Nobody in sight.*

Cal Redmond opened the door of the pickup and stepped out, a puzzled frown on his face. He gripped the door in his left hand and pulled his Glock from its holster with his right. He looked carefully into the timber on both sides of the road, and then stepped around the door and walked to the log across the road. He hesitated, head swiveling, scanning the timber. He stepped over the log and started walking slowly toward the body lying in the middle of the road.

Bud's voice stopped Cal in mid-stride. "Drop your weapon, Cal. It's over. I'm placing you under arrest." Bud walked out of the shadows and into a patch of sunlight, the AR-15 pointed at Cal's chest. "I can't miss you from here."

Cal turned slowly to face Bud, the Glock still held in his right hand. "What the hell happened here, Bud?"

"Your friends missed me."

"I don't know what you're talking about. Point that rifle someplace else, will you?"

"No. Don't think so. Cal, I told only one person we were taking the Fort Rock Road to get home. That was you. And you told the bad guys."

"Not true, but even if it was, you can't prove it."

"Well, Cal, I'll admit it's all circumstantial, but it's a lot of circumstantial, and I'll bet if we check your finances, we'll find you're on the take. Right? Either way, I'm placing you under arrest. I'll apologize later if I'm wrong."

Cal just stared at Bud, calculating his chances, thinking about the horror of a trial, his good name ruined, his sons embarrassed, his ex-wife gloating at his downfall. He took a deep breath and said, "Hell, Bud. I never intended it to go this far. Just got in too deep to back out."

Bud took a couple of steps closer and asked, "How did you get in this mess?"

Cal slowly holstered his pistol and then backed up to the log across the road. He sat down and took his Stetson off and mopped a sweaty brow with a shirtsleeve. "Looks like my guys winged you. You hurt bad?"

Bud shook his head, walked down off the bank and stood in the road about twenty feet from Cal, holding the rifle to his shoulder, aiming at Cal's eyes. "I think it would be a good idea if you put your pistol on the ground. Don't you?"

Cal thought he could see death in Bud's eyes. He grimaced and then with his thumb and middle finger, lifted the Glock and dropped it on the ground. "Kick it over here, Cal."

Cal gave the pistol a half-hearted kick with the toe of his boot, and Bud walked up and kicked it the rest of the way into the tangle of tree limbs in the ditch.

"Now," Bud said. "Who do you work for?"

Cal shrugged and said, "I don't really know. I'd tell you if I could, but I don't know."

"How do you communicate?"

"I buy throwaway phones. I get text messages from somebody who signs off as Bloodstone."

Bud waited, not saying anything.

"Jesus, what a mess," Cal said. "I just sort of wandered into this. My wife divorced me, got the house and half my retirement, and I got all the bills. Pissed me off. There I was just a few years from retirement with nothing to show for all the years.

"And then a guy calls and says it would be worth my while if I made sure none of my deputies were in LaPine on such-and-such date. It seemed harmless enough. Just look the other way. So I took the money…a lot of money…and then I couldn't get back out. And what they asked kept getting more and more serious."

"What about Crazy Charlie?" Bud asked.

"I swear I had no idea they were going to kill him. It was just supposed to be a rescue operation."

"So you did set that up," Bud said. "I kept trying to figure it out. Who, I asked myself, had the resources and the opportunity to pull that off? And then I remembered how helpful you were, how easy it was for you to decide to drive through the blast site…the crater… our crime scene. Every time I looked at it, there you were, the one constant in all of this…arranging for medevac, calling for ambulances, offering to take Chase and Harley to Lake-view, just sort of hovering like a mother hen over her brood of chicks."

"So you set me up?" Cal asked.

"Yeah. I did. I really wanted to be wrong. But here you are."

"What now?"

"You give me a way to contact this Bloodstone of yours, and I'll do my best to get you a minimum sentence. If you are good enough, you might get witness protection. But that would really piss me off since you just tried to kill me."

Cal took a deep breath and then said, "I'm sorry. I really am. When you captured Cowboy, I started feeling a bit desperate. About the only thing I did right was to not tell Bloodstone about the FBI raids on the mosques in Portland and Seattle. And he'll kill me if he finds out I knew and didn't tip him off."

Bud shook his head, and said, "Not if we find him first." He stopped and then said, "Cal, I want your backup piece. The one in your boot."

Suddenly the big redhead grinned. "Got two of 'em."

Bud tried not to smile, the tension lifting somewhat. "Okay. Take off your boots…slowly…one at a time."

Cal took his boots off and then carefully pulled a .22 Baretta from a holster strapped just above his right ankle. Then he pulled a .380 made by Hollywood Arms from behind his back. He made no sudden moves, just dropped the pistols on the ground and kicked them over to Bud.

"You think I can skate out of this? Claim I was working undercover? Give up Bloodstone in exchange for witness protection?"

"Maybe." Bud said, "I know it's better than trying to shoot your way out. That was running through you mind, wasn't it?"

Cal gave Bud a wry smile. "Decided against it."

Bud nodded. "I thought so. Now, take out your handcuffs and cuff your right wrist to a nice big limb. Then we'll talk about it."

Cal did as Bud said, and then Bud leaned the AR-15 against the stump of the tree. He sat down on the log about six feet from Cal, keyed his cell phone to record on video and said, "How do you contact Bloodstone?"

WHEN CAL STOPPED TALKING, BUD TYPED in Michelle's email address and punched send. "God bless the Internet," he mumbled.

HE HIT A SPEED DIAL NUMBER and waited for Michelle Trivoli to answer. "Bud," she said, "are you all right? Roger said you were shot!"

"Just an abrasion," he lied. "Listen, I'm sending you a video recording of Cal Redmond's confession. Cal's the local kingpin working for a drug lord who goes by the name of Bloodstone. You can get the details from the recording. Save the message and wait for a call from Dutch Vanderlin. He's the FBI's SAC in Portland. He'll give you instructions on what to do."

"Cal Redmond, as in Sheriff Cal Redmond? Good Lord! I can't believe it!"

"Believe it, Michelle," Bud said and then hung up. He punched in another number and waited for the phone to ring.

Bud heard Dutch growl, "Not now, Bud. I'm busy."

"Get a grip, Dutch. I'm busy too, and it's only going to get busier." And then he briefed Dutch about his capture of Cal Redmond,

Cal's confession, and the contact number for Bloodstone Cal had given him.

"I had Redmond send Bloodstone a text message, the guts of which is that he had captured me.

"Bloodstone sent a text back with a GPS reference and a message that reads 'Brg 2 M 2moro ltst.'

"I don't know the location, but you can figure it out." Bud read the coordinates from the text message. "And call my undersheriff, Michelle Trivoli. Tell her where to send a copy of Cal's confession. Understood?"

"Holy crap, Bud. How do you keep winding up in the shit? Never mind, I'll call your undersheriff."

Two Oregon state police cruisers, lights flashing, sirens wailing came flying up the road from the direction of Fort Rock. The two cruisers slid to a stop, one angled to the left, the other just behind and angled to the right, both cars forming a "V" blockade of the road. A tall trooper dressed in state police blues uncoiled from the first cruiser. A smaller, compact trooper, also dressed in blue, opened the door of the second cruiser, pistol extended. He shouted, "Hands up!"

"Easy boys," Bud said and raised his right arm in a sign of surrender. "I'm Lake County Sheriff Henry Blair. And this man is my prisoner."

The taller trooper glared at the smaller man and said, "Put your weapon away, George." He didn't say the words "dumb ass," but he might as well have.

The senior trooper, Jerry Swanson said, "Stay by the radio, George," and then walked up the ditch on the east edge of the road, careful to avoid the area around the dead woman.

"You okay, Sheriff?"

Bud glanced at the blood soaked bandage on his left arm. "I've been better, I guess, but I think I'll live."

"What happened here?" Swanson asked.

Chapter 34

Back at the NCIS Springdale office, Thompson leaned back in his captain's chair, the smell of a burning cigar running a distant second to his acrid comments. He was livid that NCIS had been "snubbed," as he put it, by the FBI. No NCIS agents were included in the Seattle raid.

"Hell of note," he said disgustedly to his deputy Dennis Moore. "We uncover the plot and the FBI gets all the glory."

"As I understand," Dennis said, "one of *them* was shot. Maybe we don't want that kind of glory."

"I know, I know. We don't want anyone to get shot, but we should have been included, damn it!"

Dennis shook his head and tipped the wooden visitor's chair back against the wall. "Not our jurisdiction."

"Why not? In for a penny, in for a pound."

"I agree. I wanted to be in on the raid. But honestly, we didn't bust this case. Just helped. Our cowboy sheriff provided the linchpin evidence."

Madeline Page knocked and pushed the door open. She handed a file folder to Thompson and said, "I have a bulletin for you regarding Detective Grandfield's funeral. It's set for tomorrow afternoon."

"Damned shame," Thompson said. He leaned forward and placed his elbows on the desk. "I hate funerals, Dennis, but you and I will be there. Right?"

"I wouldn't miss it," Dennis said dryly.

"Madeline, order up a big funeral wreath, lots of flowers. And I want a card that reads, 'Greater love hath no man'."

"You want the whole quote?"

"No...I think that's the gist of it," Thompson said. "And then get in touch with Mrs. Grandfield. Tell her we'd be honored if she would ride with us to the service. I'll lay on my wife's limo." He stopped. "No, don't do that. I'll call Chief Homer first."

Madeline nodded and then turned and walked through the door before the two men could see the empathetic tears that flooded her eyes.

"Well, Dennis, don't just sit there. Go find this Bloodstone asshole Cowboy wrote about." He didn't say, "And kill him," but he might just as well have.

Chapter 35

Trooper Swanson and Sheriff Blair decided to send Cal Redmond to state police headquarters in Salem. They reasoned that since they didn't know whom to trust among Cal's officers, and since they didn't have time to sort the good guys from the bad, it would be safer if Cal simply disappeared into a holding cell for a day or two.

Bud watched as Trooper George Brett expertly frisked and repositioned Cal's handcuffs. Just before Brett stuffed the lanky Cal in behind the cage of the cruiser, Bud said, "Cal. One more question. Did Cowboy work for you?"

Cal paused for a few seconds, evaluating the implications of the question and then shook his head. "No. He worked for Bloodstone...I think."

Bud pointed at the dead woman. "What about her?"

Cal's stomach bile rose in his throat and he swallowed it back down. He nodded.

"Say it, Cal. Say it out loud. Say, 'She worked for me.'"

Cal swallowed again and said, "No. They worked for Bloodstone. I only supplied the information."

"But you knew they were told to kill me."

Cal swore and said, "What do you want from me, Bud? Sure I knew it, damn it. But I hoped you would survive."

"Bullshit. You hoped they would kill me. Then you would kill them and look like a hero. That's why you came out here, isn't it?"

Cal refused to speak.

Bud looked at Trooper Brett and said in disgust, "Get him out of here before I change my mind and shoot the son-of-a-bitch."

Swanson and Bud watched as the cruiser backed down the road to a wide spot and then turned around. Bud walked to his water bottle, carried it to the log and sat down. He took a long drink from the bottle and unwrapped a power bar. Swanson sat down next to him. Bud looked at Swanson and stared back down the road at the drifting cloud of dust. "He any good?"

Swanson grimaced. "A little green yet, but he'll do."

"I'm glad he didn't shoot me."

Swanson smiled and said, "Me too. Okay, I've laid on a state police ship…a Bell to give us 'eyes' in the sky, and if they can find a suitable opening, possible extraction." He looked at the dead woman. "Our forensics team from Bend will be here shortly. We'll need to open the road when they get here."

Bud pointed to the small chainsaw sitting on the stump. "Can you run a saw?"

Swanson snorted. "I grew up in Prineville," like that was all the answer needed. "When's your tracker getting here?"

Bud glanced at his watch. "They should be here any minute."

Swanson nodded and then asked, "Who is Bobcat Larson?"

Bud shook his head and grinned. "A retired government trapper. A real character. Straight out of a mountain man novel. Bobcat claims he can track a trout in a flash flood. And my deputy, Roger Hildebrand says Bobcat is damned near that good."

The sound of a diesel engine echoed through the timber and then Roger's big crew cab pickup rounded the curve and stopped a hundred feet short of the woman's body.

A thin man in worn blue jeans, a green plaid cotton shirt and homemade moccasins, a flat-brimmed leather hat perched on his head, slid down from the cab and walked carefully up the ditch. He studied the woman from a short distance and then walked to where Bud sat on the log. "You sure done 'er, Sheriff. Double-ought buck?"

Bud nodded. "And now we need to catch her partner."

Bobcat looked at the bloody bandage on Bud's left arm, but didn't say anything.

Roger, Bobcat, and Bud left Trooper Swanson standing by his cruiser, door open, talking via radio to a helicopter that came roaring overhead, following the road. Bud led them to the red flagging and pointed out through the timber. Bobcat studied scattered blood drops and motioned Roger to his right and Bud to his left. "Keep your eyes peeled," he said almost in a whisper. "This varmint might try and circle back...take a shot at us."

The tracks led almost due west. The ground rose gently for the first mile, gaining elevation. Bobcat followed the blood trail and then found where the man had stopped and sat on an old stump. "Took care of his wound," Bobcat said to himself.

Bobcat motioned Bud and Roger over. "He's gonna stiffen up, just like a crippled animal. So I figure he'll have to find someplace to keg up. How long ago did you shoot this guy?"

Bud looked at his watch, surprised at how much time had passed since he first spotted the ambush. "Maybe an hour and a half back," he whispered to Bobcat.

Without saying anything, Bobcat nodded and pointed them back out on the flanks.

Thirty minutes later he motioned them over and pointed across a scab rock flat. "There's your varmint," he said.

Bud later figured those five short minutes would be etched in his memory forever: Roger's incredible two hundred and fifty-yard shot at a hungry cougar eyeballing Bobcat's varmint as a possibility for supper; the man screaming in terror when the big cat landed on his wounded legs; Bobcat's victory jig; the "varmint" panicking, holding down the trigger on his machine pistol, shooting big .45 caliber slugs into the dead cat until the magazine was empty.

Bud told Bobcat to hold back while they finished the capture. Out of bullets and unable to run away or shoot at them, the man simply sat on the pine needle duff, back against the bluff and waited while they walked across the sage covered flat.

Roger told the man to put his hands behind his back and then snapped the cuffs tight around his wrists.

Bud waved Bobcat over and then glared at his prisoner. "Call in the chopper, Roger. Let's get this piece of shit out of here."

"Aren't you gonna fix my wounds?" the man whined and looked at his bloody legs.

Bud's eyes narrowed and he growled, "Shut up, asshole, or I'll shoot you again."

THE BELL WHOP-WHOPPED OVER THE TREES, hovered, and slowly settled on its landing gear, peppering the men on the ground with bits of sagebrush, small rocks, and dust. Roger helped load the wounded killer in the helicopter, pushed Bud up and through the door, and then motioned that he and Bobcat would hoof it back to the vehicles. Bud thought he heard Roger shout, "See you at Saint Charles," before an armed trooper pulled the passenger door shut.

Two state police troopers met the helicopter at the Saint Charles Hospital heliport. They unlocked the handcuffs, waited until the EMTs had the wounded man on a gurney, and then cuffed each of his wrists to the rails. One followed the gurney through the entrance to the ER. The other offered Bud his hand and helped him step down to the asphalt. "You need a wheelchair?" he asked.

Bud took deep breath and then smiled. "Nope. I can make it." He stopped, looked around and almost smiled as the sun slid behind the edge of a towering, anvil-shaped thunder head perched on the Cascades. The sun set the clouds on fire with the deep purple, red, and yellow hues that constantly lured photographers to the high desert.

Bud said to the pilot, "Great day to be alive, isn't it?"

Chapter 36

NANCY'S CALL CAUGHT SONNY PULLING THE long grade out of Grass Valley on Highway 97 north of Madras. He managed to say, "Sonny" before the connection faded. "Crap," he grumbled. He toggled the overdrive button on the gear shift and punched the accelerator. The big V-8 in the SC 400 Lexus sucked him back in the seat in spite of the six percent uphill grade.

Some residents of Lake County thought it was suspicious to see an underpaid deputy sheriff driving a Lexus. What they didn't know was the car was a 1992 model that had 150,000 miles on it, or that he had paid $5,500 for it from a generous neighbor. The neighbor brought home a new Lexus, knocked on Sonny's door and said he would rather see Sonny driving the old one than trade it to the Lexus dealer.

Sonny had initially declined the offer to buy it, but the neighbor persuaded him to drive it anyway. He test drove the car north to Valley Falls and back, and when he pulled into his driveway, he had a big grin on his face. He handed the keys to the owner and asked, "How much?"

In truth, the Kelly Bluebook wholesale price was right at the asking price. Sonny talked it over with Bud and Bud had asked, "If you came driving into town in a big 4x4 pickup, would anyone give it a second thought?"

Sonny laughed and said, "Of course not."

"Then the only question is one of appearance. Why don't you get a vanity plate with '1992' on it and have some fun?"

That had been last spring right after the William Casey manhunt. And he did have fun with the Lexus. He and Asa Conner's daughter,

Carol, had driven the ninety-seven miles to Klamath Falls several times to do some shopping, have dinner, take in a movie, and then dodge the mule deer back to Lakeview. Carol had been sworn to secrecy about a seventy-minute return trip late one night.

He used the passing lane to scoot around two hay trucks that were grinding up the grade, moved to the right hand lane and let off a little for a gentle bend and then pushed his speed back to eight-five on the short straightaway just before the rest stop at the top. Sonny hit his brakes as a black and brown state cruiser emerged from the exit to the rest stop. The light rack pulsed blue and red two seconds later.

Sonny pulled onto a wide shoulder of the road, powered the driver's window down, and put both hands on top of the steering wheel.

The officer had his ticket book in hand when he stepped out of the cruiser and walked up to the passenger side of the Lexus. Sonny powered the passenger window down and tried to look composed—not exactly how he felt—just how he thought he should look.

The officer leaned down and said, "You know why I pulled you over?"

Sonny nodded. "Because I was speeding."

"That's right. You were speeding."

"Did you clock me?"

"No. That's why I'm citing you for violation of the basic rule. I'd like to see your driver's license and registration, please."

Sonny pulled his driver's license and his "carry permit" from his wallet and handed it to the state trooper. He said, "I'm licensed for a concealed hand gun. It's in the console along with the registration."

"Sit here. Keep your hands on the steering wheel," the trooper ordered, and then walked back to his cruiser and closed the door.

Sonny vacillated between anger at having been stopped—*caught*, he thought to himself, and at his own stupidity. The hay trucks he passed ground their way up the grade and Sonny could hear the gears shifting as they accelerated on top and then passed his parked car. One trucker gave him an air horn blast and leaned over so Sonny could see his middle finger salute.

It was a long five minutes before the tall, lanky trooper got out of his police car and walked back to the Sonny's Lexus. He handed Sonny's his license and concealed weapons permit, leaned in the window and asked, "Are you the same Sonny Sixkiller involved in busting up that terrorist operation in Christmas Valley?"

Sonny nodded. "One and the same."

"That Sixkiller got hurt, didn't he?"

Sonny took off his Lake County HS Honkers cap and pointed to a bald strip on the top of his head that sported a neat row of stitches, twenty in all.

The trooper shook his head. "Wow. I'll bet that hurt. You guys did a hell of a job on that one. I read the after-action report. Now... what's the hurry?"

Sonny's cell phone range, but he ignored it. "I needed to get to an area where my cell phone would work. My mother had a stroke, and I'm on my way to Yakima to see her."

"And I'm holding you up." Trooper Briggs looked thoughtful. "Tell you what: you take your call. I'm going to give you a warning, and then I'm going to break trail for you to Biggs Junction." He eyeballed the Lexus and added, "If you can keep up."

"I'll try."

Sonny returned Nancy's call. "Sorry 'bout that. I lost the signal."

"Where are you?" she asked.

"Well, I'm sitting on the side of the road a few miles shy of Shaniko with a state police cruiser parked right behind me.

He heard Nancy laugh and say, "I told you that Lexus was going to get you in trouble."

"Actually, I'm enjoying a degree of fame. I'm not getting a ticket, and a nice officer is going to provide a fast moving escort to Biggs Junction. Where are you?"

"I'm just about to Paisley. How did your hearing go?"

"Well, it was a bit strange, but Roger and I have been cleared. We can go back to work." He paused and then said, "You take your time getting to Yakima. If you want to be late for something, have a wreck. That'll slow you down."

"It sounds like you're the one who should be careful. See you in Yakima."

The trip to Biggs Junction was fast and smooth at a steady 80 miles per hour. Sonny pulled into the AM PM Mini Mart in Biggs Junction to gas up.

Trooper Briggs walked over, a big grin on his face, and Sonny shook his hand. "Thanks," Sonny said.

Briggs grinned. "Most fun I've had in a month of Sundays. Take care, you hear?"

Sonny waved as Briggs's cruiser pulled onto the highway and headed south back toward Shaniko. After a quick run to the restroom, Sonny collected the credit card receipt and drove to the Washington side of the Columbia. A black and white Crown Victoria pulled along side the Lexus and a State of Washington trooper signaled Sonny to follow. Sonny gave him a thumbs-up. The Crown Vic accelerated and pulled ahead of the Lexus, emergency lights flashing.

The brotherhood was taking care of its own.

Chapter 37

John eased Bud's battered, bullet-scarred pickup into the parking lot of the Christmas Valley lodge. He wheeled the vehicle around and then backed up to the short rail that marked the boundary between gravel and shrubs.

A small red GMC pickup followed him into the parking lot and stopped a few feet away. An older man wearing a straw cowboy hat, blue jeans, and tennis shoes jumped out and stared for a few seconds. He walked over and ran his fingers over a bullet hole in the passenger door.

John recognized him as a local, but couldn't put a name with the face.

The man said, "Saw you coming through town," by way of explanation. "What the hell happened to the sheriff's pickup? Is he all right?"

John nodded. "He was in a gun fight, but he'll be okay."

"Is he hurt?"

"Not too bad."

"Damned big holes in the sides here. Large caliber. They must have ambushed him."

John nodded.

The man started edging away, suddenly suspicious. "Why are you driving the sheriff's pickup?"

From the open door of the Lodge, Larae said, "It's okay, Dusty. He's one of ours."

Dusty. Now I remember. Owns the place with the Airedales. John smiled at the memory of two wire-haired dogs racing down the pasture fence, barking, trying to outrun any vehicles that drove the highway. Over several years, the dogs had pounded a rut into the pasture just inside the fence. When they reached the end of the pasture, they stopped, barked once or twice and trotted back to the house, proud as punch.

Dusty looked skeptical, but the fact that Larae was in uniform persuaded him to hold his peace. "Okay. If you say so."

"MacNabb" had been handcuffed to a chair and Wally was sitting in another chair about ten feet away, a shotgun across his lap. Wally grinned when John raised his eyebrows and looked pointedly at the weapon. "Citizens arrest."

Larae stood watch while John emptied the imposter's pockets, removed his belt, stripped off his boots and placed them in a big plastic bag. Using the restraints from Bud's pickup, the prisoner was secured with leg and waist chains.

He looked at Larae and asked, "We ready to go? Bud said to take him to Lakeview. Lock him up there."

"Let's do it."

By the time they helped the mystery man shuffle his way to the pickup, a dozen residents had gathered to watch the drama. And they wanted to know what was going on.

The sheriff's pickup was full of bullet holes. The windshield was starred where a bullet had punched a hole. A Lake County deputy had a Deschutes County "deputy" under arrest. And Gar, their local bottle-and-cans man was helping Deputy Holcomb load the Deschutes "deputy" into the battle scarred pickup.

A middle-aged woman walked over before Larae could hoist herself into the passenger seat.

"Officer, I'm Nadine Caldwell. I'm the North County correspondent for the *Lake-view News*. Can you tell me what's happening?"

Larae, whose training in public relations was stale as last year's news, thought for a few short seconds, and then Rule Number One popped into mind: Never talk to the press.

Larae shook her head. "I'm sorry, but this is part of an ongoing investigation. I'm sure the sheriff will have a statement for the press when the investigation is complete."

"Is he part of the terrorist ring?" Nadine pointed at MacNabb who was locked behind the Plexiglas that divided prisoners from the police.

"I'm not at liberty to say. I'm sorry, Ms. Caldwell, but we have to get going."

Larae turned and plopped her butt in the passenger seat and shut the pickup door.

John didn't say anything until they were headed north to Highway 30. "You do realize she'll call the paper and report what she saw. That's news even if the 'why' part is missing. Think about it."

"What would you have me say?"

"Nothing at all. If you aren't going to talk to the press, either say nothing at all, or if you're cornered, just say 'no comment.' That's more insulting to the press than silence."

"And you're an expert?"

"Right. I just stare them down and say nothing."

John pushed the vehicle to seventy-five miles an hour. The result was a loud snap and a new crack that ran from the bullet hole to the lower right corner of the windshield. "Uh oh," John said and slowed the pickup to sixty. "I hope the windshield doesn't blow out."

The trip lasted nearly two-and-a-half hours. MacNabb complained about being claustrophobic, and kept whining, "Can't you give me some air back here?"

When he said he had to piss, Larae turned and shouted over the wind whistling through the windshield, "Go ahead."

Carol Connor, assistant editor of the *Lake County News* was standing on the sidewalk when they pulled into the station. She didn't ask questions, just snapped pictures of the war-wracked pickup, and of Larae and John escorting "MacNabb" through the door to the sheriff's office. She scanned the images in her digital camera. When she found the one of the bullet holes in Bud's pickup, she thought, *Yes, that'll make a dandy front-page photo.*

Karen Highsmith booked MacNabb while District Attorney Howard Finch hovered behind her, his tie askew, blond hair looking like it had last been used for a mop. At Howard's insistence, the list of charges included "Public Indecency."

Temporary Deputy Sheriff Lonnie Beltram and Acting Undersheriff Michelle Trivoli placed their pistols in a lock box near the cell block door and pushed MacNabb into a cell. He grumbled about wanting to call his lawyer, but they ignored him and took the restraints off his wrists and ankles. Beltram was disappointed when he didn't fight them. Karen locked the cell door and they retreated back down the hallway.

Michelle and Lonnie retrieved their pistols and walked back up front. They were surprised to find Carol Connor chatting with Howard in Bud's office. Howard was sitting behind Bud's desk, Carol in a visitor's chair. John Bernard and Larae Holcomb were leaning against the wall, arms crossed, staring daggers at both Howard and Carol.

Michelle took charge and said, "Let's move this to the conference room."

Karen Highsmith walked outside and joined a group of Lakeview citizens staring at Bud's damaged pickup. A number of them were aiming digital cameras, snapping pictures of bullet holes and damaged windows. The owner of the Coffee Pot, a woman Karen knew as Betsy—"Bet" to her friends—said, "Karen, what in the world happened? Where's the sheriff?

Karen nodded to herself and thought, *If the newspaper can hear the news, then I guess I can tell a few friends.* And so she told them what she knew. Within the hour, pictures and homegrown stories about the great adventures of Sheriff Blair were streaming through cyberspace.

"OKAY," HOWARD SAID WHEN THEY WERE all seated, "I asked Carol to join us. She already knows Bud was wounded. And she knows you arrested someone posing as MacNabb. Her North County reporter sent her a heads-up and some photos via the Internet. So, I think facts are better than speculation. As the chief law enforcement officer for Lake County, I'm asking you," he pointed at Larae and then John, "to brief us on what's been happening."

Larae muttered, "So much for rule number one."

There was a knock and Judge Lynch poked his head around the door. "Am I late?"

John nudged Larae and whispered, "Who's he?"

"I don't know," she whispered back.

"Come on in, Judge," Michelle said. "We haven't started yet. Let me introduce you to Officer Beltram, who is filling in until Roger and Sonny return to duty. And this is John Bernard, and Officer Larae Holcomb."

"Ah," Lynch said, "our undercover agent in Christmas Valley." He walked to Larae and offered his hand. "How's the ankle?"

Larae started rise, but Lynch said, "Don't get up. It's okay." She couldn't help it—she was charmed by the sincere warmth of the silver haired rancher turned county judge.

She said, "I'm healing up."

Lynch offered his hand to John and asked, "How do you fit in all this?"

"I'm an NCIS agent tracking an AWOL sailor." Which wasn't exactly true, but the real reason was too complex to explain quickly. And John wasn't exactly sure he had any legal standing anyway.

"Well, welcome to Lake County." He turned to Carol. "How's your dad doing? I hear rumors he had prostate surgery."

Carol nodded and said, "Yes. He called and said he was doing just fine."

Howard watched Lynch and was once again amazed at the man's memory. But Howard knew Lynch was genuine. He really did like and care about the people of Lake County.

Howard cleared his throat and waited until the Judge was seated. He reached out and pushed a small digital recorder into the center of the table. "Do you mind if I record this?"

Larae looked disgusted. "Yes. I do object. I won't talk to the press. We're in the middle of an ongoing investigation. And that's all I'm going to say."

Michelle spoke up and said, "And I don't think you'd pull this kind of stunt, Howard, if Bud was here. So as Lake County undersheriff, and the interim sheriff until he gets back, this interview is over. We'll issue a press release within the hour."

Judge Lynch laughed, and then looked at Howard. "You know she's right." He stood and looked at District Attorney Finch. "Are you coming, Howard? Let's let these young people do their jobs."

Carol Connor was fuming, but she was too professional to let it show.

Michelle softened and said, "Carol, I know Bud and your father work together. How about you and I do the same?"

Carol shook her head in disgust. She didn't swear, but then she didn't have to. "I can write that," she said disgustedly. "You don't need to send me a formal press release."

Michelle nodded and then said, "But we will issue a general press release, and send a copy to the *Lake County News*. It's protocol."

Carol didn't say anything. She just closed her note pad and left the room.

Judge Lynch said, "You didn't make any friends there, Sheriff Trivoli."

"I know. Now if you two," she pointed at Howard and Judge Lynch, "want to stay. I'll ask John and Larae to brief us."

Larae said to no one in particular, "Rule number one rules the day."

Chapter 38

DELL BEBE HAD BEEN FURIOUS WHEN Dutch ordered him back to Portland. "I've got work for you to do," Dutch said, "so get on the plane."

"I need to watch Bud's back," BB argued.

"He has his officers and that NCIS fellow to do that. I need you to babysit Cletus."

Two hours later, BB was home. An hour after that the same two burly agents who had picked him up in the first place escorted Cletus to BB's apartment.

BB opened the door and said, "Hey, little buddy, how you doing?"

Cletus didn't say anything until BB had thanked the agents and closed the door.

Cletus looked at the apartment and said, "So this is how the big time detective lives. Not bad, my man, not bad." And then tears started pooling in his eyes.

BB wrapped his big arms around Cletus and patted his back, like a father trying to comfort a child.

"It'll be all right, Cletus. The bad guys will never know."

Cletus sniffed and pushed himself out of BB's arms. "Yeah, I know. But I'm still scared."

He walked across the room to the gas fireplace and studied the photo of Brian Dell BeBe, Marine. "He looks like he be having more fun than me. Where is he?"

BB said, "Iraq."

Cletus turned and stared at BB for a good five seconds before asking, "You worry for him?"

BB nodded. "Just like I worry for you."

Cletus shook his head and then tried for the old Cletus swagger. "You should see this foxy chick I met at the FBI place. Man, I changed my mind. Don't wanna be a big city detective. I'm gonna be an FBI man."

BB smiled and shook his head. "Next you'll want to be a cowboy or a fireman."

"Hey...don't you be making fun of Cletus. I can't help it if I see career opportunities other people miss. 'Sides, I think I'd better just stick to the import-export business. This information stuff is getting too heavy."

"So the FBI is on to your scam, huh?"

Cletus shrugged. "I have been 'advised' to...what's the word? To limit...yeah, that's the word...to limit my information business to the FBI and the Portland city police. That's you. I was also informed that," and he deepened his voice and got a stern look on his face, "you will not 'inform' other federal, state or county or city people. Just the FBI."

BB grinned. "Caught up with you didn't they."

"Puts me out of business, I guess."

BB said, "You hungry?"

Cletus nodded in the direction of the kitchen. "You cook?"

BB shook his head. "Nope. Just coffee and donuts."

On the ride down the elevator to the parking garage, Cletus asked, "How long you gonna keep me? I got business to take care of."

"If everything goes right, I'd say just until this afternoon." BB stepped into the garage and said, "You go to church, Cletus?"

"No way, man."

BB nodded. "I thought so." He pointed in the direction of his classic red Corvette and said, "Get in. Let's take a little ride. I want you to meet a good friend of mine, the Right Reverend T. J. Wildish."

Chapter 39

AMANDA SPEARS WAS SITTING AT HER desk in Springdale, staring vacantly at a blank computer monitor, not really working on anything. She had just read a copy of Special Agent Tobias Warren's letter of resignation. It was full of recriminations and accusations that his senior partner was "a loose cannon," "failed to follow Homeland Security direction," etcetera, etcetera...and that he could no longer in good conscience work for NCIS.

Her first thought was, Up yours, Toby. Her second thought was Toby's father, Montana's Congressman Warren would raise hell with NCIS generally and with her in particular. Even if there wasn't a word of truth in Toby's letter.

She wadded the letter up and dropped it in her wastebasket. "I don't need this bullshit right now," she grumbled.

"Don't need what?" Abe asked as he slid into a neighboring desk chair.

"Toby resigned. Called me incompetent, a loose canon. Implied I'm a rogue agent. Hell, I don't need this."

"Good riddance," Abe said. And then he asked, "Did you hear about your buddy Sheriff Blair down in Lake County? The word's out that he got himself shot in a gun battle."

"How bad?"

"Don't know," Abe answered.

Amanda scrolled through her cell phone list and pushed the Call button for the Lake County sheriff's office.

Karen Highsmith answered Amanda's call with a testy "Lake County Sheriff's Office."

"This is NCIS Agent Spears. Do you remember me?"

"Yes, and if this is about Bud, all I can tell you is that Bud is being treated for a non-life threatening gunshot wound at Saint Charles Hospital in Bend. That's all we know right now. Why don't you call back tomorrow?"

The news put Amanda in a blue funk. That Bill Thompson could even suspect her of betrayal was beyond belief. Add the murder of Detective Grandfield, the injury to Gino Maretti, the shooting of her favorite sheriff, and the resignation of her junior partner and she was almost overwhelmed by the futility of it all.

"I can't retire," she muttered to Abe, "but maybe a quiet police department out in the boonies would be a nice change."

Abe smiled and then said, "Yeah, maybe in Lake County."

She laughed, "Yeah…someplace like that." She was quiet for a few second and then said, "Hell, why do we risk our necks? Drug lords become billionaires, their mules pass back and forth through our southern border like it wasn't even there, and we don't do a damned thing about it."

Her desk phone rang and she picked up the receiver. "Spears."

Moore said, "Amanda, Agent Payne just called. The FBI found the U-Haul that moved Pettibone's records, and they found the driver and his helpers. They appear to be clean…just day workers. But they took the FBI to Pettibone's storage unit. They got a search warrant and broke in. Found a lot of Pettibone's records. Payne said the records are a gold mine."

Amanda was suddenly energized, her sour mood swept away by the news. "Wow! Nice work. What did they find?"

"Well," Moore went on, "they identified a Seattle drug lord who goes by the code name Bloodstone. Pettibone must have been doing some digging on his own. Anyway, the FBI found an address for Bloodstone…on Bainbridge Island."

"Terrific!" Amanda said.

"It gets better. Bloodstone is former Congressman Kevin Ross."

"The guy who was caught feeding cocaine to his young female aides?"

"That's the one. Remember? His daddy got him probation in exchange for a resignation? Anybody else would have gone to jail. Anyway, to get back on track, the FBI plans to hit his place within the hour. And, Amanda, NCIS's anti-terrorist team is invited to the party. They rendezvous here in thirty minutes."

Abe recognized the gleam in Amanda's eyes when she said, "Gather the team, Abe. We get to arrest former Congressman Kevin Ross."

AN ENTHUSED DAN WITHERSPOON INSTRUCTED HIS NCIS Silverdale analysis section to find the closest cell tower to Bloodstone's address. "Denny told me the FBI has identified this guy as former Congressman Kevin Ross. We are to monitor any calls from that location...outgoing or incoming...cell or land line. Keywords to scan for: Bloodstone, Ortega, Pettibone, Blair, Sheriff, Lake County, and all of the usual triggers relating to drugs and terrorists. You know the drill."

Twenty minutes later, just as Witherspoon was lighting a cigarette out in "the garden" as he euphemistically called the open-air smoking patio, Kathryn, his number two, jerked the door open and said, "You'll want to see this, Dan."

Two minutes later, Witherspoon called Dennis Moore. "We got something really hot."

Moore didn't ask what, just said, "Meet me in the SAC's office."

THE MEETING BETWEEN THE FBI, NCIS and the Coast Guard didn't go as planned. The report of a phone call between Bloodstone and Raul Ortega delayed the raid.

Agent Payne held a sheet of printer paper in his raised right hand. "So, what this tells us," he said to the twenty or so people crowding the conference room at NCIS Springdale, "is Kevin Ross, aka Bloodstone claims to have captured the sheriff of Lake County and is inviting Ortega to, quote, handle it personally, end-quote."

"Is that true? Do they actually have the sheriff?" Bambi asked.

"No, but Bloodstone believes one of his minions will deliver Blair to Bainbridge Island early tomorrow morning."

He picked up a second printer copy and held it aloft. "And this is a text message intercepted by our good friends here at NCIS." He walked to a white board mounted on the wall, and picked up a red marker. He wrote, "C U 2MRO."

"Do we know that's from Ortega?"

"No," Hoosier said, "but we do know it is from the fine state of Sonora, Mexico. And according to DEA and AFT and CIA and NSA and the Lord knows who else, that's where Ortega hangs his hat."

Dudley, always one for quick action asked, "Why not go now? We take down Bloodstone and then wait for Ortega to show up. Bloodstone might do a runner on us otherwise."

"We'll plan the takedown, then stake out Bloodstone's house and wait. D.C. says the risk of losing Bloodstone is out-weighed by the chance to take Ortega. We already have watchers on the way."

Bambi snorted, "Yeah…and they'll stick out like sore thumbs. No offense, but no matter how you guys try to blend in, you still look like FBI agents. You just can't help it."

He looked at Bambi's jogging outfit, noted her trim runner's build, the short cropped hair, and had to admit she might be right. "Suggestions?"

Bambi pointed to Dudley's ponytail and earring and said, "Me, Dudley Do-Right and Abe. We know the Island, and we don't look like cops."

At dusk Abe, Bambi and Dudley parked Dudley's small pickup in the driveway of a vacant summer house that was screened from the road by a thicket of shore pine. Abe backed the pickup into the driveway, nose out, ready to roll. Bambi and Dudley settled in to watch the only street into Bloodstone's house.

Bambi poured coffee from a thermos and handed Dudley a steaming travel mug. "You want some, Abe?"

"No," he said. "I think I'll take a look around."

He geared up, slipped a whisper mike in place, stuffed night vision binoculars into a ruck sack and said, "Thirty minutes."

He stepped silently around the back of the dark house and found what he was looking for—a rough path that paralleled the shoreline.

Abe had been gone twenty minutes before Dudley said, "Uh-oh. Here comes trouble." He pointed to a private security sedan coming up the street.

"Well, let's move in then," she said. She hopped out of the vehicle, grabbed a duffel bag from the bed of the pickup and walked up the front steps of the house. The security light over the front door lit up and she pretended to search her pockets for the key to the door.

An older man stopped the car in front of Dudley's pickup. He stepped out using the car door as a barricade. "What are you doing here?"

Dudley slowly uncoiled from behind the wheel of the pickup and stepped out. "The Hamptons," he said, using the name on the roadside mailbox, "said we could use the house for a couple of days while they're gone."

Her back to the driveway, blocking sight of the door, Bambi worked furiously with a lock pick, cussing under her breath, until the lock clicked quietly into place. She exhaled slowly, picked up the duffel bag, opened the door and flipped the foyer lights on. "You coming?" she said to Dudley.

"Well, I guess you're okay. The Hamptons let family stay sometimes, but they always let us know ahead of time. Guess they forgot."

"Thanks for being so conscientious, officer," Dudley said. "We know you have a tough job keeping an eye on things."

The older man nodded, a hint of suspicion lurking in his eyes, and then he said, "You have a good time." He backed out of the driveway and turned around. Dudley noted that he did not drive in the direction of Bloodstone's house.

Chapter 40

Bud was in the Saint Charles ER for two hours. Although John Bernard had dismissed the injury simply as "a good Purple Heart wound," the young ER doctor had insisted on an x-ray of the left arm. "The bullet was pretty close to the bone," was all the explanation she offered.

While they waited for the x-ray results, Bud asked Roger to find a Wal-Mart or a Freddie's and buy him a shirt and a pair of pants, some clean socks, and new underwear. "These seem to be a bit bloody."

Roger sailed out through the curtain and Bud watched the IV drip feed the tube leading to the back of his right hand.

"Gotta stay out of these places," he grumbled.

An RN bearing a clip board wanted to know the date of his last tetanus shot. He couldn't remember. The RN returned a few minutes later with a syringe. "This is good for ten years," the nurse said and jabbed the needle in Bud's right arm.

"On a scale of one to ten, how would you rate the pain from your wound?"

Bud told him, "About a six, I guess."

The RN handed Bud two pills in a paper cup and water in a second paper cup. "Take these."

"I can handle it," Bud growled.

"Yeah, but why bother? Take the pills."

Roger returned with a Wal-Mart bag in time to watch the MD suture the wound, pad it with a neat wrap-around bandage, and place a nifty blue sling around Bud's neck. The doctor asked, "You fish?"

Bud nodded, and she slipped the suture clamp in a baggie and handed it to him. "My dad uses these to take hooks out of his fish. Besides, we throw them away, and this pair cost you about a hundred dollars." She also handed him two prescriptions, one for an antibiotic and one for pain relief.

"You check in with your doctor when you get back to Lakeview," she said. She turned blue eyes on Roger. "I know these tough guys. They won't take care of themselves. He needs to rest that arm for a few days. You make sure he does."

Roger grinned. "Yes Ma'am, I surely will."

Bud offered his hand to the doctor and said, "Thanks. You folks run a first class operation. Don't mean to be a grump."

The doctor smiled at the rough-looking sheriff. "You didn't even come close to winning the prize. And I suspect a gunshot wound would make me grumpy myself." She shut off the IV drip, pulled the stint and slapped an adhesive strip over the pinprick.

"Are you responsible for our other gunshot victim?"

"If you mean, did I shoot him, the answer is yes."

"Was it necessary?"

"Yes, yes it was. How's he doing? I need to question him."

"I think he's out of surgery and in recovery."

An RN pulled the curtain back and stuck her head into the room. "Doctor, you're needed in Room 16."

Bud said to Roger, "Get out of here while I change."

Five minutes later, Bud emerged wearing a new denim shirt and blue jeans. Most people would never identify the dark spots on his boots as dried blood. He spotted a nurse and held out a bundle made from his bloody pants and shirt. "Where can I dispose of these?" he asked.

BUD AND ROGER RODE THE ELEVATOR to the third floor. They spotted the hospital sign with a list of room numbers and an arrow pointing left.

Trooper Swanson was sitting in a chair in front of the last room in the hallway, eyeing the elevator door, alert for intruders. Bud nodded in appreciation at the shotgun Swanson held across his lap, muzzle pointed away from the throng of busy nurses and meal carts.

"That must be it," Roger said.

Swanson eyed Roger's uniform and Bud's nifty, blue sling. "Here to question my prisoner, I suppose," he said when they walked up.

"Yes, we are," Roger said.

Bud said, "This is Officer Hildebrand."

Swanson nodded at Roger, but didn't offer to shake hands. He looked at Bud's sling and asked, "How's the arm?"

Bud glanced down at the sling and shook his head. "I've had better days, but I'll survive. How's my prisoner?"

Roger caught the proprietary emphasis of "my prisoner," and stuffed a smile. Bud's still on the prod, he thought.

ALL THEY LEARNED FROM THE WOUNDED man handcuffed to the hospital bed was his name: Allen Pinkerton, the name of his lawyer: Jerome Bradshaw, and the name of his business: Central Oregon Yards and More.

"I won't answer any questions until my lawyer gets here," Pinkerton huffed.

"You do realize," Bud said, "you're being charged with murder, attempted murder and assault on a police officer. And you are being investigated as an accomplice in a terrorist plot. That'll get you the federal needle. Give us some answers and you might get a life sentence instead."

"You killed Aimee," he snarled at Bud. "I'll get you for that."

"No," Bud said, "you'll get the needle first."

"I'm not saying another word until my lawyer gets here."

"Good enough," Bud answered. "I've got all I need anyway." He looked at Roger and said, "Let's get out of here."

BUD WOKE WHEN ROGER'S PICKUP SLOWED for the short stretch of road through the little town of Paisley. His mouth was dry, he was hungry, and his arm was starting to throb. In the east, an autumn moon was riding the night sky over the black bulk of Abert Rim.

"Musta nodded off," he said to Roger.

Roger stifled a yawn and said, "You been out for over an hour. I think you need some rest."

"Maybe we all need some rest."

"Yes. It's been a rough couple of weeks," Roger said. "You know Boss, I've been thinking. Do you know how hard it is to spend illegal cash? You can't really buy anything big with it. All you can do is make small cash purchases. And you can't run it through a bank account. Big sums attract attention.

"So I got to thinking about Pinkerton's landscape business. A lot of that work is paid in cash. And you can simply make up customer orders. It might be a good way to launder some money."

Bud nodded. "Yeah, it could be. The FBI might want to take a look at Pinkerton's business records. I'll call Dutch in the morning."

Forty minutes later, Roger pulled into Bud's driveway. "Call me when you want me to pick you up. I'll stay in town tonight. But you sleep in before you call me." He handed Bud a duffle bag. "Your gear...equipment belt, weapon, ID, back-up...it's all there. Oh, and I turned your cell phone off so you could sleep. You might want to check for messages."

Bud slid out of the passenger seat and said, "See you in the morning." He set the duffle on the gravel of the driveway and slammed the pickup door. He could hear Molly bark from the back yard as Roger drove out of the gravel driveway and headed for town.

The security light flooded the back yard when he opened the gate. Molly pointed her nose at his wounded arm and whined while she tried to beat him to death with her tail. He closed the gate and said, "I'm okay, old gal. I'll bet you could use something to eat."

He opened the metal cabinet that stood sentry by the back door and dumped a scoop of dry food in her dish. She looked at him to see if it was okay to eat. He scratched her behind the ears and gave her a weary smile. "Go for it," he said.

Molly was crunching and scattering dry dog food on the back porch when he closed the door and headed for his living room. He dumped the duffle alongside his recliner and clicked on his reading lamp. He eased into his recliner and then pulled the duffel closer to the chair.

He reached over and unzipped the bag, digging for his cell phone. In a few seconds the phone booted up and posted a message. He had six voice messages. He skipped the messages and hit the speed dial for Nancy's cell.

When she answered, he said, "You still up?"

"Yes. Roger called Sonny. Are you okay?"

"Well, let me see. All my parts are intact, so I guess you could say I'm 'right as rain,' or 'fit as a fiddle.'"

"I'm serious, Bud," she barked. "How badly are you hurt?"

"A bullet cut a groove in the meaty part of my left shoulder...on the outside of the arm. A pretty young doctor stitched it up and sent me on my way."

"You're not in the hospital?"

"No, I'm home. On a more important topic, how's your mother?"

The catch in her voice told him she was working hard to keep from crying, but she soldiered on. "She had a bad stroke. Verna was with her when it happened, thank the Lord. Verna called 911 and they got her to the hospital right away. The doctor said that if stroke victims get to a hospital within the first thirty minutes, a new medication can stop and even reverse any damage to the brain. So...she has a chance."

Nancy stopped talking for a few seconds and Bud waited for her to regain her composure. "Oh, Bud," she cried, "Mama didn't even know me."

HIS FITFUL SLEEP WOVE DREAMS OF fire-spitting machine pistols, bleeding corpses, cougars, helicopters, and an army of cold-faced assassins that he shot over and over only to see them get up and shoot at him again.

The bed sheets were soaked with sweat and his heart was pounding when he awoke.

"Damn," he said when he looked at his bedside clock glowing in the dark. "Six-thirty. Pain pills must have knocked me out."

He shuffled his way to the bathroom and turned on the shower before he realized he'd have to settle for a spit bath. "Damn," he said again for no particular reason. Except he had killed a woman, his shoulder hurt like hell, and his personal life was upside down again.

He brushed his teeth and stared at the hollow-eyed face in the mirror. He noted a scattering of gray hair in his sideburns. "I wonder when that happened?"

He splashed cold water on his stubbled face, slipped into a bathrobe, and padded barefoot to the kitchen to start his morning coffee. Molly scratched at the back door and whined, but he ignored her and walked back to the bedroom to fetch his cell phone.

Dutch answered on the third ring. "You up, Dutch?"

"Yeah, I am. You can sleep well because the FBI is looking out for you."

Bud said. "Roger and I arrested an Allen Pinkerton yesterday. He's in the custody of the Oregon state police."

"And...?"

"He's the same guy who killed Crazy Charlie. He and a woman named Aimee...that's all I've got on her...dressed up as EMTs, drove a stolen ambulance to Cowboy's ranch, and then slipped him a shot that stopped his heart. They work for somebody who goes by the code name Bloodstone."

"We know about Bloodstone. What about the woman?"

"She was killed in the shootout."

"Are you okay? Word is out you were shot."

"Just scratched me. Doctor stitched it up and I'm home now. But that isn't why I called. I think you need to check out Pinkerton. He runs a business called Oregon Yards and More. Roger thinks Pinkerton may have laundered some money through the business."

"Thanks for the tip. We'll check it out. Gotta' go, Bud."

Chapter 41

Bambi watched the street for Bloodstone while Dudley strapped a camera to the trunk of a small tree, lens pointed back up the road.

Once turned on, the camera provided constant video feed to NCIS headquarters via satellite. "Good for day or night," Springdale technicians had told them. "You just turn it on, point it where you need it, and the camera does the rest. We can run it remotely from here after that."

A dark blue Dodge Charger with tinted windows sped by, heading in the direction of Bloodstone's house.

"Did you get that?" Bambi asked.

"Yes."

A man's voice came quietly through his ear piece. "Springdale, here. Good shot. We'll run the plates. Back soon."

Thirty minutes later, Abdul Abraham McKenzie, NCIS, whispered in their earpieces, "I'm coming in. Meet me at the back of the house."

"What's with the lights?" Abe asked when Bambi and Dudley came around the side of the house.

"We're guests of the Hamptons," Bambi said.

Abe chuckled when Dudley related the story of their encounter with a local security man.

"So we have to leave some lights on, and a TV going to keep up the pretense."

"Good," Abe said, "Now here's what I saw. First, there's a motion sensor on the trail…maybe a hundred feet from the house. Second, there's a trip wire right at the edge of Bloodstone's clearing.

He doesn't have any landscaping...just a clearing. Right now the place is lit up like Times Square on the Fourth of July. I saw a dark blue Charger come in. One man...Caucasian...salt-and-pepper crewcut...six-feet tall...maybe a skosh taller...forty-five or so...a lean one-seventy to one-eighty. Fit looking guy, military maybe. He was carrying a black duffel bag about four feet long. It looked heavy."

"Body guard?" Dudley asked.

"I don't know. I saw two other guys walking the perimeter...in the yard lights, no less. I can't figure out what they hoped to accomplish."

"Good targets, maybe. Are they armed?" Bambi asked.

Abe said. "I didn't see any weapons, but I'd bet on it. This is a residential neighborhood. I would think the open display of weapons would have local police pounding on the door."

"Any other way out, other than the road?" Dudley asked.

"He's got a boat house on the south side of the main house, and a ramp that leads down to the water. I checked it out. There's a big Zodiac...maybe twenty-feet long...with twin outboards. I didn't stick around long enough to read the horsepower on the engines, but they are big. That's a very fast boat, for sure."

"Any communication antennas on the house?" Bambi asked.

Abe shook his head. "I couldn't see the north side, but I didn't see anything on the roof."

Abe briefed Springdale via secure satellite phone. They heard him say, "Okay, we'll wait. Bring 'em on in."

"What?" Bambi asked when he hung up.

"The FBI team is going to hide their van here...in the Hampton's RV garage. They'll be ready to roll when we give them the go sign. We, on the other hand, get to camp out tonight. Bambi, I want you watching the driveway. Dud, you take the north perimeter. And since I know where the sensor and the trip wire is, I'll take the south perimeter. Stay alert. It could get interesting in the morning."

The buzz of a float plane woke former Congressman Kevin Ross at first light. Still in his pajamas, he grabbed a pair of binoculars and pushed through a set of French doors out onto the third floor balcony. He focused on a blue and white Beaver circling downwind, and watched the plane settle gracefully on the surface of the Sound.

He walked back into his bedroom and punched a call button. "Frank, get your ass out of bed. Use the boat to pick up our guest, and get everybody up. I want 'em awake. You hear me, Frank?"

Frank said, "I'm on it, Boss."

Abe watched with interest as a burly, dark haired man, maybe forty or forty-five years old, ran to the boat house, slid open the big door on the ocean side, and walked around the side of the building, out of Abe's sight. A minute later, the Zodiac eased down the ramp to the water, the man seated at the console, and holding what looked like a garage door opener in one hand.

When the Zodiac was afloat, the man pushed a button on the remote and unhooked the cable from the bow of the boat. He slid under the wheel, cranked the starter and backed away from the shore when the big four-cycle outboards coughed and fired up.

Abe's whisper mike suddenly crackled to life. "Where are you, Abe?"

"Amanda?"

"Yeah. I'm joining the party. What's going on?"

"Our buddy Bloodstone is sending a red Zodiac out to a float plane which is tied to a mooring buoy about fifty yards off shore. As soon as I can see who gets picked up…that is if it's Ortega… I'm calling in the cavalry."

"How do I find you?"

"Are you at the Hampton house?"

"Yes, with our FBI friends."

"Why don't you wait and come in with them, Amanda." It was more command than question. She needed to understand that Abe was in charge.

"You sure? I might be able to help."

Bambi cut in, almost snarling. "Yeah, he's sure, and so am I. The bad guys don't know we're here, and we want to keep it that way."

There was a good ten second pause, and then Amanda said, "I guess you're right. I'll ride in with the cavalry."

Abe turned back to the spotting scope. Two men climbed into the big raft and held it against the plane's float. A slender man dressed in a black North Face windbreaker, blue jeans, and white tennis shoes backed out of the plane and down to the float. When he turned to step into the boat, Abe identified Raul Ortega. "Gotcha, you murdering son-of-a-bitch," he whispered.

Abe waited until the Zodiac eased away from the plane and turned for the shore a short fifty yards away. As it grounded on the narrow sandy beach, he used his cell phone to call the FBI team leader. "Ortega is here. Roll 'em! And send in the Coast Guard. Ortega is wearing a black windbreaker, blue jeans, and tennis shoes. We want him alive."

Abe whispered into his mike, "Time to take the perimeter guards out." He used the bulk of the boat house for cover and then, pistol in hand, simply walked around the corner and said to a sleepy looking man, hands in his jacket pocket, shivering in the cool morning air, "Don't move and don't call out or I'll blow a hole in your head."

He walked the man into the boat house, cuffed the man's hands behind him, wrapped two quick ties around the man's ankles, and stuffed an oil-stained grease rag in his mouth. The only equipment Abe found on the man was a small walkie-talkie. Abe turned it off and then crushed it with his boot.

"You be a good boy, and you might live," he said.

He heard Dudley whisper, "North side is secure."

KEVIN ROSS LED THE COLOMBIAN TO his third floor bedroom and office.

"Where's the asshole who messed up my Northwest operation?" Ortega asked without preamble. "I'm going to kill him...slowly."

"Patience, Raul. He'll be here in a couple of hours."

They walked out on the balcony and watched as the pilot untied the float plane and climbed back into the cockpit. The engine fired up and the plane began a slow taxi back toward the middle of the channel.

"One of yours?" Ross said to Ortega.

Ortega shook his head. "Charter plane," he said in his flawless, unaccented English. "Let's go back in. We need to talk."

The increasing noise of a helicopter beating down the Sound drew them back to the balcony. Bremerton naval base wasn't more than ten minutes by helicopter from the island, so helicopters weren't all that unusual. But this one sounded like it was getting awfully close to his house.

Both men watched the approaching helicopter with growing uneasiness. Their worst fears were confirmed when a Coast Guard cutter made a high speed turn around the point and headed for the float plane. The Coast Guard helicopter made a straight run at Ross, right at eye level.

"You son-of-a-bitch," Ortega snarled and pulled a pistol from the right pocket of his windbreaker. Ross started backing up, hands held up in a defensive posture. "I didn't do it, Raul. Somebody sold us out."

Raul hesitated and Ross suddenly turned, took four running steps, and jumped off the balcony, out over the water.

Ortega ran to the railing and aimed a shot at Ross just as the concussion of an explosion rolled up the stairway. He heard people shouting, "Hands in the air. Get down on the floor." And then more shouting, followed by a blast that sounded like a shotgun. He identified the voices of his body guards crying "Don't shoot! Don't shoot. We give up."

"Cowards," Ortega muttered. He looked at the balcony and knew he didn't have the nerve to make such a jump. So he hid in the master bathroom.

That's where Amanda found him, hiding behind the shower doors. "Come on out, Raul, or I'll shoot you where you stand."

Trembling either from fear or from rage, he rolled back the frosted glass door and tossed his gun on the floor. "Don't shoot," he pled.

He started to step forward, but the toe of his left foot hooked the raised lip of the shower and he stumbled toward Amanda, arms out, trying to catch his balance. She reacted to what she thought was an attack, so she shot him in the head. Twice.

Later she would swear he lunged at her. She offered to take a lie detector test, but no one cared enough to take her up on it. Ortega's gun, on the other hand was linked by ballistics to the death of a DEA agent in Sonora, Mexico. That was a lot more interesting.

BAMBI AND DUDLEY STOOD ON THE shore, pistols in hand grinning at an agonized Kevin Ross. His leap into the Sound had been long enough, but at low tide, there just wasn't enough water to absorb a three-story jump. He floundered chest deep in the water, legs buried up to his calves in mud. The mud might have been a good thing, but it was only a thin blanket for the rocks.

"Get me out of here," he begged, "My legs are broken."

"Not me, Congressman," Bambi said. She looked at Dudley. "You do it. I'm not getting wet for that asshole."

"Me either," Dudley agreed. "Let's wait for high tide and see if he washes ashore or drowns."

Abe walked up and said, "You guys knock it off. We'll slide the Zodiac over and pull him out. You," he pointed at Bambi, "keep him covered."

The tally, when things calmed down and the drug thugs were restrained and locked in the FBI van, was: one injured Bloodstone; one dead Ortega; one dead thug who lost in a shoot-out with the FBI; two Colombians who worked for Ortega, two inept perimeter guards, and Bloodstone's right-hand man, Frank.

One of the FBI agents found a basement room blocked by a heavy steel door and a combination lock. Frank gave them the combination. The room was stacked full of cardboard boxes stuffed with money, lots of money—most of it American twenty-dollar bills.

Frank was more than willingly to cooperate. According to him, the dead man was hired by Bloodstone to kill Ortega and his two *compadres*, and had, in fact, already killed the assassin who blew up Pettibone's yacht.

"That guy is…was…a contract killer. Kevin was going to take over Ortega's operation. He used the cowboy sheriff to lure Ortega up here. Listen, I'll help you," Frank said, "if you'll help me."

An ambulance rolled up to take Kevin Ross, with a two-man FBI detail riding shotgun, to a local hospital. Ross would later be transferred to the University of Washington Hospital because of the severity of his injuries. A forensics team moved in and began a painstaking examination of the house, grounds, and boathouse. It would take forensics twenty-four hours to process the scene.

BAMBI, DUDLEY, AND ABE STOLE QUIETLY back up the path to the Hampton house. They were careful to not trigger the sensor or the trip wire. Abe pointed out the motion detector and opined that were it a newer generation detector he might steal it. "But not this piece of junk."

While Dudley retrieved his camera from the tree, Bambi made sure there was no trace of their entrance or occupancy of the Hampton's house. She killed the lights, turned off the TV, and locked the front door. They stowed their gear in the bed of the pickup, and with Bambi in the back seat, headed for Silverdale. An older man in a sedan with security company decals on the doors drove slowly around the corner. Dudley honked and waved. The man waved back.

Chapter 42

Bud used his electric shaver and washed up while his coffee maker wheezed and burped and trickled a thin black stream of fresh coffee into the pot.

The mundane acts of making coffee, shaving, and getting dressed were soothing to Bud's raw nerves. The chorus from an old song, "Little things mean a lot," came to mind.

"Yes," he said aloud, "yes they do."

He put on new pair of jeans and a blue, short-sleeved sport shirt. He found he had to sit down to pull socks on his feet, but he won that battle, sore arm and all, and walked through the house to the kitchen.

Molly was sitting on the back porch when he opened the door, tail beating a steady rhythm.

"You hungry?"

She yelped a canine "yes."

He stepped into a pair of old Wellingtons and opened the locker.

She quivered in anticipation when he poured a scoop of dry food into her dish, but she didn't move until he said, "Go for it."

He walked through the back gate and down the driveway to his roadside mailbox. A red pickup heading to town slowed, and the driver honked and waved at the sheriff. Bud recognized the driver as a local BLM employee. He couldn't remember her name. He waved back.

The mailbox was stuffed with a dozen advertisers, a Cabela's catalog, a credit card offer, an electric bill, and a personal letter from his dad. He stuck that in his shirt pocket.

He carried the mail through the back gate in time to see Molly chasing the last pellet of dry food. It had fallen in the space between the locker and the wall, and her tongue just wasn't long enough to reach it. Bud dumped the mail on the kitchen table and walked back to the open door to watch Molly scratch and dig for that last morsel.

He chuckled and said, "I know you're not starving, so what's so special about that one?" But he pivoted the locker on one corner and opened a space big enough to let her at the pellet.

"Satisfied," he asked? Molly grinned as he pushed the locker back against the wall of the house again, and nudged him with her head.

A mower was cutting a lawn two houses over, and Bud could smell fresh cut grass.

Suddenly the day was looking up. "Going to be a warm one, Molly."

AT 8:30, LOOKING LIKE "WALKER, TEXAS Ranger" minus the beard, Bud drove his personal vehicle to the station. He slipped the soon-to-be-famous blue sling around his neck and stuck his arm in the cloth *Just to keep the critics at bay*, he decided.

Karen Highsmith peeked up over the booking counter and a smile bloomed on her face. "Good morning, Bud. How are you?"

"Right as rain, fit as a fiddle, raring' to go. Why I could wrestle alligators, storm the ramparts, and...I don't know what else."

Michelle came laughing up the hallway. "And run out of clichés is what else."

She walked over and gave him a peck on the cheek and a hug, careful not to squeeze his injured arm. "You're alive. That's the important thing." She stepped back and surveyed his face. "You had anything to eat?"

"Just coffee, but it was really good coffee."

"Chief Hildebrand just called. Said he was at the Indian Village and wanted to buy you breakfast or at least a cup of coffee."

"Well...I guess I could do that. Where's the rest of the crew?"

Michelle lied smoothly, "Roger and Lonnie are headed for Adel to look into some cattle rustling."

"Again?" Bud exploded. "I thought we put a stop to that."

She smiled and said, "Must be some new rustlers."

"Shit," he muttered. "And Larae? Where is she?"

"Shopping. She needs some things for her apartment."

"Well, hell, and I thought we were running a police department."

Karen came around the booking counter trying hard not to let a grin ruin things. She squeezed his right arm and stood on her tiptoes to give him a kiss on the cheek. "Run along, now. Go see the Chief and have a nice breakfast."

Bud said, "I'm suspicious of you two. What's going on?"

Michelle said primly, "You go eat breakfast. We've got a sheriff's department to run here."

A puzzled Bud Blair walked out the door and started down the street to the Indian Village when a twinge in his left shoulder reminded him of the prescriptions in his shirt pocket. He turned and crossed the street to the drugstore.

A pretty young woman smiled sweetly and said, "Good morning, Sheriff. Can I help you?"

Bud fished the two prescriptions out of his shirt pocket and pushed them across the counter. "I need to get these filled."

"We'll have them ready in about thirty minutes. Is that okay?"

Bud frowned, "Yeah…that would be fine."

"Good. How is your arm?"

Not, how did you hurt your arm, but how is the arm. Something is going on here. Grapevine must be busy this morning.

He said, "Right as rain…" and walked out of the store.

Gus was waiting on the sidewalk when Bud came strolling down the street to the Indian Village. Gus shook Bud's hand and said, "You ready for some breakfast?"

Except for a couple of tourists, the front of the restaurant was empty of customers. "I got us set up in back," Gus said and led him to the banquet room.

When he opened the door to the big room, thunderous applause broke out. Bud stopped in surprise, gawking at the packed room, and Gus pushed him none too gently forward and pointed to a chair in the center of the head table. Bud was stunned and then he could see his officers grinning and pointing to blue ribbons pinned to their lapels. He scanned the crowd, familiar faces everyone, and saw they were all wearing blue ribbons. He glanced down at his blue sling and then grinned.

Bud could see a big homemade sign taped to the back wall declaring, "Sheriff Blair, Lakeview's Own!"

A chorus of "For He's a Jolly Good Fellow" broke out as he sat down.

Commissioner Lynch, seated to Bud's right tapped a water glass with a butter knife trying to get the crowd's attention until Bud thought the glass would break.

Finally, the crowd hushed enough for the judge to say, "Lake County has always been blessed with good, honest, and honorable sheriffs, but none have outshone the dedication to duty exemplified by Sheriff Henry Bud Blair, Lake County's own, hero of the hour."

The enthusiastic crowd interrupted Judge Lynch with applause and a noisy chorus of "Amen."

The judge stood and waited until the noise died. "Deputy Hildebrand, would you turn the television on."

Bud watched as a big, flat screen TV mounted high on a side wall of the banquet room showed a FOX News Alert banner streaming across the bottom of the screen: *The FBI announced today the capture of Bloodstone, a major drug dealer and suspected associate of terrorists.*

In the upper right hand corner of the screen, a picture of a haggard Bud Blair, taken at the time of the bomb incident shared the screen with a FOX news anchor. "Well, Brett, it looks like the sheriff of Lake County, Oregon has done it again. What do you make of it?"

"John, a reliable source is telling us the sheriff found a coded diary kept by one of the terrorists...a drug runner named Robert

Clark. The sheriff succeeded in breaking the code and tipped off the FBI. Based on information from the diary, the FBI raided two Muslim mosques yesterday, one in Seattle and one in Portland. The raids apparently uncovered huge supplies of arms, ammunition and explosives...all aimed at supporting terrorist acts against the United States. There is no word from the FBI as to the actual number of weapons or the types of explosives found. But approximately twenty-five people have been arrested. This is a major disruption to drug trafficking and terrorist organizations in the Pacific Northwest."

"Any word on what the terrorists were targeting, Brett?"

"The FBI isn't sharing everything they know about the intended targets, but John, the Puget Sound area is home to several naval installations including the Bremerton Naval Base, so that area is what is called a target rich environment. Any of them could have been the target."

"Thanks, Brett." John looked into the camera. "We'll have more coverage later in the show. What a remarkable man Sheriff Blair must be." The anchor paused, and Bud's picture was replaced by a video of mob-filled filled streets. "In the Sudan, rioters..."

Roger caught Bud's disgusted look and shut the TV off.

Bud could feel every eye staring at him, waiting for him to say something. Finally he rose to his feet and looked at every face, one at a time. The judge sat back down.

"In every age," Bud began, "our people have faced danger from marauders and brigands. The brigands of our era are terrorists...some homegrown...some from foreign lands. What they ultimately intend I can only guess at. But don't call me a hero.

"Yes, my officers and I will be here as your shield and your frontline spear chuckers. That's the nature of our chosen profession. We keep the peace against all enemies...foreign and domestic. Officers Hildebrand," he searched for and found the others, "Highsmith, Trivoli, Beltram, Holcomb, and Special Agent John Bernard, please rise. If I'm a hero, then I owe it to these fine young people. And to Sonny Sixkiller who can't be here today."

The four officers of Bud's force rose, Larae balancing awkwardly on a walking cast while a smiling John Bernard held her arm. Applause once again filled the room.

Bud waited until the room quieted. "But the real heroes are those good, solid, honest citizens who daily go about the business of raising families, running businesses, paving our highways, making our lumber, and growing our food in spite of the brigands." He raised his coffee cup in salute. "I give you my heroes, the people of Lake County and the United States of America."

The thunder of applause and cheers was so loud people outside the restaurant stopped to listen.

Bud sat down and said, "And now I want to eat some breakfast."

But the speech making wasn't over quite yet. After coffee cups had been refilled and breakfast orders taken, Mayor Gladys McKnight rose and said, "Our sheriff is much too modest." She pointed to the blue ribbon pinned to the collar of her suit jacket. "By the power invested in me, and by the blessing of the City Council, we proclaim Sheriff Bud Blair a Knight of the Order of the Blue Sling. And further we proclaim the next seven days as Sheriff Blair Week.

"For the next week, Sheriff Blair may not spend any money in our city. Gasoline for his vehicle, food for the freezer, dinner out, what ever he wants is to be paid for by the council."

Again the applause was nearly deafening. Bud caught Michelle's eye and she winked.

When the noise settled down to the chatter of seat mates, and the clink of silverware on plates, Gus nudged Bud. "Nice speech, but you didn't tell us anything about what happened."

Bud mumbled around a mouthful of toast, "All in good time, Gus."

Roger slipped a folded paper napkin under the edge of Bud's plate. "Read it after breakfast."

In another twenty minutes the crowd thinned out. People with businesses to run stopped to shake Bud's hand and say, "thank you" before going to work. A few pointed to their blue ribbon and asked, "How is your arm?" All were dying with curiosity about the woman Bud had shot, but they all tactfully left their questions unasked. Carol Connor stopped by Bud's chair and said, "I suppose an interview is out of the question."

Bud smiled and nodded. "You'd be right. I'm thinking you can find enough on FOX for a story."

She nodded and smiled as she held out her hand, thinking of the impact the pictures of Bud's bullet punctured pickup was going to make on national TV. "I'm glad you're okay, Bud."

"How's your Dad doing?"

"Asa is Asa," she said. "I think he could lose an arm and explain how good his other arm was. But he did call and tell me he is doing all right."

"Give him my best."

Finally, just Bud, Gus and their officers were left sitting with Judge Lynch and Mayor McKnight. Bud unfolded the napkin and read Roger's message. "Well," he said, "It looks like I'm suspended," he glanced at Lynch, "with pay," he emphasized. His officers laughed and Lynch smiled. "Pending," Bud went on, "a review of yesterday's incident in which a citizen lost her life."

"How long is the suspension?" Lynch asked.

Bud shrugged. "I don't know. For as long as it takes, I guess. The state police will conduct the review. And before you ask, Roger will be acting sheriff, Michelle will continue her duties as undersheriff, Lonnie will work full-time, a situation I hope will continue permanently, Judge, and Larae will work out of this office until her ankle heals and she can return to full-time duty."

Bud stopped and then he smiled at them all. "Good luck to all of you. I'm going to Bremerton for Detective Grandfield's service, and then I'm going to take some much needed time off. Don't call me unless it's about the review." He handed Roger his weapon. "As prescribed by ORS something or other."

"Oh," and one more thing, Bud added, "Larae, how would you like to housesit for me and feed Molly while I'm gone."

Larae grinned. "You bet I will. My apartment is nice, but I need a little more room to move around in."

John Bernard stopped Bud on the sidewalk and waited until the others had walked around the corner. "Well, that blows my cover."

"John, it was already blown and you know it."

"You got a uniform that's fit to wear?"

"One left…hanging in my closet. Why?"

"Because in about an hour a nice military Q-200 is going to land at the Lakeview Airport. It's our ride to Bremerton for Grandfield's funeral."

Chapter 43

GRANDFIELD WAS HONORED BY NAVY FIGHTER planes roaring overhead in the missing man formation, a nice eulogy by the Police Department Chaplain, and "Taps." Torn with grief, Julie Grandfield, could only respond to Maretti's condolences with, "You got my husband killed."

Maretti ducked his head and mumbled, "I'm sorry."

Ruby Goldstein, Gino's constant companion for the past few days was incensed, but Gino squeezed her left arm in a vise-like grip, silently telling her to let it go.

John found Abe, Dudley and Bambi, and then enjoyed a round of quiet, good natured insults, punctuated by a hug from Bambi who said, "You asshole. Where have you been?"

Bud pushed through the throng of well wishers and sympathizers to where Maretti stood talking to a tall uniformed officer who was patting Maretti on the shoulder. Bud heard the officer say, "Don't take it personal, Gino. She's just upset over Grandfield."

Bud said, "Am I interrupting?"

Gino turned to look at Bud and then said, "The high sheriff himself. It's good of you to be here. Nice funeral, wasn't it. Let me introduce you to my old partner, Milo."

Bud endured a bone crushing hand shake from the big officer who smiled and said, "I been hearing about you for the last two days. 'Bud did this, Bud did that,' and I think I watched you on TV until my eyeballs burned."

Gino winced and said, "He's been my babysitter for the past couple of days. And this nice lady is Ruby Goldstein who really got things rolling on the Cowboy-Pettibone case. Ruby, meet the famous Bud Blair. Looks like the bad guys winged you, too, Bud." He raised the cast on his left arm.

"I heard about your wound," Bud said. "When you going back to work?"

"Don't know. The doc says I won't ever be able to straighten out my arm again, and I damned well won't ride a desk, so it's kinda up in the air."

"You do any fishing?"

"If that's an invitation to Lakeview, I might just take you up on it. I don't fish, but I drink a little beer."

They both chuckled. Bud said, "I'm on administrative leave. Why don't you come down and spend some time at my cabin with me? You can drink beer and I'll fish."

"Give me a call when you get back," Gino said.

"Does that include me?" Ruby said quietly in Gino's ear.

Gino shook his head. "It's strictly a guy thing, Ruby."

Amanda eased up beside Bud and said, "The team would like to meet you," and pulled him away to a waiting limo.

By the time they poured Bud back on the plane for a return trip to Lakeview, he was feeling no pain.

Epilogue

A MONTH LATER THREE MEN CASUALLY watched rod tips for signs of fish nibbles as a soft evening breeze gently rocked the fourteen-foot aluminum boat anchored next to a weed bed in Dog Lake. A small black Labrador was curled in sleep on a piece of carpet in the bow of the boat.

Gino Maretti, left arm in a cast, pointed across the lake to the A-frame cabin. "Somebody's pulling in your driveway, Bud."

Bud watched through binoculars as a woman stepped out of a new Toyota SUV and walked to the door of the cabin. "I'll be damned. It looks like Amanda Spears. I wonder what she wants?"

Dell BeBe smiled. "Maybe she wants your body."

"Shut up, BB." Discussions of Bud's love life were verboten. Two weeks earlier, Bud helped Sonny and Roger load Nancy's household goods into a U-Haul truck.

The one private conversation between Bud and Nancy sadly convinced him Nancy would never be back. Not as an emergency dispatcher. Not as his wife.

She had tears in her eyes when she said, "I can't do it, Bud. I love you, but the thought of not knowing every day if you'll come home alive…well, I don't think I can live with that. And my mother needs me." She accentuated her determination by handing him the engagement ring he bought earlier in the year.

"Well," he said to BB and Gino, "what do you think? Shall we go see what she wants?"

"Nah," Gino said, sipping the last suds from a bottle of Heffy, "Let her swim out."

BB laughed and Bud shook his head. "Don't you like her, Gino?"

"Oh, hell yes. That's a foxy lady. I just don't want to talk shop with her. Hey…before I forget…for some good news, Agent Warren resigned. I heard that before I decided to run down and kill some fish with my buddy, Sheriff Blair."

Bud's cell phone rang and he unbuttoned his shirt pocket. "Forgot to turn it off," he apologized. "Yeah?"

"Bud, this is Amanda. Is that you across the lake?"

"Yeah. What do you want?"

"Well, that's friendly. Look, I resigned. I'm just taking a slow trip through the West. Thought I'd stop and say hello."

"You what? You resigned?"

He could hear a giggle in her voice. "Yep. I'm a free woman."

"I'll be damned."

HUGS AND HANDSHAKES TAKEN CARE OF, with Amanda's whispered "I'm sorry about Grandfield," in Gino's ear, they just mainly stood and stared out at the lake for several long seconds until Molly barked and tried to jump up on Amanda.

"Get down, Molly," Bud said without any heat. "Sit."

Molly sat, and Amanda knelt down to pet her. Molly held out a paw for Amanda to shake. "Nice dog, Bud," she said. "And a nice cabin. You build it?"

"Yes," and without knowing why added, "I built it to stay sane the year after my divorce."

She studied the sage green A-frame, fronting the lake. "Nice," she said again. "And did it?"

"Did what?"

"Keep you sane," she smiled.

"Hell, I'm not sure I've ever been sane."

That brought the expected chuckles, and Bud moved Amanda up a notch on his scale of approved characteristics.

"You guys catch any fish?"

BB laughed and said, "What…with bare hooks? Bud doesn't use bait. He just uses beer."

"Well, in that case, I brought some steaks. I see a barbecue in your future."

BB caught Bud's eye and nodded at Amanda. "She brought steaks?" he mouthed with raised eyebrows.

Bud gave him a surreptitious single digit salute and shook his head in disgust. Two weeks dumped, and already BB was trying to fix him up.

While Gino fired up the barbeque and Amanda worked on a salad, BB and Bud opened a big Cabela's carton hiding in Bud's garage. Bud stripped the plastic wrap and tried to lift a big steel fire pit free of the box, grunting from the effort.

"Here, let me help," BB offered.

They wrestled the fire pit to the gravel drive between the small garage and the cabin. "That's pretty nice," BB said, admiring the cutout silhouettes of deer, fish and elk running around the circle of polished steel. "Your arm still sore?"

"Yeah. I can use it, but it seems like I'm always bumping it. Let's get a fire going."

EVENING SHADOWS TURNED THE LAKE A shiny slate color, and the high desert temperature dropped steadily, hinting that winter was lurking around the corner, waiting to bite them with cold days and wind-blown snow. Stomachs full to aching, they sat around Bud's new fire pit and stared into the flames.

Bud said, "Good steaks, Gino. Maybe you can start a career as a chef."

"And what about the salad?" Amanda demanded, a grin tugging at the corner of her mouth.

BB raised his whiskey glass. "Here's to the salad."

"Hear, hear!" Gino said.

"A toast," Bud offered. "To dear friends. Old and new."

They sat beside the fire until the whiskey and wine were gone and the night chill had seeped into their bones. It had been a nice quiet party, fellow police officers swapping stories, catching up.

Amanda entertained with descriptions of Bloodstone bolting from his office and leaping off the balcony into the sea. "Only thing is, he forgot the tide was out. He wound up taking a three-story jump into about three feet of water. Broke both legs. We had to haul him out before he drowned. Dudley thought we should just wait for high tide. We think he was trying to get to a beached Zodiac. So now he's busy ratting out his criminal buddies, trying to beat a murder rap."

"And," Bud said, "you got Ortega."

"That," she said emphatically, "put a definite speed-bump in my career path. I know in my mind it was a good shoot. He lunged at me, so I shot him. But in my heart, I wonder if I didn't want to kill the son-of-a-bitch and just waited for an excuse."

And then she found herself talking about losing her enthusiasm for chasing terrorists and drug dealers, "One and the same these day," she ended gloomily.

"What about you, Gino? What are going to do?" She asked, changing the subject.

"I'm going to run," Gino said. "There's this nice lady in Bremerton, a nice rich widow who wants to partner with me. She wants to start a detective agency."

"And what's wrong with that?" Amanda challenged.

Bud and BB nearly rolled out of their chairs in laughter.

"Nothing, but she keeps telling me she loves me…keeps hinting we should get married. Hell, I've tried that twice, and I don't want to try it again. At least not with her," he added.

"Ruby Goldstein. Right? The one you saved?"

"One and the same. I'm almost sorry I did."

There were appreciative chuckles, and BB said, "I know what you mean. I've been married once and divorced twice. And that's once too many."

"Divorced twice?" Amanda asked.

"Yeah. First you divorce the husband from his wife. That's once. Then you divorce him from his house and half his retirement. That's twice."

"Men," she said disgustedly."

"No, young miss, it's just reality. You know what I'm gonna do about it? Nothing. I'm just gonna retire and move to Lake County. It's dangerous down here, but the city has gotten dull. Need something to spice up my life."

"You're not serious?" Bud asked.

"Serious as sin. Did you know, my old friend, I turn fifty in two months. I'm gonna hang it up. That's why I bought a piece of ground next door to you."

"In town?"

"No. Right there." BB pointed to a piece of ground just beyond Bud's cabin.

"I'll be damned." The thought of BB not doing cop work just didn't compute, but he'd known BB long enough to hear the finality of his words. And having him as a neighbor was appealing.

Gino shook his head. He lifted his left arm out to his side. "I'm being forced out. Well...that's not exactly accurate. I've been given a choice, a desk or disability retirement. Shit, I'm no good as a desk jockey, so I guess I'll just retire. Maybe I'll move to Lakeview along with you," he said to BB.

Bud groaned. "I don't think I could take it." But privately he was glad BB and Gino had decided to like each other.

It got quiet and then Amanda asked, "What about you, Bud. What are you going to do?

He sipped his drink, only his second actually, and a weak one at that. He looked up at the sky, spotted Orion coming up in the east, and looked back into the fire. He said, "I really don't know. I've had a half dozen job offers from NCIS on through the alphabet, good paying jobs. But when I'm reinstated as sheriff, I'll probably stay right here in sleepy little old Lake County."

"Honky, *if* they offer you your job back, you take it," BB growled. "Now where we gonna sleep?"

Amanda chose to roll out her sleeping bag on a pad in the back of her Toyota 4-Runner. BB pulled a heavy piece of foam and a big sleeping bag from the trunk of his red Corvette. He announced his intention of sleeping on Bud's small dock. "I sleep best on the water," he explained.

With a wave of his hand, he intoned, "Sufficient onto the day," and walked down to the lake, Molly padding quietly behind him.

Gino chose the recliner, and Bud, stifling minor guilt pangs, yawned his way to the loft and was asleep before his head hit the pillow.

A MAN WATCHED UNTIL THE FOUR law enforcement officers had gone to bed. He keyed his cell phone and hit Send. A sleepy voice said, "Yes?"

"I found her, *Jefe*."

AT A SILVERDALE UPS STORE, JOHN Bernard, aka Gar, aka Stone Fly, sent a registered letter to Crazy Charlie's parents with a cashier's check for $20,000. *What the heck*, he thought. *I don't know where Charlie got it, but it was his. Besides, there's no such thing as dirty money.*

He walked around the corner to where his pickup and attached trailer filled two parking places. He hadn't fed either parking meter, so a conscientious meter maid left him two parking tickets instead of one. He tossed them both in his glove box, and then grinned. "I wonder if they'll chase me all the way to Christmas Valley?"

EARLIER THAT MORNING AN ATLAS MOVING van parked in front of Ron Grandfield's house in Bremerton, and four burly men began packing and loading household goods. Young Widow Grandfield's purse held a ticket to take her from SeaTac airport to Phoenix. Her parents were waiting to drive her home to Sedona.

She took one last look around the living room, picked up the plaque with Ron's citation for heroism and stuffed it in her carryon. Then she turned and walked out the door and down to a waiting limousine. Chief Homer held the door for her, and Bill Thompson gave her a sympathetic look as she settled in the seat opposite from him. "I'm glad you decided to let us take you to the airport."

She nodded, fighting tears again. She had discovered she could handle the hard things in life, but not sympathy. "Thank you," she said quietly.

IN YAKIMA, NANCY SIXKILLER SAT BESIDE a hospital bed, watching her mother sleep, and thinking about Bud Blair. The thought of disappointing Bud was stronger than her sense of personal failure, but she couldn't find the courage to face a daily life that meant not knowing if her husband would return home alive at the end of the day. "Go with God, Bud," she whispered. "Go with God."

Author's Note

I knew the setting for *Spider Silk* and for *Stone Fly* intimately, so my assertion that I have walked the ground of my characters was accurate insofar as where those tales are set.

In Bloodstone, however, I've taken some liberties with the setting. I have been to Bremerton, but the area called The Heights is fiction. Every city I'm familiar with seems to have such a place, so it didn't seem unreasonable for Bremerton to have one as well.

My description of the Bremerton city police station is purely fictional, as is the description of the NCIS headquarters in Silverdale.

As for Poulsbo Harbor, I spent parts of two days and one night aboard a forty-seven-foot Kroger moored there, so the accuracy of that place is skewed only by my memory.

Kevin Ross's house on Bainbridge Island is simple fiction—and so is Kevin Ross.

Thompson's mansion is modeled after one I visited years ago on Queen Anne Hill in Seattle. That one is a cozy thirteen thousand square feet, has thirteen suites, and—yes—a tunnel to a four thousand-square-foot carriage house at the bottom of the hill. The real one faces Puget Sound while my fictional one faces Lake Washington.

As for the rest, trust me—I've been there.

ROD COLLINS has done a little of everything: teacher, newspaper editor, logger, truck driver, soda jerk, construction worker, wildland firefighter, fire lookout, aerial observer, and business consultant.

More important, he is a devoted husband, father, and grandfather. And, like Louis L'amour, he has walked the land his characters walk.

Rod is also the author of the award-winning business reference guide: *What Do I Do When I Get There? A New Manager's Guidebook;* and award-winning novels: *Spider Silk* and *Stone Fly*—Sheriff Bud Blair mysteries set in the high desert of Eastern Oregon.

Rod's books can be purchased at **www.brightworkspress.com**